Malcolm Hamer is a s[...] worked extensively in [...] 1971 he founded his own agency [...] represented many top sportsmen, among them golfers such as Johnny Miller, Sam Snead and the young Severiano Ballesteros. He is an enthusiastic golfer himself, although these days he no longer plays off a single-figure handicap. As a writer, his pieces have appeared in a wide variety of magazines and newspapers, including *The Sunday Times* and the *Observer*. His recent books include *The Ryder Cup – The Players* and a *The Guiness Continental Europe Golf Course Guide*, as well as two previous Chris Ludlow novels, *Sudden Death* and *A Deadly Lie*. Together with his wife, Jill Foster, he has published a successful series of guide books, *The Family Welcome Guides*. They live in London with their daughter, Polly.

Praise for previous Chris Ludlow golfing thrillers:

'A bright debut in the sports-thriller genre' *Daily Mail*

'[The author] has used his inside knowledge of the professional game to create a very readable thriller involving murder and devious off-course machinations with a magic putter' *Sunday Telegraph*

'An unusual sports thriller' *Oxford Mail*

'A subtly wrought piece of infinite charm and depth' *Time Out*

Death Trap

Malcolm Hamer

HEADLINE

First published in 1993
by HEADLINE BOOK PUBLISHING

First published in paperback in 1994
by HEADLINE BOOK PUBLISHING

10 9 8 7 6 5 4 3 2 1

ISBN 0 7472 4162 7

Typeset by Avon Dataset Ltd, Bidford-on-Avon
Printed and bound in Great Britain by
HarperCollins Manufacturing, Glasgow

HEADLINE BOOK PUBLISHING
A division of Hodder Headline PLC
Headline House
79 Great Titchfield Street
London W1P 7FN

To Jill

Many thanks to
Larry and Vivian Martin
for all their help

Chapter 1

The cat got languidly to his feet from the drive in which he'd been bathing in the early evening sun. He padded through two bars of the wrought-iron gate and came to be stroked. Just the muscle movements of the words 'Hello, cat' set my bruised face protesting. The pain couldn't spoil, though, this moment of peace on my walk down a quiet tree-lined Surrey lane. Moments of peace had been rare in recent months.

The cat belonged to a house built in stockbroker Tudor style. The owner had probably turned me down for a job in the past few weeks; there were not many City firms which hadn't done that.

Up to now my life had been pretty comfortable; too comfortable by half, according to some of my friends and family. Then all the slings and arrows had arrived in one unexpected salvo. I had lost both my jobs, all my slender reserves of capital and most of my confidence.

Much of my time had been spent as a salesman for a firm of stockbrokers, a small company which had retained its independence, and still relied on the business provided by a caucus of wealthy private clients. The chairman of Norton Buccleuth, Andrew Buccleuth, described me as a specialist in the leisure market and this allowed him to give me a long rein. I needed that because I was also a caddie on the professional golf circuit.

The consequent juggling of my time in order to serve my two masters required some extremes of ingenuity on my part, the good will of my clients and, above all, the indulgence of Andrew Buccleuth. It helped that he was the archetypal golf nut, who would rather discuss the merits of the latest brand of putter any day than the prospects of a new issue on the stock market. Golf magazines always seemed to be more in evidence in his office than copies of the *Investor's Chronicle*.

Everyone had known that times were hard in the City. The sweet days of eighties prosperity, of champagne nights in the bars and of five, sometimes six-figure bonuses at the end of the year, had gone. The talk was of the tightening of belts, of leaner and fitter industries; clichés run smoothly through their paces by well-fed politicians with a dozen or two non-executive director-ships to keep them going in those dark days.

'They are always the last to know', it is said of cuckolded husbands and I had no inkling at all that my job was on the line. I had noticed that Andrew was not his usual bonhomous self, but had put that down to the struggle to keep the turnover of the company at a respectable level. Most of us in the office had marked the arrivals and departures of various bands of quiet and sombrely dressed gentlemen, whom none of us could identify. Perhaps Andrew was bringing in some new partners to keep the Norton Buccleuth ship steady.

He certainly was and there was a price to pay. Several jobs, including mine, had to go.

It was the last Friday in April and I returned to my desk after a moderately short lunch with my journalist friend, Toby Greenslade. Toby is the golf corre-spondent of the *Daily News*, a down-market tabloid newspaper which anyone can read from cover to cover in half the time it takes to travel by tube from Knightsbridge to Hyde Park Corner. Toby should really be the wine correspondent for the *News* as he spends more time appraising the products of the world's vineyards than he does in assessing golfers. A moderately short lunch with him means from noon to three, during which time he covers a fair amount of ground; in terms of wine, that is. A Californian sparkler was followed by some Alsace and an excursion to New Zealand for some *merlot noir*.

Even though I was drinking more mineral water than wine I could not keep up with Toby.

'Young Rollo's doing well,' he said. 'Started with a sixty-six. Lying fifth.'

Rollo Hardinge was then my boss, the golfer whose well-laden bag I carried along the fairways of Britain and Europe. He was blessed with all the golfing talents; there was power in abundance, a delicate touch when required and a smooth and considered putting stroke. He was also arrogant and sensitive in turn, mercurial, randy and, because of his rich father, immune to worries about money. He was infuriating and great fun and provided yet more evidence that left-handers could be as crazy as goalkeepers. Rollo had received an invitation to play in an American tournament and had grabbed it eagerly. With typical confidence he had said that if he won it he would be invited to play in the Masters Tournament at Augusta, the first of the golfing year's four major championships.

'The boy could win in America, you know,' Toby said unkindly. He knew that I had wanted to accompany Rollo but that my City job would not have allowed it; an important company in the leisure industry was about to make its stock-market debut.

'Toby, I wish you wouldn't call him a boy. He's twenty-five. You sound like one of those patronising and inarticulate football managers.'

'Yes. And if he's successful in the tournament I shall

3

say "the boy done good". It's what my readers understand, dear boy.'

Our often repeated discussion about the standard of sports reporting was interrupted by the arrival at our table of a journalist friend of Toby's. He carried a bottle of port and I made my excuses and left.

I should have stayed and ordered another bottle.

When I walked into the dealing room the usual clatter of telephones, the whirr and ping of the fax machines and the shouted exchanges of the salesmen seemed strangely muted. A sign of recessionary times, I thought. I realised just how accurate my assumption had been when I got nearer to the block of desks which I shared with three other salesmen.

At first sight I hadn't registered the scene in front of my eyes. Why were two security men, in their drab grey uniforms, standing in embarrassed, if watchful, silence alongside my three colleagues? Why were they packing the contents of their desks into black plastic bin liners? With a shock I saw that two of the same plastic bags lay across my desk.

'Welcome to the dole queue,' Hugh Charleson said bitterly. 'We're all on our way out. And pronto.' I could see that he was close to tears. With a heavily mortgaged house in Kent, a weekend cottage in Norfolk and two children, he needed a job more than most. 'Andrew would like to see you,' he added grimly.

Suddenly bereft of my usual energy I took the lift instead of the stairs to the chairman's office on the floor above. Andrew's secretary, Veronica, the steely guardian of his business hours, nodded me towards his door without a word. I knocked, entered and saw the chairman gazing through his wide windows at the City landscape. His tall figure, in its smart but habitually rumpled suit, seemed more stooped than usual, as if he were trying to assess the line of a putt on a particularly tricky green. With his beetling brows and jowly cheeks he looked more than ever like a bloodhound who knew he was about to go into quarantine for six months.

He waved me to a chair at the side of his desk and asked me about my golf. I was sure that my conventional reply did not register with him at all. He was as ill at ease as I had ever seen him, an essentially kindly man who had to take jobs from people he no doubt regarded as friends.

Andrew straightened a small sheaf of papers which lay on his desk, turned his head to stare out of the windows again and said: 'Chris, you know what's going on, I'm sure. I have to make some job cuts. There's no easy way to say this, but my new masters have forced all this upon me.'

'New masters?'

'I've sold most of the family interest to a Swiss company. We've had some heavy losses, just like many other firms. The turnover just isn't there. There's so little trading, people are frightened and they're sitting on their money, that is if they've got any left to sit on. I don't need to tell you. Anyway, it seemed the only way to keep the firm going, so I've brought in some new investment. For their part, they want . . .'

'. . . a leaner, fitter operation,' I said ironically.

Andrew Buccleuth sighed and straightened his sheaf of papers again. He continued: 'I've tried to make the surgery as painless as possible. There are people I desperately wanted to keep. Poor Hugh Charleson, heaven knows how he'll cope if he doesn't get another job quickly. And there are others. You, of course, Chris. They wanted to know why you've had so many days off. You're a part-time employee in their eyes. You had no chance.'

'But my "days off" have brought in plenty of business,' I protested. 'Just because I don't punch a time clock . . .'

Andrew shrugged miserably. 'That doesn't wash with them. Conformity is all. I don't like it but at least the company will survive.' He took a deep breath as though extra oxygen were needed to help him say the unpleasant words that he now got out as quickly as he could. 'All I can offer you, Chris, is three months' salary. You have to clear your desk and be out by five o'clock. Veronica has a cheque for you outside.' He paused, searching for some way to offer comfort. 'I'm sorry. It's all so bloody uncivilised. I'll do everything I can for you. We'll play golf soon.'

Despite Veronica's conventional words of regret as she handed me my envelope, I imagined I saw a glint of triumph in her grey eyes, as watchful as always below a heavy line of green eye shadow. I knew that she considered Andrew's treatment of me to be indulgent. She'd agree with her new bosses' judgement of me: all that time off, all those golf days. Well, her moment had come.

Chapter 2

When I left the offices of Norton Buccleuth that Friday evening, I consoled myself that I did not have the commitments of Hugh Charleson. After all, I had a second job, as caddie to Rollo Hardinge, who seemed destined for stardom on the European golf circuit. If he made a lot of money I would survive quite adequately on my percentage of his winnings.

The only shadow on the horizon had been cast by some investments I had made in the leisure market. They were secondary stocks that I judged to be very healthy wagers; I had been so confident that I had even borrowed money from the bank to finance their purchase. Like millions of other investors and businessmen I had not bargained for a world-wide recession. The shares were now worth about one fifth of what I had originally paid for them. No fool like a professional. I could not take the risk of waiting for sunnier days to return; the shares had to be sold and the bank repaid. I thanked my stars for the redundancy cheque; at least I was back to square one, even if I had no reserves of capital whatsoever.

The unaccustomed luxury of lying late in bed on Monday morning was enhanced when I heard the sports news on the radio.

'And now to golf. The British player, Rollo Hardinge, won the Florida Classic by two shots yesterday. This is the young left-handed golfer's first tournament victory and has earned him a place in next week's Masters Tournament at Augusta.'

I yelled with delight and jumped out of bed in my excitement. The telephone rang in the hall and I guessed that it would be Toby.

'Great news,' he said. 'I trust you were listening to the wireless.' Toby's anti-technology stance had become more extreme as the newspaper industry embraced modern electronic techniques.

'We'd better have a quick one to celebrate. See you in the White Hart at noon, dear boy.'

Toby's invitation was stated briskly enough to sound like a command and I was about to say that I had work to do, when I remembered that I hadn't and said I would be there.

I made a few calls to various friends and acquaintances in the City to see whether any jobs were on offer and met little but gloomy predictions of job losses to come rather than job opportunities. The best responses I had were no more than half-hearted promises to 'have lunch sometime' or 'get that game of golf organised'.

My liquid lunch with Toby raised my spirits as much as it exercised my right arm and we were at one in predicting great things for Rollo Hardinge when he returned to the European golf tour. Why should I worry about grabbing another job in the City when a long and promising and undoubtedly lucrative summer as Rollo's caddie lay ahead? We chatted comfortably about some of the more appealing places we would visit in our respective roles on the golf circuit: Crans-sur-Sierre, Paris and Biarritz, Villa d'Este.

My level of euphoria was still sky high as I tried to do a few domestic tasks in my flat. With my concentration impaired by several pints of Bass and an attempt to keep one eye on a Gary Cooper western in black and white, it was not a successful effort. I was relieved when the telephone shrilled and delighted to hear Rollo's voice, clear and bright from Florida.

After congratulating him on his victory and discussing the renowned Augusta golf course I asked him when he would be back in Europe. 'You'll be back for the Spanish Open? That track at Valencia is a real brute, but you'll enjoy it.'

'No, I'm afraid not, Chris. I'm going to hang on in America. Try to play the tour full time. I'm exempted into virtually every tournament; it'll do my golf the world of good.'

'Oh,' was all I could say. Goodbye euphoria.

'I'm sorry, Chris. I feel I've let you down. But you'll get another bag to carry, if you want it. Anyway, you're earning a fortune in the City. I'll be over for one or two tournaments. The Open of course. See you then.'

I didn't want to embarrass Rollo by telling him that I had lost my City job; it smacked of moral blackmail and he had his own career to think about. But this second hefty kick from the fates in the lower abdomen made me realise that I would now have to give some serious thought to my own future.

'What about the Ryder Cup?' was my parting shot. 'You won't get many points if you're full time in the States.' (Qualification for the European Ryder Cup team is based on a player's results in European tournaments in the ten months preceding the biennial fixture.)

'I'll have to rely on a wild card. If I do well over here . . .'

Rollo was right; the Ryder Cup captain has the prerogative to select up to three wild cards from outside the Order of Merit and if Rollo continued to play with such success he would probably make the team. I just managed to wish him luck. As I put the phone down I experienced an almost physical surge of bitterness at this reverse.

Rollo did indeed attend the Open but not with me as his caddie. He brought his new caddie over from America. And I didn't blame him. She was a long-limbed Californian girl with a flawless skin, a dazzling smile and the sort of carefree grace that makes you look, look again and then smile right back. I couldn't compete.

By the time of the Open Championship in July I was confident that I would have another job in the City. During the next few weeks I scoured the appointments pages in the newspapers and in the financial magazines and wrote hundreds of letters. But many companies did not even acknowledge my application and I did not receive a single invitation for an interview.

In my desperation I even attended a network marketing conference. It was at a London hotel and turned out to be yet another of those American techniques for selling products direct to the public. We were addressed by a large and eager American lady who told us how networking was organised and how much money we could make; then by an engineer who took us through a range of 'personal security' products; and finally by a tall, middle-aged American who ran the British company and spoke about the 'wunnerful opportunities that lay in store for us and the wunnerful people back home who devoted their lives to his wunnerful company'. A messianic gleam came into his eyes when he spoke about the huge amounts of commission we could earn by selling the products.

When he began a rambling simile about life being akin to a room with dozens of doors, each of which could be the opening to great success, my own eyes turned towards the door marked exit which I immediately used.

It had been a thoroughly depressing evening. As I walked towards the Underground through the drizzle of the late evening I began to understand the hopelessness of a man who feels he'll never get another job.

Chapter 3

My walk had now brought me to my destination, the house of my new boss, a young professional golfer called Ben Massey. I was looking forward to my dinner with him; he was good company as well as a good golfer.

It was at the Open that I first met Ben Massey and it was for Ben I caddied when, halfway through the championship, I took over his bag from his elder brother, David.

At the time I wondered how they could possibly be brothers, so unalike were they. Ben had the perfect build for a golfer; at a shade under six feet tall he packed a lot of power into a solid frame. Like many golfers he had hands like small shovels and forearms the size of most people's thighs. I learned that in his youth he had done a lot of weight training to build himself up. Ben looked like a cruiser-weight boxer who had beefed himself up in order to move into the heavyweight class. In contrast, David was a real heavyweight, built to an entirely different scale. Although only two or three years older than Ben, I noticed that his waistline was already beginning to expand; whereas Ben had neat and regular features, David had a rather fleshy nose above thick, slightly drooping lips which gave his face a sullen look.

These differences were explained later when I found out that they were stepbrothers. Then the hoary old debating points about heredity and environment tripped through my mind; nature or nurture, the debate would continue until the crack of doom.

Ben Massey's pretty Victorian house – announced by a small sign as Myrtle Cottage – now came into view and as I walked towards the front door I saw a black BMW sitting on the edge of the drive. I knew that Ben had recently acquired a Mercedes, as befitted his new financial status. Although the golfing pundits as yet adjudged him to be young and promising, rather than an established presence on the tournament scene, he had already won nearly a million pounds. Then I remembered that David Massey owned a black BMW but he was one of the last people I wanted as a fellow-guest at dinner.

Quite a chunk of Ben's new income had clearly been invested in his house. Myrtle Cottage had been extended here and there and the alterations had been done with a sure hand; no aesthetic vandalism was discernible. The house had a sizable garden, full of mature trees which formed a natural alliance with the woodlands beyond. I knew that there was a golf course on the other side of the trees and that the house was only half an hour's drive from Heathrow. Ben had planned a sensible location for his home; such is the international scope of golf these days that professional golfers seem to spend half their lives in airports.

The old-fashioned bell-pull didn't seem to produce any sound so I knocked hard on the gleaming brass lion's head knocker. The lack of a response made me glance at my watch to check that I wasn't early. I bashed on the door again. Right day, right time, but still no reply. I assumed that on this beautiful evening Ben was probably in his back garden. I knew that Ben had no pets, so I could walk around the house without fear of an attack by some ravening dog.

I went through a gate and strolled quietly along the side of the house. There was no one in the conservatory and I called out Ben's name as I reached the lawn. There was no answer and I walked round the edge of the grass and saw that Ben had made himself a practice putting green and dug a bunker alongside.

There were a couple of tables on the terrace at the back of the house. A mug and plate, the remains of tea and sandwiches, and several crushed cans of lager lay on one of the tables. If the housekeeping was a bit below standard on the terrace, it was well up to scratch elsewhere. As I peered through a window, I saw a very bright and clean kitchen; Ben was either unusually meticulous for a bachelor or he had a conscientious cleaner. Two cast-iron casseroles sat on the hob. My dinner, I hoped. There was, however, no sign of David or my host.

I walked a few paces to the right to some french windows, cupped my hands to give myself better vision and surveyed a sitting room which stretched the depth of the house. There wasn't any sign of life there, either.

Or was there? I thought I could see a foot protruding from a chair which faced away from me. And was that an elbow resting on the arm of the chair? The light was not particularly good inside the room since the shutters on the front windows were closed. I pressed my face against the pane of glass and strained to see more. It was a foot, the size of which confirmed to me that one of my dinner companions was David Massey. I guessed that he'd given Ben's reserves of lager a searching examination and was now out cold. I pounded on the window and cursed him for not waking up.

I reckoned that David Massey was the reason that a fair proportion of my face and body hurt like hell and was beginning to turn into various and interesting shades of blue, black, purple and red. Suddenly I had a great urge to kick in the window and get at the bastard. But it was Ben's house and he probably would not see my point of view.

The night before I had been well and truly beaten up. Unfortunately I had been close to the state that David Massey was now in and unable to defend myself. Although I was staggering drunk, I could remember the details well.

That morning I had flown into Heathrow after a very successful three-week foray into Europe with Ben. He had played wonderfully consistent golf and had reaped his rewards with second places in the Dutch Open and the Scandinavian Masters, and fifth place in the Belgian Classic. He had returned home nearly £100,000 richer and I had benefited to the tune of nearly seven grand.

I had sought out Toby Greenslade and a long lunch was followed by a few sharpeners, as Toby called it, at around five o'clock. By ten o'clock I had degenerated into a state of near-speechlessness and semi-collapse. To my surprise, a cab driver had taken pity on me and had dropped me at my flat. Cabbies normally avoid drunks and who can blame them, but the recession had taken away such little freedoms from most people, even cab drivers.

As I fumbled irritably with the lock on the front door — I could hardly gauge where the door was, let alone the lock — someone called to me from the garden.

''Scuse me, mate, can you give us a hand?'

I gave up the unequal struggle with the lock that was gyrating at such high speed and stumbled down the path towards the voice. The first blow was at the back of the neck, swiftly followed by a jarring kick under the right knee.

Christ, I thought, muggers, and they're serious about

it too. I tried to yell but my effort was stifled by a blow in the mouth and a hefty smack on the side of the head. I hoped that someone might intervene but the constant rumble of traffic from the nearby road overlaid the noise of battle.

My assailants were serious, but they weren't muggers. This was physical violence on a comprehensive scale. It felt as though there were ten of them but, as far as I could make out in the semi-darkness, there were three men each determined to leave his mark. I landed a few solid short punches of my own and was rewarded with some grunts of pain, but as the fists and feet rained on me my only recourse was to roll into a ball and try to protect the delicate parts: the face, ribs, kidneys and groin. I don't think I passed out but I wasn't truly aware of when they ran off. I lay on the ground, both shocked and hurt but also relieved to find that I was alone and that my nightmare had passed.

I've never believed that drunks can become suddenly sober, but the shock of the attack seemed to counter the alcohol in my system and I felt the pain in every bone and muscle.

My first thoughts were why and who? It didn't take an analytical genius to provide the answers. David Massey was the obvious villain; because I had done the same to him at the Open Championship. I'd hammered a very percussive tune on his ribs and he'd ended up in hospital. He clearly wished to do the same to me.

I peered through the windows of Ben's house and reflected that at least I would now have a chance to clear the air with David. If only he'd wake up and let me into the house. And where the hell was Ben?

It was particularly annoying to find no welcome after the huge effort of will it had taken to transport my battered body from Putney to Ascot. I had passed the

17

night in a semi-delirious state, the effects of a day on the booze compounded by the beating I had taken. At dawn I gave up the struggle for sleep, defeated by the impossibility of finding a position of any comfort and by the need to relieve a bursting bladder. My head felt as if someone had levered it open during the night. I tried to sit upright and failed; the pain in my back, where I had been kicked long and hard, was too intense. In the end I rolled carefully out of bed, lowered myself on to the floor and crawled on all fours towards the bathroom. I managed to perch on the lavatory and then roll off afterwards. To my horror I saw that my urine was coloured by blood and realised that, despite my efforts at defensive action, some of the blows had got through to my kidneys and had caused some bleeding.

I wondered how much harm had really been done. A look in the shaving mirror did nothing to cheer me as I saw a lid drooping over a half-closed left eye and swellings and weals scattered across my face. I wouldn't apply for any modelling jobs that week.

Certain of my impending death, I arranged to see my doctor. Later that morning, after a couple of hot baths, I was able to limp around the flat and I even tried a few stretching exercises. I was sure that nothing was broken but decided to keep my afternoon appointment anyway. James Cheyney is a cheerful, red-faced man, who is only a few years older than me but cultivates a sonorous and rather sardonic manner which puts several years on him.

The inevitable delay in Dr Jim's surgery nearly made me late for my train to Ascot. I had been naive enough to think that a four o'clock appointment meant exactly that, but doctors do not play by the same rules as the rest of us. I had spent half an hour thumbing through women's magazines learning how to cope with the menopause, straying husbands and dinners for sixteen. Where were the golf magazines, for heaven's sake?

Jim was busily writing when I walked into his office. It took me some time to lower myself into an armchair and he looked up as I was halfway down. His initial look of surprise quickly turned into a smile.

'Well, well, Chris. You've either given up that silly game of golf and started playing a real game like rugger or you've had an evening out with some money brokers. What happened?'

As I talked he helped me off with my clothes and gently pushed and prodded at my body.

'Nothing broken as far as I can tell. You'd better have some X-rays. Go down to St Luke's. As for your kidneys, drink plenty of water; they should be okay in a day or two. If not, come and see me again.'

At least I still had some medical insurance. Norton Buccleuth had paid the fees up to the end of the year.

My trip on the fabled Network South-East to Ben Massey's home coincided with the beginning of the commuter rush out of the city. Across the aisle of seats, although he was trying to hide his face with the *Financial Times*, I spotted a broker I knew, Mike Slater. Three weeks before I had written to Mike to ask if his firm had any jobs in the offing. So far, I had not had a reply. I abandoned my seat and tapped on the copy of the *Financial Times*.

Startled, he looked up and said, 'Chris? Is it you? What on earth have you been up to?'

'Oh, a slight accident. But what I'm up to is looking for a job. Do you know of anything?'

He looked embarrassed. 'I'm sorry, old boy. Times are hard. Worse than ever, I'm afraid.'

He diverted me by telling me of mutual acquaintances who had lost their jobs or gone broke. The conversation petered out into desultory generalities and Slater eventually left the train with a promise to keep in touch. Fat chance, if he couldn't be bothered even to reply to a letter.

At the back of Myrtle Cottage I stopped my window-peering and hammering and tried to apply some logic to the situation.

Perhaps the garage would give me a clue? I walked round to the other side of the house. The roll-over doors were open and Ben's Mercedes had gone. Ah, maybe Ben was out choosing wine for my dinner. I tried the door from the garage into the house. It was unlocked and I entered the utility room, walked past the washing machine, a large freezer and a boiler and down a corridor and into the kitchen. There was no smell of cooking.

'Look, David, wake up,' I said none too quietly as I opened the door to the sitting room. 'Let's clear the air before Ben gets back.'

He didn't stir. His head was slumped forward on his chest and I grabbed a handful of his thick black hair and jerked his head upright.

David Massey and I would never clear the air. A black hole was all that remained of his left eye. Dried blood and flesh and what looked like small shards of bone lay behind him on the armchair. Stooped over him, I stayed motionless for a moment and then gently laid his head back in its original resting place. I tried to smooth his hair, a useless gesture since it was unkempt at the best of times.

I felt sick, gagged and swallowed hard. I had to do something. Get the hell out of there seemed a good idea. Instead I decided to do what mother had taught me — phone the police. I looked about me for a telephone, saw one on a window seat at the far end of the room and moved towards it. As I passed the mirror above the fireplace I looked up and saw an unfamiliar face in the mirror. It was puffy, one eye was almost entirely closed and there were red weals, scraped skin and darker shades of blue/black to be seen. It was my face. I stopped and anticipated the deductions of the police: I'd been on the wrong end of a fight with David Massey and taken my revenge. Simple.

I had a quick look at Massey's hands and saw that there wasn't a mark on them. But he'd orchestrated the attack on me, hadn't he; and I had taken my revenge. Simple.

But maybe I had an alibi. There was the visit to Dr Cheyney and Mike Slater had seen me on the train.

My next thoughts were of Ben. Where was he? His absence was enough to make him the prime suspect. Had he finally lost control in the face of his stepbrother's provocation?

I couldn't believe that he was capable of murder. There had to be an explanation. There'd better be, or I was out of a job again.

With that selfish thought I dialled 999.

Chapter 4

I waited in the kitchen for the police to arrive, sipping at a cup of tea. I couldn't stay in the same room as the dead man, but couldn't think of anything but him and the scene of our first meeting at the Open.

For some time after the double blow of my dismissal from Norton Buccleuth and my loss of Rollo Hardinge to the lucrative environment of the American golf tour, I remained optimistic about finding a new job in the City, despite the recession. I was still just the right side of thirty and was reasonably experienced. In the old days my golf handicap of two would certainly have got me a job, but not in the cold climate of the nineties.

The lack of response to my formal applications for jobs did not worry me so much as the apologetic but definite rebuffs from my City acquaintances. With one or two exceptions, they had become amazingly difficult to meet for a drink or a chat, were usually 'in conference with a client' and were invariably 'desperately busy'. Invitations for a day's golf, and I had been a popular choice because of my low handicap, were noticeable by their infrequency, except from others of the City's unemployed.

Even my friend and neighbour of many years, Mrs Bradshaw, an elderly lady whose energy belied her years, was not around to offer her company. She had gone off on a lengthy cruise with a group of friends, during which they were to combine visits to many of the

world's cultural hot-spots with a series of on-board
bridge tournaments.

At first I enjoyed the sudden release from my daily
routine; it was a treat to lie in bed and listen to the radio
and not have to put on a suit and go to work. But I
missed my involvement in professional golf. If you can't
be out there on the course actually hitting the shots and
holing the putts in an important professional event, the
next best thing is to be standing by the player's side and
helping him to win. I had brought a few winners home
in my time and those memories would never dim. But I
wanted to have the chance to add to them.

Calls to some of the other caddies to discover if any
of the pros were looking for a new bag carrier elicited
nothing much of interest. Those golfers who curse and
moan their way along the fairways of Europe, ill-
tempered and mean-spirited, invetcratc throwers of
clubs and insults in the general direction of their
caddies, were of course open to offers. But not from
me. And the younger players were usually too broke to
offer a proper wage and tended to rely on friends to
caddie for them, or carted their clubs around themselves.

I went to one or two tournaments as Toby's guest but
the pleasure of being there was muted since I was not
properly a part of the event. I had no role except to chat
to Toby and his cronies and to deplete the sponsor's
seemingly limitless supplies of food and drink.

By the time June came round I realised that my
overdraft had reached its limit. Money had become a
serious problem, especially since the mortgage and other
payments on my flat took over a thousand pounds a
month. I negotiated another bank loan, for which Toby
stood as guarantor. He also managed to persuade his
sports editor to give me a little work as a golf reporter. I
attended a couple of amateur tournaments and a

women's professional event on behalf of the *News*. My reports ended up as a couple of lines in a corner of the sports section, which was probably just as well.

Toby was his usual generous self and was ever available to buy me drinks and meals. But there is a limit to how much hospitality you can accept. I became uncomfortable; Toby knew it and laughed it off. He reminded me of the support he'd had from me in times of stress — usually caused by one or more of his women.

At least my golf prospered. I had the time to spend on the practice ground and became a genuine two-handicap player again. I augmented my meagre pocket money by playing skins games with a pair of retired stockbrokers. They were only in their mid-forties. In our skins game we each put up £5 per hole; if there was no outright winner the money was carried over to the next hole. We were then playing for £10. The money mounts up until it is won; you then begin again with £5 units. With units gained for birdies, sandies (up and down from a bunker in two shots) and other awards, it is possible to win useful sums. After I had won over £200 from each of them in one week, I noticed that they sought other playing companions. I didn't blame them; who wants to play golf with a hustler.

My finances reached crisis point in July, when I received the dread summons from my bank manager. He cross-examined me about my job prospects (he was not impressed when I told him I had a casual job three nights a week at a local bookshop) and told me that no more money would be advanced.

'Have you no family who can help?' Mr Tomlinson asked with apparently genuine sympathy.

'No.' I had no intention of asking my father for help. He would certainly have responded but would have taken his chance to encourage me into the family firm.

It had always been his wish that I work for his highly successful computer software concern and I couldn't take his money and disappoint him yet again. I hadn't told him that I was unemployed.

'When do you intend to pay us back?'

'As soon as I get another job.'

'And when is that likely to be, Mr Ludlow?' the bank manager asked as he leaned back in his chair and clasped his hands over his generous belly. 'When we last spoke you were confident of getting another job. But a casual job in a bookshop hardly fills the bank with confidence.' Why was he talking in the abstract about his sodding bank? It was he who had no confidence in me. 'We haven't seen any money entering your account in the last several weeks, only money going out. Now, Mr Ludlow, we have to be very circumspect about lending money to people in your situation. You must reduce your loan by, let's say, a thousand pounds, within thirty days.'

The bastard. 'Thirty days,' I said angrily. 'How can I do that?'

'Well, you could put your flat on the market. If you do that we can give you a little more time. I notice that you've fallen way behind with your mortgage payments. The last thing we want to do is to repossess your flat, but soon we will have no option. I'm sorry, Mr Ludlow, but these are difficult times,' he said piously.

'Yes, difficult times. Made even more bloody difficult by the attitudes of banks like yours. What's the point of repossessing someone's home? What's the point of throwing them out on the streets or on the uncertain mercy of the local council? Of destroying people's self-respect, their dignity, their hope.' I was shouting by this time. My own frustration was pouring out at the injustice of it all.

26

'You lot were glad enough to hand the money out when times were good but where is your support when times are bad?'

'We cannot stand by, Mr Ludlow, and allow you to overreach yourself. The bank . . .'

'You've allowed hundreds of thousands of people to overreach themselves,' I interrupted, 'because of your greed. Greed which fed on your customers' greed. Just as you were greedy enough and stupid enough to lend billions to Third World countries, when a ten-year-old could have told you you didn't have a hope of getting it back.'

Mr Tomlinson was now standing in a vain effort to halt the tirade. I carried on regardless.

'And now you're turning the screw on people like me.' I was also on my feet. 'No doubt you hope to recoup some of the money you've pissed away in the Third World from my misfortunes and the misfortunes of others like me. Got a cosy little arrangement with a local estate agent, have you, Mr Tomlinson, to divvy up the profits?' I finally ran out of breath.

I headed for the door, having well and truly burned my boats.

To my amazement I received a letter from the bank on the following morning; three months' grace on the mortgage was offered and my loan was extended for a further three months.

Two days later I received the bad news about my car, a six-year-old Porsche with over a hundred thousand miles on the clock and a fine collection of envy scratches on the bodywork. If the car were to pass its MOT test the estimate was £1200 to do the essential work. I drove it back to the flat, parked it, locked it and walked down to the nearest pub.

The Open Championship began during the following

week and I was going to be a part of it come hell or high water. The final qualifying round was played on the Sunday and the tournament proper started on the following Thursday. The event, in all its splendour and excitement, was to be played on one of the great links courses on the Kent coast; a barren and wind-blasted stretch of land which looked fit for nothing. It is one of the most unrelenting challenges of a golfer's skill.

I decided to make my way down there, join the queue with the rest of the unattached caddies and try to secure a bag to carry for the week.

My lack of money dictated that I hitch-hike to Kent and, on Monday morning, I stood on the A3, a small bag at my side, and raised a thumb hopefully. At last I had become a real caddie, one of the old school who slept in hedges and − the truth of it hit me − gambled or drank away every penny he earned. Mournfully I reflected that the new breed of caddie, who carried the bag of a superstar, could earn well over a thousand pounds a week.

I eventually got a lift along the M25 from a salesman who, in reply to my polite inquiry about his job, told me in minute detail about all the types of paint he sold; sorry, that he marketed. He was infinitely preferable, however, to the television service engineer who took me along the M2 into Kent and told me in intricate and intimate detail about his sex life.

Chapter 5

I caught a local bus for the last few miles of the journey to the course and headed for the caddie master's hut near the first tee. All the accoutrements of the Open were in place: the huge grandstands around the final hole and at many other points on the course, especially behind the short holes; the tented village where the equipment manufacturers display the latest in golf technology; the massed ranks of the hospitality tents from whence many invited guests fail to make their way on to the course, content with the television pictures and the generous supply of food, drink and convivial company; and all the scaffolding and the miles of cable which are needed by the television companies to cover the event. Service vehicles were edging their way between the avenues of tents, buggies with officials were swooping from point to point and, out on the rolling fairways, where every blade of grass had been tamed to its statutory length, were the people for whom the whole spectacle had been mounted – the players. They were out in force, trying to assess the course, to discover its strong and weak points, to woo it and perhaps conquer it.

The atmosphere, even on a practice day, was intoxicating, like a large glass of vintage Krug on an empty stomach. I longed to be a part of it as never before.

I spotted the caddie master, Bob McGuinness, at the door of his hut and strolled over. He is a likeable Scot who, despite living in Kent for several decades, retains his original Borders accent.

'Good day to you, Chris. You're not looking for a bag, surely? I thought you'd be with one of the top boys.'

'Not this year, Bob. Rollo stayed over in the States and I didn't make any other arrangements. I've been very busy with my other job.' I couldn't bear to admit that I was unemployed. 'But I thought I'd have my usual week at the Open. So what's going?'

'Nothing much. There's a pro from Yorkshire who's been let down by his caddie. Bill Lloyd, he came through the qualifying.'

'What's he like?'

Bob made a rolling motion with his right hand. 'So, so. He's been around a while. He might make it through to the final rounds if he listens to you. He's on the putting green, in the brown sweater and the red cap.'

The red baseball cap was the only patch of colour to be seen on Bill Lloyd, a man of medium height with a pale face and glasses. Wispy strands of fair hair straggled from under the stained cap. His brown corduroy trousers showed a stretch of dark sock above scuffed black shoes.

I smiled at him and asked if he needed a caddie.

'Yeah,' he grunted, 'as long as you don't charge an arm and a leg.'

'Fifty quid for practice days, seventy-five for the real thing and five per cent of the prize money if you qualify for the final two days.'

After some haggling, Lloyd pointed at his bag and told me we were off the tee in twenty minutes. Would I get him some chocolate from the professional's shop? He didn't offer me any money to make the purchase. Oh well, a few of his golf balls could always make up the discrepancy if he made a habit of it.

Lloyd had the charm of a New York cab driver but he
was a reasonable golfer with an economical swing and a
neat method. I wondered whether he had the power to
sustain his game when the wind blew, as it surely would
at some stage. To add to my misgivings, I realised that
his reading of putts was woeful, an impossible handicap
on the mammoth greens with their severe undulations
and racy surfaces. Some of the slopes were enough to
give you vertigo.

For the first four holes I tried to give him some advice
about the pace and lines of his putts. He paid little heed
and finally said: 'I'm the pro and you're the caddie. I'll
ask for your advice if I need it.'

We spoke little thereafter and Lloyd told me to be at
the practice ground at 7.30 the next morning.

I had to find a bed for the night and a cheap one. I
had twenty-five pounds in my pocket and no credit
cards, which had been withdrawn by the bank some
weeks before. Lloyd refused to pay me my first day's
fee.

'You'll get it at the end. That'll make sure you turn
up, won't it?'

That was clear enough and I went in search of Toby
Greenslade. He should know of a likely billet for a poor
and hungry caddie. He did; it was the sitting room floor
in the house he and a few journalist friends had rented
near the course. I stayed there for the rest of the
championship.

On the morning of the first day of the Open I awoke
after a very short sleep. My eyes were gritty and runny
from lack of rest. Toby and his friends were incapable
of going to bed before 3 a.m., but how could I
complain? On the contrary, I was grateful to have a
roof over my head; I had no wish to ape the old-style

31

caddies completely by sleeping under a hedge.

I padded towards the kitchen to make some tea. While I waited for the kettle to boil, I picked up a large bundle of newspapers which lay in the hall. Most of the nationals were represented.

The *Daily Post* lay on top and I turned to its back page.

'European Stars in Punch Up' blared the headline and the report began:

Two of European golf's finest, the volatile Spanish ace, Ramon Gonzales ('the Ram' to his friends) and the tough British Masters champion, Nick Spencer, amazed spectators at the swank Memorial Tournament in New Jersey last weekend. The two stars, certain to be team mates in Europe's Ryder Cup side in just over a month's time, scuffled after the first extra hole of their play-off for the trophy. Officials had to separate them and Spencer was reported to have said, 'I'll fill that spick in before he's much older.' Let's hope he doesn't do it during the Ryder Cup.

As I finished the article Toby walked in.

'Good God, what are you doing up?' I asked.

'Couldn't sleep. Too much brandy, dear boy. Should know better. Any tea?'

With eyes squinting Toby looked at the *Post*, pronounced it a load of rubbish and subsided into a chair.

'The wind's getting up,' he said.

I looked out at the great gobbets of cloud that were staining the window-framed sky before moving briskly on. I reckoned that my work with Bill Lloyd would be confined to two rounds. He would be very lucky to qualify for the final two days, when the field is reduced to about seventy players.

My prediction was accurate. Bill Lloyd was sunk by the extra demands made by the strong gusts and especially by the fierce finish to the course. Three par-four holes of over 450 yards into the prevailing wind, with a short hole of 240 yards playfully inserted amongst them, proved too much for a club professional. His short game gave way under the pressure and his putting became more and more wayward.

My own few attempts to encourage and counsel him met with baleful glares and his habit, after playing a shot, of throwing his club in the general direction of me or his bag didn't add to the pleasure of working for him. I had known dogs with better manners.

Lloyd's two rounds in the mid-70s ensured his early journey home to Yorkshire. After he had signed his card he told me to wait by the caddie master's hut.

'I'll change my shoes and bring you your money. Two hundred-odd quid for the privilege of having a golf bag carried. I'd have been better off with the mother-in-law as a caddie,' he muttered.

I would not take the bait, but smiled and wished him better luck in next year's event. The important thing was to get my money.

I chatted for a while to Bob, the caddie master, and realised that Lloyd was taking a very long time to change his shoes. Perhaps he was having a drink; unlikely, I thought. With suspicions stirring I walked rapidly back towards the players' changing rooms. A security guard barred my way. Caddies are not allowed anywhere in the clubhouse and certainly not in the players' changing rooms.

I brandished my watch at him and said: 'I nearly

walked off with my governor's watch. He's off back to Yorkshire, he'll be livid.'

'If that's the prat with the red cap, it serves him right. You've missed him anyway, he went off towards the car park a few minutes ago. Good riddance.'

Bill Lloyd certainly knew how to win friends. But I didn't wait to discuss his merits with the security guard; I ran around the corner of the clubhouse towards the competitors' car park. I knew Lloyd's car, since I had put his clubs away two nights ago. It was a Volvo estate car; in brown, of course.

The car park was earmarked not only for competitors but for officials as well and contained several hundred cars. I ran down the rows and tried to spot Lloyd's car. Bloody hell, I wasn't even going to get my measly couple of hundred quid. I was on the brink of giving up the search when I glimpsed the red cap about fifty yards away. That was him.

I crouched low behind an adjacent line of cars and sprinted towards him. As I got level with him he was leaning into a Volvo. I crept around one more car and came up behind him just as he sat in the driver's seat and reached out to swing his door shut. Grabbing his arm with my left hand, I pulled hard and then slammed the car door with my right. With a satisfying thud the heavy door trapped his arm and he yelled with pain. I leaned a bit harder on the door.

'Where's my money, you miserable shit?'

'You aren't worth that sort of money,' he said. A foolish remark when your arm is firmly trapped in a car door by someone you owe money to; someone who really needs that money.

I pushed a lot harder on the door and said quietly through the gap: 'Would you like me to break your arm?'

Lloyd saw the force of my argument and nodded towards his coat which was lying on the passenger seat. 'Take your fucking money. My coat. Inside pocket.'

I released the door and, as he groaned with pain, reached in and took the car keys. Just a spot of insurance. I walked around the car, opened the passenger door and extracted two hundred and twenty pounds from Lloyd's wallet. His face was even whiter than usual.

'What about my tip, Mr Lloyd?'

His answer was predictable and I took another twenty pounds anyway. I slammed the door, opened the back of the car and took six new balata golf balls from his bag. After handing him his keys I brandished the balls at him.

'Payment for all the chocolate I bought you,' I said. 'You should give it up, it's bad for your complexion.'

I stepped quickly out of the way and took refuge behind a neighbouring car just in case he tried to run me down.

Lloyd weaved off between the rows of vehicles. The adrenalin which had been pumping round my body subsided and I sat on the bonnet of a nearby car, with my heart thudding and my head and shoulders drooping. What a way to earn a living.

A middle-aged man walked by, paused and asked me if I needed any help. I thought of asking him for a job but merely reassured him that I would be okay in a moment or two. Thank God nobody had witnessed my fracas with Lloyd, though it would probably have done more damage to the tight sod's reputation than to mine.

I have rarely felt so cast down by the misery and petty meanness of man. My natural resilience had almost ebbed away and Lloyd's attempt to do me out of my meagre fee was almost the final plug pulled. His was the nastiest of a whole series of rejections.

But a wallow in self-pity is unsavoury at the best of times and serves no useful purpose. So, I stood upright, shook my head and practised a smiling confident face. I would go and find Toby and buy a bottle of fizz for us to share. I could hitch-hike back to London tomorrow.

Chapter 6

In order to avoid the worst of the crowds I cut diagonally across the car park and around the back of a row of hospitality tents. As I was about to round the corner of the last one I heard two voices, loud and angry. I paused and considered whether to turn away; I could do without intruding on someone else's argument. I'd had my fill for one day.

The quieter voice said: 'All I ask is that you keep my clubs clean. That's the first thing. It's also the caddie's responsibility to make sure that there are only fourteen clubs in the bag, David. How the bloody hell did you manage to put two sodding putters in the bag? Fifteen clubs. It's just as well I saw them on the first hole. Fifteen clubs. A two-shot penalty, in the Open, for God's sake.'

The louder, rougher voice replied: 'Stuff your putters, and your two shots. And you.'

'Thank you, David. I take it that ends our business relationship.'

I had edged around the corner by this time and recognised one of the participants in this set-to as Ben Massey.

The next words came from David, who didn't seem keen to prolong his caddying days. 'You bastard. I've had you up to here. Fucking superstar.'

David saw me as I came fully into view around the tent. Two women who were carrying trays of sandwiches were watching with great interest from a safe distance.

37

David pulled something out of his back pocket — a Stanley knife. 'Your golfing days are over,' he said.

I've seen many partings of the ways between golfer and caddie, some of them in the middle of a round, but never one as bitter as this. Raised voices and some not very original insults were the rule; a knife fight was a new one on me.

'Stop it,' I yelled. As I moved towards them I took my jacket off and wrapped it around my left arm. It was cotton and wouldn't give me much protection but it seemed the right thing to do.

'Keep out of this,' screamed David, but I kept on going, dived under his flailing right arm and knocked him on to the grass. He was big and powerful and I didn't fancy my chances in a long fight. He'd probably got away with bullying other people all his life and I knew that I had to dent his confidence in his strength straight away. As he started to struggle upright I jabbed at his eyes with my fingers and knew from his screech that I had made contact.

I guessed that his next move would be a sweep with the knife. Over it came and I used both hands to grab his wrist. He was thumping me with his other hand and it hurt. Despite my efforts to twist his arm he wouldn't drop the knife. In the end I sank my teeth into the fleshy part of his hand and bit as hard as I could. Not your Clint Eastwood, but effective. He screamed and dropped the knife and launched himself at me. His elbow caught me a glancing blow on the nose. Christ, it was agony and tears sprang from my eyes.

That was when I lost my temper. All the frustration and bitterness poured out of me and swamped the powerful if cumbersome body of David Massey. My memory of what happened is only shadowy but I think I wanted to kill him.

When two security guards and a policeman finally wrenched me off Massey I had him pinned against the corner of a tent and had pounded him senseless.

Quite a crowd had gathered and, as the policeman, breathing hard, fumbled some handcuffs out of his pocket, there were some muttered cries of 'bloody lunatic'. I realised that they meant me.

Two members of the St John's Ambulance Brigade were tending David Massey by this time and he was beginning to groan. Ben Massey looked down at him and said, 'He'll live. Unfortunately.' He saw the policeman about to snap the handcuffs on me and intervened. 'You should save those for my brother. He was about to carve his name on me with that Stanley knife. This guy saved my bacon. So you leave him alone.'

'It's still grievous bodily harm, sir.'

'You'd prefer to be dealing with murder? Because you might have been if it weren't for him. I mean, look at the size of my brother, will you.'

All of us ended up in the mobile police station which was situated on the course. All, that is, except David Massey who had been carted off to hospital. I asked for and got some painkillers because both my hands and my nose had suffered damage.

After many questions and statements, including accurate ones from the two girls with the sandwiches who had seen and heard the whole incident, Ben Massey told the police that he would not press charges against his brother, as long as no action was taken against me.

The police, despite their protestations, were obviously relieved to be rid of us and contented themselves with giving me a severe warning. They were there to enjoy the golf.

They gave us an escort through a substantial

gathering of reporters who were waiting to shout questions at Ben Massey. The Open Championship not only attracted the world's golfing press, but also more than a smattering of tabloid journalists who were there to uncover anything of interest about the sporting superstars; the more unsavoury the better.

We kept our heads down and said the usual 'no comment' into the microphones which were thrust in our faces. We were having a very tough passage as we pushed and shoved our way towards the waiting police car.

'Is it true that your brother tried to kill you?' yelled one intrepid seeker-after-truth in Ben's ear.

'Don't be bloody stupid,' Ben shouted, his patience clearly frayed.

'But he attacked you with a knife?' shouted another.

'Just a disagreement. There was no knife,' lied Ben.

An American voice broke through from the ring of reporters. It came from a broad-shouldered man with jet-black hair and a droopy moustache which was noticeably lighter in colour.

'You European golfers seem to make a habit of brawling,' he drawled. 'Do you think you'll all lose your tempers when you get beat at the Ryder Cup?'

As we were at last pushed into the back of the car I took a long look at the American's sardonic face and suddenly realised what was odd about him. His moustache was its natural colour, his hair was decidedly not.

We bumped across one of the service roads and Ben said, 'You used to caddie for Jack Mason, didn't you? And Rollo?'

I nodded.

'Who are you carrying for tomorrow?'

'No one. We missed the cut.'

'Do you fancy a job with me?'

'Not half.'

'Is five hundred pounds against seven and a half per cent of my prize money OK?' It was more than generous and, with a handshake that made me jump with pain, the deal was done.

'What about your brother?'

'My stepbrother. I'll take care of him. I'll see him in hospital tonight. He won't bother either of us.'

'Take care of him?'

'In the only way he understands.'

I looked hard at Ben, taken aback by the fierceness of his tone.

He relaxed and smiled. 'Money,' he said. 'He's only interested in money. See you on the practice ground at nine-thirty.'

I got out of the police car and walked down a side road to Toby's rented house. All the lights were on but only Toby was there to greet me.

'Where are the others?' I asked.

'I sent them off in hot pursuit of Ben Massey. But Christopher Ludlow, caddie and pugilist extraordinaire, will give me a little exclusive for my rat-faced, intellectually challenged editor.'

'No, he won't.'

'Oh, come on, Chris. Have a glass of fizz. I'll only have to make it up otherwise.'

'That's what you usually do, isn't it?'

'Now then, walls have ears. Just a few quotes.'

'How about "Down-at-heel caddies brawl for young star's favours"? That's the level of the *News*, isn't it?' I said nastily.

'OK, OK. But I need a strong story to counteract the *Daily Post*'s effort.'

'Oh? What's that?'

'An old chestnut about Ross Bentley. Read it tomorrow, I won't spoil it for you.'

Ross Bentley was one of the best-known golfers in Europe and the most successful Ryder Cup captain ever. Under his leadership Europe had regained the Ryder Cup in the mid-eighties and never relinquished it; he was about to take the helm for the fifth time. He had been one of the most accomplished golfers in the world during the decade or so from 1972 when he won the first of his two Open Championships; he had confirmed his quality by becoming the first Englishman to win the Masters at Augusta.

Not only had Ross Bentley managed to earn great sums of money during his years of prominence but he had invested it wisely. People said that this was mainly due to his wife, Louise. They made an idyllic couple and complemented each other perfectly. Bentley was lively and gregarious, with a restless and inquiring mind that gave him an opinion on everything and a fine facility for expressing those opinions. He had always had lots of charm and his great success as a sportsman had added immeasurably to his presence.

Louise was the daughter of a Parisian banker and she brought considerable wealth to the marriage and, even more important, a sharp intelligence. Beautiful and elegant, Louise had overseen every aspect of Ross Bentley's career. She had applied a smooth patina to his rougher surfaces; for example, she taught him to speak French and to appreciate good food and wines. They led the sort of cosmopolitan life that the previous generation of golfers could never have imagined. Among their various properties were houses at Cap Ferrat and in Belgravia.

Locker-room gossip had it that Bentley originally had no wish to captain the Ryder Cup but that Louise saw it as a chance to rejuvenate his earning power as a professional golfer. Despite his journalism and his work as a golf course designer, the big money endorsements had been diminishing. Louise was right again, as Bentley once more became one of the pre-eminent figures in European golf as a result of his Ryder Cup successes.

The only thing missing from their marriage was children.

Under pressure from Toby I eventually gave him enough information about my encounter with David Massey to make a story, anodyne though we both knew it would appear to his voracious editor.

Toby noticed me wince as I unscrewed the top from a bottle of mineral water.

'Serves you right for trying to drink that poison,' he growled. 'Pour some champagne down your throat and pour that water over your hands. Actually, I've got a better idea − for your hands, that is.'

Toby disappeared into the kitchen and I heard a door slam and a muffled curse. He reappeared with a packet of frozen peas.

'It's about the only thing in the freezer,' he complained. 'Wrap this around your knuckles. It will reduce the swelling. Honest. I use them for really bad hangovers. On my head, that is.'

He was right. Bliss.

Toby was right to describe the story in the *Daily Post* as an old one; it went back over two decades. But it still had some potency. 'Shadow in Ryder Cup Captain's Past' was its banner headline, followed by, 'Ross Bentley's 1972 Open victory a fraud, claims US source.'

I read on with great interest as the report explained

how Bentley, playing in the penultimate pair on the final day, had scored a brilliant final round of sixty-six to win the Open Championship by one shot from the American player, Scott Hampson.

A film, recently discovered in the offices of the American TV company, Univision, shows Bentley's final putt which won the 1972 Open. The British golfer marked his ball and then moved his marker sideways to clear the line for his playing partner. BUT HE FAILED TO REPLACE HIS BALL ON THE ORIGINAL SPOT. The penalty for such an infringement is one shot and Bentley would therefore have tied with Scott Hampson and been involved in a play-off for the Championship over eighteen holes.

Comments, both for and against Bentley, then followed and the most sensible came from a member of the rules committee of the Royal and Ancient Golf Club, the body which, together with the United States Golf Association, governs the game.

The rules committee at the 1972 Open Championship were made aware of Bentley's alleged breach of Rule 20 a few days after the end of the Championship. Since the tournament was over and the player had not placed his ball any nearer the hole and since his final putt was one of less than a foot it was deemed equitable to allow his score to stand.

Toby glanced at the report, sniffed and deemed it 'very old hat to the cognoscenti'.
'Well, I didn't know about it,' I protested. 'And

technically Bentley should have been docked a shot. And how do we know how Hampson would have reacted? A birdie on the last hole to tie the Open is one thing, a birdie to win is another.'

'Hampson would have blown it anyway. He was never in Ross Bentley's class. The R & A were quite right to do a Nelson. Can you imagine the impracticalities of bringing everyone back for a play-off? A load of nonsense,' Toby pronounced in magisterial tones.

'What really interests me,' he continued, 'is why the story has reared its head again. It was over twenty years ago. Who cares? There are better stories about than that. Even the *Post* can't be struggling that badly, surely.'

'Someone obviously wants to embarrass Bentley,' I ventured.

'Why?'

'The Ryder Cup? The source was American, wasn't it?'

'As I've remarked before, for someone so young, you hold very cynical views.'

Chapter 7

Any embarrassment over our first bizarre encounter was soon dispelled by Ben Massey when I met him on the practice ground the following day to take up my new job as his caddie.

'Hi, champ,' he greeted me cheerfully; and then continued in a much quieter tone, 'Thanks for everything yesterday.'

I grinned and asked him how his stepbrother was faring.

'He'll be out later today. A broken nose, slight concussion and two cracked ribs. Couldn't have happened to a nicer fella.'

Ben now had a grin as wide as a Muirfield bunker.

'The two of you don't get on, then?' I asked, rather foolishly.

'He's been the bane of my bloody life since we first met. Anyway, more of that later. Let's not spoil a nice day. Let's get to work. I want to get up with the leaders today.'

I watched Ben limber up with some pitch shots and short irons; he then progressed to the medium and long irons and hit a few full shots with his three-wood. He had a completely orthodox swing; a wide arc and a finely balanced finish gave him both power and grace. It was lovely to watch.

He certainly got closer to the leaders during that third round. He played as if a great weight had been lifted from his shoulders, as it had, in the shape of fifteen

47

stone of belligerent stepbrother. At one stage during the final round on the following day he got to within two shots of the lead with some fluent and courageous golf. A few mistakes over the final nine holes put him into a tie for sixth place, and his game impressed me immensely. One of Ben's great attributes was his ability to enjoy himself even when the heat of competition was at its fiercest. And I enjoyed every moment too and earned a generous bonus of £3,500.

It was a heartening performance and, although the championship was won by an Australian, European golfers filled eight of the first fifteen places, a distinctly good omen for the Ryder Cup.

Ben's splendid form continued in Europe and our efforts brought him nearly a hundred grand. My share enabled me to look my bank manager in the eye again, not that he wanted to get that close after my recent harangue. Above all, Ben's successes had qualified him for the Ryder Cup team; at the tender age of twenty-two he was about to be tested in the most intense and dramatic form of matchplay yet devised in golf. I would be at his side to savour every morsel of the drama.

Now that dream was unlikely to come true. My run of good luck had ended. The shrill notes of the siren heralded the arrival of an ambulance. Someone banged loudly on the door which I opened to men in various uniforms; ambulancemen, policemen and all the paraphernalia required to record and analyse the scene of a crime.

A policeman in plain clothes took me firmly by the arm and led me into the kitchen.

'I'm Detective Inspector Colley. You must be Mr Ludlow.' He looked around the kitchen. 'Is there any tea on the go? I'll do it. You sit there. It must have been a shock. Tell me about it.'

He busied himself with the kettle and looked in and out of cupboards in a search for sugar. With his mug of tea at last in his hand, he leaned comfortably against one of the kitchen cupboards and tried to lead me in a logical sequence through my story.

I had time to study him and saw a man of about my own age, tall and solid-looking, with a square face and closely cut fair hair. He looked fit and alert, his blue eyes sharp and clear. He had a habit of rolling his head on his shoulders as if to ease some stiffness there. Perhaps he was a swimmer or pushed weights.

Although I had anticipated some pointed questions, they were couched in a reasonably friendly manner. Or was he just softening me up? I tried to put the idea out of my mind; I had clearly been watching too many detective series on television.

'I take it that you're not a professional boxer as well as caddie, so how did you collect the battle scars?'

I explained about the previous evening's fracas and the Inspector came over and looked more closely at the damage.

'Can I see your hands, please sir?' He turned them over and felt the puffiness over the knuckles. 'You got in a few blows of your own, then.'

'Not enough to make any difference.'

'Too many of them, eh? Did you report the incident to your local police?'

'No.'

'That's a pity,' Colley said thoughtfully.

'There wasn't much point,' I said quickly. 'Nothing was broken. I made a visit to my doctor just to make sure.'

'You seem philosophical about it all, Mr Ludlow. You're used to violence, are you?'

'Not at all.'

'Have you any idea who might have done you over?'

'No,' I lied.

'Just a casual mugging, then. Part of the rough and tumble of big-city life. The men saw you were drunk and took their opportunity.'

'I suppose so.'

'How much did they steal from you?'

'Well . . .' I hesitated. 'I, erm, had very little on me. I'm just a caddie and don't have much on me at the best of times and I'd spent everything I had.'

The Inspector looked at me carefully, a watchful smile on his face.

'What about the money your caddying earned you in Europe in the last few weeks? What have you done with that?'

'All in the bank, to help pay my debts.' At least that was true.

'And you didn't extract a few hundred, just to have a good time.'

'A hundred. And I spent it.'

'What about credit cards?'

'They're cancelled, for the time being.'

'Wise man,' the Inspector said without any conviction.

Once again we went over my movements throughout the day and Inspector Colley took a note of my doctor's telephone number and that of Mike Slater.

Seemingly satisfied with my answers he changed tack and started questioning me about Ben's whereabouts. There was nothing I could tell him. While I'd been waiting, I'd carried out a rapid inspection of the upper floor which had revealed nothing much except that he had left in a hurry. A pair of trainers lay in one corner and there were some discarded clothes on the bed. A couple of drawers of a handsome elm chest were half open. This lack of order was in marked contrast to the rest of the house. Ben was a tidy person; even his books were in alphabetical order, and there were many of them, in marked contrast to most professional golfers of his age who confine their reading to golf and girlie magazines.

'It's usually someone in the family,' Colley said wearily, 'and this time it's pretty obvious who the culprit is. Ben's a really promising golfer, isn't he? What a shame.'

'He couldn't murder anybody, let alone his brother. Well, stepbrother, to be accurate.'

'Not even a brother who tried to do some amateur surgery on him with a Stanley knife?'

I looked startled because I hadn't mentioned the incident at the Open Championship and Inspector Colley's face wore a look of triumph. 'I read the papers, Mr Ludlow, especially the sport. There wasn't much brotherly love between those two, was there? More than the usual sibling rivalry, made much worse by their being stepbrothers, I suppose.' He paused. 'How are we to guess what went on between them, what dark currents flowed?'

He refilled his mug with tea and sat down opposite me at the table. 'I drink too much of this stuff. I ought to drink more water, so my wife says, or herbal tea.

'Anyway, I believe that you were the knight in shining armour who rode to Ben Massey's rescue. Is that right, sir? And you put the young David in hospital. Is that right?'

Apart from the look of satisfaction on Inspector Colley's face, I thought that I also saw a hint of contempt.

I tried to explain. 'Yes, I lost my head completely. I was at a very low ebb and I took it out on him.'

'Well, it's all turned out very well for you but not so well for David Massey. You've got your meal ticket and your rival is dead.'

'He wasn't a rival, Inspector,' I said with some heat. 'He was just a bloody embarrassment to Ben.'

'Nastier policemen than me, sir, would make out a very good case that David Massey had you beaten up yesterday in revenge for what you did to him at the Open. You have already shown that you have a violent temper and you took your chance to even matters up when you found David Massey here.'

'That's a load of crap.'

'Yes, probably. I hope your alibis hold up.'

So did I.

Inspector Colley grinned and rolled his head a couple of times from side to side. He was conscious of my gaze and said: 'A bit stiff. Rugby training.'

He got up and said briskly, 'We'd better ring the next of kin. I assume there's a mother or father somewhere.'

'I only know a mother. She lives nearby. There's an address book by the phone.'

Inspector Colley left the room and I tried to collect my thoughts about the tragedy. I did not like the drift of Colley's questions but, as long as the pathologist didn't change his mind about the time of death, I could comfort myself with the thought of my alibis. Thank God I had spoken to Mike Slater; I had been tempted to ignore him and concentrate on the discarded copy of the *Daily Telegraph* appointments section which I had found on my seat. Above all, I could not believe that the intelligent Ben Massey, his future career potent with promise, would commit a murder. But since when did intelligence come into it? I supposed that I might have done David Massey a serious injury at the Open if I hadn't been hauled off him by three other men, and I'm

not a total idiot. But that was a far cry from putting a
bullet through another human being's head. And Ben
seemed to be always in control of himself; even in the
heat of the last round of the Open he retained his poise.
He seemed above it all, almost serene.

There had to be another explanation and it lay with
David. He was a nasty piece of work. How many
enemies did he have? Plenty, I would guess.

Inspector Colley put his head around the kitchen
door. 'She's on her way. Mrs Massey. She sounds like a
determined lady. I wanted to go over there to break the
news, but she insisted on coming here. She only lives a
few minutes away, apparently.'

'Did you tell her?'

'Only that there'd been an accident. To David.'

Chapter 8

On Mrs Massey's arrival I followed Colley into the hall to see a slim woman in dark shorts and a pink T-shirt being admitted by one of the uniformed policemen. It was easy to see that this was Ben's mother. With a slight jolt I realised that I knew her by sight; I had seen her amongst the spectators at the Open because Ben had gone over to chat to her. At the time I had assumed that she was a girlfriend, perhaps a shade old for a man only just in his twenties, but I had wholeheartedly approved of his choice.

The second sight of Mrs Massey, even in these unpromising circumstances, confirmed my first impressions. She was just a few inches over five feet in height but her slender legs gave an impression of greater stature. Even in her casual clothes she looked chic; and her features, framed by tight and curly black hair, kept you looking. Especially into her dark eyes, bright with intelligence and with a very slight oriental shape to the corners.

'Suzi Massey,' she said briskly. 'Where's David? What's wrong? Why are all these people here?'

I was glad that Colley had the rotten job of telling her the news and he did it as gently as he could. He tried to lead her into the kitchen but she shrugged him off.

'Tell me. Now.'

'I'm very sorry, Mrs Massey, but David is dead.'

'Dead?' she repeated softly, as if in wonder. 'How?'

'He's been shot, I'm afraid.'

'You said an accident.'

'I'm afraid we suspect murder.'

I looked away as I saw Suzi Massey's eyes cloud over and she now allowed Inspector Colley to steer her to a kitchen chair, into which she collapsed with a thump.

'Oh, Christ. The poor boy, he never had any luck. Where's Ben? Is Ben all right? I need Ben. Where is he?'

'That's the problem,' said Colley. 'We don't know. And we very much need to talk to him.'

Suzi Massey immediately understood the implication of Colley's words. 'If you're suggesting Ben had anything to do with this, Inspector, forget it. Ben wouldn't harm a soul.'

'I'm sorry, Mrs Massey, but we have to eliminate him . . .'

'Yes, yes,' she interrupted, 'but you don't understand. You wouldn't believe what Ben put up with, ever since they were boys. He used to take the blame for David's antics a lot of the time. And never complained. No, no, not Ben.'

'But he's disappeared,' Colley said quietly, 'and in a hurry, too. And his passport seems to have gone with him.'

Suzi Massey slammed her fist on to the table and said fiercely: 'It isn't Ben. Why should he? He has everything to look forward to. There's nothing mean or rotten about him. If it had been the other way round . . .'

'What do you mean?'

'What I mean, Inspector, is that Ben is everything that David never was. Poor David was trouble all the way, lazy and mean-spirited, a thief and deeply jealous of Ben. Talk about sibling rivalry. Christ, David took it on to a new plane. He tried to demean everything Ben did. He even stole the golf trophies he won as a boy. We tried to help him, to show we loved him, but he never responded, never improved. And I don't think he ever would have.'

'Can we do anything to help?' Colley asked sympathetically. 'Contact anyone? His father, for instance, he must be told.'

'No, I'll do that,' Suzi said. 'He's at a conference in Madrid. It's best that I tell him.'

Suzi asked to see David's body and, after some hesitation, Colley took her into the living room.

While they were next door I leafed through Ben's address book which Colley had left on the kitchen table. I jotted a few numbers down, including Suzi Massey's, that of Ben's agent and any names that sounded like those of possible girlfriends. If Ben had bolted he was likely to have bolted into sympathetic arms.

The door to the kitchen opened and Suzi, white in the face, collapsed again into a chair. I offered her tea and she asked for whisky. David Massey's body was being taken out of the house as I went in search of alcohol.

I decided I could do with one myself and joined Suzi in a Scotch. There was plenty available since I had found a gallon bottle of the stuff in a corner of the living room. I remembered that Ben had finished well up the field in the Scottish Open that year and the Scotch was one of the sponsor's products. It was hardly touched; it needed a few evenings at the tender mercy of Toby Greenslade to make a proper dent in it.

Suzi seemed to notice me properly for the first time. 'You're Ben's new caddie, aren't you? Chris? Yes, he talks about you. Where is he, Chris?'

I couldn't help her any more than she could help Inspector Colley, who, with a diffidence appropriate to the circumstances, had questioned her about Ben's likely whereabouts. We were both to make formal statements on the following day and Colley offered me a lift to the nearest railway station.

Suzi intervened: 'I'll drop Chris off. I go past the station.'

'Are you sure you want to drive?' asked Colley. 'I don't want to be rude, but are you fit to drive?'

'Oh, come on, Inspector, one whisky?'

'No, Mrs Massey, I didn't mean the whisky, more the reaction to . . .'

'Yes, of course. Thank you, Inspector.' She managed a smile. 'I'll be fine.'

As we moved through the hall Colley asked me if I had all the phone numbers I needed from Ben's address book. For a rugby player he was quite intelligent.

So off we went in Suzi's little white Citroën. After a few hundred yards she asked me if I fancied a quick drink. I realised that not only would I like a quick drink but I would very much like to have it with Suzi Massey. I was badly in need of food too since nothing solid had passed my lips since midday.

We were soon sitting at a table in the lounge bar of an archetypal thatched Surrey pub. The fact that much of the interior, under the low ceilings, was authentic told me that the big battalions of the beerage had been kept well away from it. There wasn't a plastic beam nor fake log to be seen.

'Nice pub,' I said.

'Yes. It's been in the same family for nearly two hundred years. How about beer and sandwiches?'

'I'll do it.'

'No. Let's spend some of Garfield's money. He's got more than you.'

'Who's Garfield?' I asked, though I knew.

'My husband,' Suzi said, without any discernible warmth.

We were halfway through our pints of Tetley's when the sandwiches arrived, great doorsteps of wholemeal bread with several inches of filling in between.

'Dainty, aren't they?' she said with a smile. Not much conversation ensued as I attacked the mountains of food. Suzi took a couple of bites and then put her plate to one side.

I decided that it was foolish to avoid the issue of David's death and Ben's disappearance and questioned Suzi as to where he might be in the hope that she might tell me something she would not tell the police.

'Search me,' she replied. 'I don't think there's a special girl at the moment. He's playing the field, as young men so arrogantly put it. I suppose he's quite a catch, isn't he?'

She realised what she had said and her head dropped. 'God, I hope he's okay.' There were tears in her voice and I turned my stool slightly so that I could hide her from the rest of the room. Suzi looked up, grabbed a napkin, put it to her face and said, 'I'm all right. Don't worry. He'll contact me, or maybe you, as soon as he's ready.'

'Me?'

'Yes. He's got a high opinion of you. Because of your support and advice when he's playing and, of course, because you rescued him from David. He feels he knows you and that you wouldn't let him down.'

'Anybody would have . . .' I started.

'No, they wouldn't, not these days. They'd have looked the other way and afterwards have said how awful it was. "Don't know what the country's coming to," they'd say, wouldn't they?'

Suzi recommended I try the cider because it was made on the premises. It was murky, as dry as a bone and had a marvellous flavour.

'As you probably know, I had Ben before I met Garfield. We got married about fifteen years ago when Ben was seven and David ten. Garfield had been through a very messy divorce. His ex-wife was an alcoholic and that's why he got custody of David. I felt sorry for him and I think he did for me. We sort of fell into marriage and we hoped the boys would get on well, be company for each other.'

'But they didn't?'

'No. There was trouble from the start. You see, Ben was intelligent and he was also gifted at sport. David was not; he was lazy and overweight, even at the age of ten. And he didn't like the competition. I can understand that. There he was, the apple of his father's eye and getting all the attention he wanted when along comes a stepmother. She takes a lot of that attention away from him. Not only that but she brings along another boy who can do all the things he finds difficult. No wonder there were problems.'

'Did your husband transfer his affection to Ben, the talented younger boy?'

'Not specially. After the gesture of taking me on for better or worse I think he tried to ignore Ben. He was just interested in me. Couldn't keep his hands off me in the early days. In marked contrast to now, I might add,' she said with a laugh.

I wondered whether Suzi was chatting so openly about her personal life because of the terrific shock she had just suffered or if she was marking my card very heavily. I hoped it was the latter.

I asked what Mr Massey did for a living and learned that he was an accountant with a large international firm.

'He's away a lot. They do a lot of business in Europe. It suits me.'

60

'So, a less than perfect marriage?'

'Well, he's been good to me in many ways. All the trappings are there; a comfortable home, plenty of money, holidays abroad, the theatre, dinners, etc. But I sometimes think of him as the hollow man; there's quite a lot missing. For instance, I've hardly ever seen him read a book or heard him discuss one. He takes one book – one, for Christ's sake – on our summer holiday.

'And I would like to work. I actually have a brain. But he likes me to be at home all the time. He sees me as a typical suburban hausfrau. He likes me to wear lipstick and a nice frock for when the conquering hero returns. He actually buys ghastly frilly underwear for me. Black, of course.'

I had a swift salacious vision of her clad only in her black frillies.

Suzi looked intently across the table at me. 'Forgive me, Chris, I've probably embarrassed you and I've certainly embarrassed myself. Rattling on like the agony column in a women's magazine. I'm sorry. Inspector Thing was probably right, a terrible shock plus alcohol is a recipe for carelessness, not to mention grave indiscretion.'

'What about Ben's father?' I asked her, in an effort to smooth things over. 'Does he keep in touch?'

'No, not really,' Suzi said vaguely.

Before I could ask her anything more on the subject, she got up and said she'd drop me at the station. As I prepared to leave she pressed a card into my hand and her lips firmly to my bruised cheek. 'Here's my number.' I didn't tell her I already had it.

Chapter 9

The tabloid newspapers swooped on the story like crows on a rotting carcass. It took little time the following day for the connection to be made between a dead man called David Massey and a rising young star of the golf world. When the police stated that they were hoping to interview the dead man's stepbrother, Ben Massey, the national newspapers were in full flight.

Even before the real hue and cry began, I received a telephone call from Ben's agent, Hugo Prince. He called himself Ben's business manager and the more grandiose title was not inappropriate since he provided an efficient service for him and a few other golfers in deciding their schedules, booking flights and hotels and in resolving other logistical problems. He had played golf to a reasonable level and I dimly remembered partnering him a decade or so ago in something like the West of England amateur championship. He understood golf but his business background was in insurance broking and whether he would have the skill and, above all, the guts to make the important endorsement deals which Ben might soon require, was as yet unproven. The odds were that Ben would soon be lured away from Hugo by one of the international super-agents. That is, if Ben were still around to play professional golf. I realised, with a shock, that this was also open to doubt.

Hugo's deep voice wished me a good morning and apologised for calling me so early. It was after nine o'clock, so I was certainly not offended, except perhaps at the assumption that the unemployed, and caddies are put in that category however busy they might be, lie abed for most of the morning.

'Chris, I spoke to Ben's mother and she told me that you found David. But not Ben. Have you any idea where he is? He's supposed to be playing a pro-am in Torquay tomorrow.'

Hugo is a man who has a clear idea of his priorities.

'If I were you, Hugo, I would get a substitute. Even if Ben shows up, you'll find Inspector Colley of the Surrey police will have first call on his time.'

'Shit. Let me know if you hear anything, won't you, Chris. *Ciao*.'

I decided to call Suzi Massey on the pretext of asking if she'd heard from Ben. My motives were partly to reassure her that I really would stay in touch and lend her some support and partly much more self-interested than that.

Suzi seemed to be in perfect control of herself. She said that her husband had arrived from Madrid and that they were about to go down to Camberley police station to make a statement and identify David's body. As I put the telephone down it rang immediately and I was summoned to the same place to make my own statement.

As I began to make myself a cup of tea, the telephone rang again. It was the golf correspondent of the *Post* to ask me where Ben Massey was. 'How the hell should I know?' I slammed the receiver back on its rest, wondering how many times I would be asked the same question today.

I grabbed a jacket and headed for the door. As I closed it, the telephone began to ring again. With a reflex action I turned back, realised that my slavery to the intrusive instrument could be put to one side for the moment and carried on walking. An enjoyable couple of hours was spent in the neighbouring shops, where I looked at books, records, cheese and wine amongst other things, without buying anything beyond a loaf of bread. It is surprising how well the self-denying ordinance of giving up credit cards works. I would have the bread with a soup I'd made out of left-over vegetables. Perhaps I'd make a lentil curry for dinner. In a way I was quite enjoying creating pauper's recipes. I felt delightfully thrifty and smugly virtuous.

When I returned, Toby Greenslade was sitting in his car outside my front gate. As he got laboriously out of his vehicle, he did an extremely theatrical double-take when he saw the multi-coloured hues of my bruised face.

'You didn't kill him this time, did you?'

'Kill who?'

'David Massey, of course.'

'I should have guessed you'd be on my trail.'

Toby pointed at the stick of bread that I was carrying. 'I can offer you better than such frugality for lunch.'

'Judging by the way you oozed your way out of that car of yours you, Toby, desperately need some frugal living – several months of it.'

'Not if I can help it. Good living didn't do Churchill any harm. Abstemiousness didn't suit him and it wouldn't suit me.'

'He had a few minor problems to keep him spry and up to the mark.'

'Yes, and so have I. Ben Massey. What's the story?'

By this time Toby was steering me back down the street towards an Italian restaurant which we both liked.

'Only one course,' I said firmly.

'You have what you like; linguine, fegato and then some cheese for me.'

'Taken your doctor's cholesterol warning to heart, then?'

The head waiter took my jacket and loaf of bread from me and we settled in our seats. Toby immediately asked me to tell him 'all about Ben Massey'.

'Ben's just twenty-two years of age, a shade under six feet tall and a future star,' I said facetiously.

'Come on, Chris. David Massey is dead, Ben Massey is missing. You are Ben's caddie. Apart from his mother and his girlfriend you are the most likely person to know something.'

'I found the body.'

'My God, he found the body.' Toby said the words slowly and with an emphasis that would have done justice to Olivier in his prime. 'My friend, Christopher Ludlow, found the body and did not have it in his soul to confide in his dear, struggling journalist friend.'

'I'm not talking to anyone about it, except the police. I've got to be discreet for everybody's sake, not least Ben's.'

'Discreet. If my lickspittle scrote of an editor could hear this conversation, he'd have a terminal coronary. He doesn't hold with deadly sins such as discretion and integrity.'

'I've nothing to tell, Toby, not even to you. Yes, I found the body and told the police and I'm due at Camberley police station in just over an hour to make a formal statement and therefore must shortly be on my way.'

'I'll drive you and then you can have some cheese.'

In comparison with the ordeal of submitting myself again to the eccentricities of Network South-East, Toby's was an attractive offer despite his appalling driving.

'I'll drive,' I said, as he settled the bill.

As we walked towards his car, Toby scrabbled in his pocket and produced a page of typewritten manuscript. It looked like a press release.

'This arrived on the editor's desk this morning. It's probably from some crank, who thinks we'll pay him a lot of money. We get a lot of this sort of rubbish. The legal boys won't let us touch it. Yet. It's from an unknown source. And of course libel is a sensitive issue these days. The papers have taken a caning, what with that bloody pop star who took the *Post* for a million in damages and that nasty business with the Duke of Whatsit. So we need some real facts. But read it, it's interesting.'

'Why don't you read it to me.'

'Heading – "Ryder Cup Captain Disowns Illegitimate Child". It goes on: "Fans of the celebrated Ross Bentley, winner of golf's British Open Championship and the Masters, and the current captain of the European Ryder Cup team, will no doubt be surprised to hear that he has an illegitimate child, a child that he has never acknowledged.

"His wife, Louise, will probably be surprised, too, since the handsome and successful couple are childless and have many times expressed their regret about this unhappy state.

"The child was born a couple of years after he married the lovely Louise and just before his major golfing successes.

"Perhaps randy Ross cannot recall all his bedroom exploits. But sources close to the illegitimate child's family are now ready to jog his memory." '

Toby and I discussed the matter as we threaded our way through heavy traffic towards Camberley. Whereas Toby dismissed it as a hoax, dreamed up by someone who wanted to take a newspaper for a bundle of money, I was not so sure.

'Why did the writer go to all the trouble of circulating the national papers and then fail to ask for bids?' I demanded. 'From your paper, for instance.' Toby grunted and I continued: 'There's something odd about that piece. I can't quite put my finger on it, but there's a false note somewhere. It almost reads like a gossip column item, but not quite.'

Toby was dismissive. 'The product of a fevered imagination. It must be someone who wants to make a few grand on the side — paid in the grubby notes in which my editor specialises.'

'But do you think it could have happened? What was Ross Bentley like in those early days? It says this was before his major successes and after his marriage. So, we're talking about the end of the sixties, early seventies?'

'Yes, he got married in about 1967. He was very young and so was Louise, and he won the Open in 1972.'

'So you were a fully-fledged golf correspondent by then I suppose, Toby?' I asked teasingly.

'No, dear boy, I was not. I was just out of short pants. Well, I was making the tea in my first job at a local West London paper.'

'Ah yes, you remember it well.'

'So I do. Because I had a foothold in the profession I'd always wanted to join. Full of youthful enthusiasm, full of hope and spirit.'

'You bring tears to my eyes.'

'Well, what you young chaps don't realise is that it was a fantastic time. The whole of Britain seemed to be on a high. Being British was the most fashionable thing in the world. It was the swinging sixties, Mary Quant, the Beatles. And of course we reinvented sex.

'I was just a young reporter, my boy, on a pittance. All I ran to was half a pint of bitter and a grapple in the back row of the local flea-pit.'

'So you didn't know Ross Bentley then?'

'No, but I began covering golf three or four years later and remember that he had a bit of a reputation, amongst those in the know, as a skirt chaser. He wouldn't have found much resistance. He was good-looking and self-assured, brash, a young man who was perfectly in tune with his age and I think he knew he would be a huge success. He was very discreet, though. Well, who wouldn't be, with a wife like Louise. An absolute stunner, a beauty and with brains too. You've seen her around, Chris, and even now I tell you, I wouldn't mind.'

'No, but she probably would. And she had money as well?'

'Pots of it. What a package.' He shook his head at the thought.

'So it's possible that Bentley slipped up, so to speak.'

'Well, yes, but why should he have done? Women were on the pill, abortion was legal. He sure as hell wouldn't have risked Louise finding out. No, no, it's a hoax. There was never a hint of any scandal at the time.'

We dropped the subject for the time being. Toby went in search of a drink while I made my statement to a detective sergeant at Camberley police station.

Towards the end of the interview, Inspector Colley strolled in to say that he had no news of Ben and to ask if Ben had been in touch with me. He congratulated me on the lovely colours on my face and said that he would continue his inquiries.

'It would appear to be very obvious. Especially when we found this note. It was in the waste bin in the kitchen. That was careless of you, Mr Ludlow.'

I looked blankly at Colley as he dropped a crumpled sheet of paper on the table in front of me. A few lines had been written in pencil: 'Chris. Sorry to let you down like this — I had to get away after dealing with David. I just need a few days to think. Tidy up for me, will you.'

It was signed by Ben but I had certainly not seen the note before, as I insisted to Inspector Colley.

He wore an expression of weary disbelief. 'Really? Well, you would say that, sir, wouldn't you? But to my unsophisticated eyes it looks horribly like an admission of guilt, wouldn't you agree? And it seems to indicate that you were involved, that you were to follow on and try to dispose of the body. Was that the plan? But you bottled it and called the police instead.'

Colley was leaning on the table in front of me, his eyes locked on mine. The situation was full of absurdities, but there was a desperate feeling in my stomach and I realised that I was afraid.

But I looked him steadily in the face and said, 'That's utter bloody nonsense. If Ben and I conspired to murder David, do you really think we'd leave notes for each other and that Ben would disappear from view? And how would I dispose of the body? I didn't arrive by car. I'd look pretty obvious walking down the road with a shovel over one shoulder and a body over the other. Somebody might possibly have noticed.'

'You could've used David's car. The keys were in his pocket.'

'But I didn't know that. I wasn't even certain that the BMW was his. Didn't any of the neighbours see or hear anything unusual? Someone must have heard the gunshot.'

'They're used to that. There's rough shooting nearby. As for any unusual people in the area, no. It was the usual case of people walking their dogs, that's all. People keep to themselves here, it's not like *Coronation Street*, you know,' Colley said dismissively.

'What about the gun?' I asked snappily. 'Have you found that yet?'

Colley shook his head wearily: 'Should I call you Morse? No, we haven't found a gun. Anyway, we'll leave it there for the moment. It'll all become clear when we've got our hands on Ben Massey. At the very least your alibis more or less show that you were not present when the murder took place.'

'What do you mean? More or less.'

'Is Mr Slater a close friend?'

'No. Why?'

'He seemed very vague about whether he'd seen you or not. He thought he had and he thought it was on Tuesday evening. But we had to press him quite hard.'

I was left to wonder what I had done to upset Mike Slater, but I had other more immediate problems than that.

Chapter 10

During the next few days it seemed that most of the investigative and gossip-garnering resources of the national newspapers were concentrated on golf. There was, above all, the continuing saga of the Massey family. I was not only the prime suspect's caddie but I had also found the body; fortunately no mention had been made of Inspector Colley's arcane suspicions of my role in the murder. Nevertheless, as a means of self-defence, I kept my answering machine on at all times. Many an old story was taken off the shelf and dusted down for the titillation of the readers; there were tales of drunkenness and disorder, which would not have raised an eyebrow if attached to a bunch of rugby players on tour, but which brought forth a jarring note of moral disapproval when coupled to a sport like golf. More disturbing were vague reports of drug abuse by young golfers on the circuit; reports certainly did not name names but usually began, 'Sources close to the professional game accuse . . .'

There was more coverage of the scuffle between Ramon Gonzales and Nick Spencer at the Memorial Tournament in America. This took the form of 'exclusive interviews' with the protagonists in two rival tabloid newspapers. It was predictable stuff, pitched at just below the level of a school playground argument. No doubt the players' respective agents had extracted handsome payments.

One of the more interesting articles appeared in a

middle-of-the-road newspaper, whose able golf correspondent took a wider and more balanced view:

> The disappearance of the talented young Ben
> Massey, a golfer of enormous potential and with
> a seemingly sound and equable temperament,
> in mysterious and regrettable circumstances,
> prompts one to ask some serious questions about
> the nature not just of contemporary golf but of
> sport as a whole.
> Young people in sport today, as in pop and
> show business, can earn sums of money which
> were probably inconceivable to the generation
> which went before. Is it any wonder that this
> unhinges some of them from reality, that the
> pressure (and I apologise for calling upon an
> expression which is over-used and abused by every
> sportsman and sports commentator) becomes too
> much?
> We in the media must shoulder a lot of the
> blame. The current stories in the Press about the
> unseemly behaviour of a few golfers – brawling,
> drunkenness, anti-social behaviour and drug
> abuse – are just a part of a supremely unhealthy
> concentration on the activities of the rich and
> famous. No wonder that some of them crack
> beneath the squalid and obsessional gaze of some
> parts of the media. When the integrity of a fine
> champion such as Ross Bentley is questioned, as in
> the ludicrous accusations that he 'cheated' in
> winning the 1972 Open Championship, it is time
> to call a halt.
> The game of golf has been fortunate in
> maintaining its very high standards of behaviour.
> It is big business, but has never allowed itself to be

dragged down into the over-commercialised mire in which sports such as football, boxing, motor racing and even cricket and athletics find themselves.

Let us hope that golf is one sport that remains true to itself.

There was certainly food for thought in that article and the writer, in my view, was absolutely right in his summation of Ben Massey. He was equable; he was self-controlled; and I did not believe that psychological cliché that such self-control is achieved at great cost, that there must be an inner fire raging. Ben seemed to be naturally calm.

As I was experiencing these brilliant insights into his character, the answering machine clicked and whirred and I heard Toby's robust tones. I interrupted his opening salvo of 'get up, you idle and disgusting unemployed loafer' and was told to meet him in one hour at the offices of the *Daily News*.

'You're on the payroll, my boy. As a freelance researcher.'

'Into what?'

'Ross Bentley.'

'Fine. But why me?'

'Because you'll do it well, under my tutelage, of course. But naturally my editor sees a further advantage. He will have Ben Massey's caddie on the strength and can keep much better tabs on that story, too.'

'Well, I'm not sure I like the sound of it, Toby, but I need the money.'

'Oh, how often have I heard that old refrain,' he said unsympathetically. I hurriedly shaved and dressed and headed for the Underground.

The project which Toby outlined was simple and distasteful. His editor had instructed him to go right back through Ross Bentley's career and dig up all the dirt he could find, with a particular concentration on whether the story of an illegitimate child could be true. 'The problem is that every newspaper got that press release about Bentley. But there's been no follow-up, nobody asking for large sums of money. So what's the game?' asked Toby.

'Mischief? Revenge?' I suggested.

'Maybe, but my low-born oaf of an editor wants to beat everyone to the story. No slimy stone must be left unturned, no septic sore left unpicked, no seedy bed linen unsniffed, no scurrilous rumour ignored . . .'

'Yes, okay, Toby, okay. You're not over-keen.'

'Here's three hundred quid in advance for your expenses,' he said roughly. 'Use it wisely. The carefree days of lavish expenses are over. Every penny must be accounted for. We will now plan our research.'

We did the planning in a wine bar near the office and Toby had a clear idea of the possible sources of information. He was going to approach Ross Bentley's existing family (there was only his mother and a sister), the golf club where he had served as an assistant professional and the various manufacturers who had sponsored the young Bentley.

'What's the cover story?' I asked.

'An in-depth profile for one of the magazines. You're my research assistant.'

'Who was Bentley's coach in the early days?'

'Coach? They didn't have coaches in the sixties. They learned from the head pro at their club. After they'd got through cleaning the members' golf shoes, re-painting old golf balls and doing club repairs, the poor sods were lucky to get half an hour's tuition a week. It wasn't

organised at all in those days. Ross was with Fred
Burgess down in Brighton. A hard task-master and
nosy, too. He'll have plenty to tell.'

Toby handed me several files in a plastic carrier bag.

'Press and magazine cuttings. Go through them and
see if anything strikes you. Any names or faces that
might be important.'

'Fine. What else?'

'You've got the privilege of interviewing Ross and
Louise Bentley. I know them much too well and they'll
fob me off, you see. I wouldn't dream of pressurising
them about anything because I've got a special
relationship with them and I want to preserve it. But
you, young Chris, can pose as a keen and dynamic
researcher who may be willing to hang on his every word
but is also ready to ask searching questions.'

'I can hardly ask him about his sex life, can I? He'd
throw me out.'

'Quite. Just keep your ear cocked for any evasions,
any signs of discomfort. Despite appearances to the
contrary, you're a bright bloke, you can do it. And
make sure you interview them in their home and then
keep your eyes open.'

'What for?'

'Evidence,' Toby said vaguely, waving a hand. 'Oh,
and here's one other thing, the autobiography. As
turgid and time-serving a piece of ghost writing as you'll
ever read. It makes the rules of golf seem exciting.'

During the following day I read through the sheaves of
press cuttings about Ross Bentley. Mostly they covered
his tournament successes and the vicissitudes of his
Ryder Cup career. He had played during a time when
the Americans had carried all the big guns. The match,
played every two years and alternating between Britain

and the USA, had been won with monotonous ease by the Americans during the seventies and early eighties, even when the British team had been reinforced by European golfers. There had been one tied match during this time but I noticed that despite the relentless defeats, Bentley's Ryder Cup record was outstanding. In seven successive fixtures he had played nearly forty matches and had only lost eight times. It was a testimony not only to his skill but also to his spirit that he could perform so well in such circumstances. Luckily his assumption of the Ryder Cup captaincy had coincided, in the middle of the eighties, with a great flowering of European golfing talent and the Americans had been defeated four times in a row.

I found very little about his life away from the golf course. There was a photograph of him at Buckingham Palace, in the traditional morning dress, when he received his OBE. He was flanked by his parents and had his wife by his side. I could see what a beauty Louise had been in those days – and, as Toby said, still was.

Various telephone numbers for Ross Bentley had been provided by Toby and I began to use them. I was rather nervous because I am aware of the suspicions which sportsmen harbour of journalists, even of golf writers like Toby, who are welcome in most circles. They are well-founded suspicions since journalists are cavalier in the way they distort other people's comments; if they are short on facts, they see nothing wrong with a little invention.

A telephone answering machine greeted me at Bentley's home number and referred me to the office from which he ran his golf course design business. A woman answered my call and told me that Mr Bentley would get right back to me.

To my surprise Bentley did so within the hour. 'So, you're helping Toby,' he said briskly. 'An article about the Ryder Cup, is it?'

'Well, yes, but we want to give it a bit more depth than usual. Your views on the modern game, the future of the Ryder Cup and so on. And a few questions about your career.'

'Toby knows as much about my career as anyone. It's all on record.' He sounded impatient and continued, 'Don't think that I'm going to talk about the '72 Open. I've said all I want to say on that subject. I made a technical and meaningless error on the last green and was totally exonerated by the Royal and Ancient. End of story.'

'No, no, we're not interested in that,' I said quickly.

After a short pause, Bentley said, 'OK, since you're helping Toby, come along tomorrow, otherwise we'll never get around to it. The Ryder Cup is only a few weeks away and I've got to look at some courses I'm building in Spain. Time is the one commodity which is scarce. Let's meet for coffee. Eleven o'clock? I'll see you in the Rochester Hotel, just off Sloane Square. Will that suit you?'

Mindful of Toby's instructions to get inside Bentley's home, if at all possible, I said hesitantly, 'Could we meet at your home? It is meant to be an in-depth piece and it would be nice to say a few words about your house. And perhaps I could chat to Mrs Bentley for a few minutes, too.'

There was another pause and then Bentley said, 'We like to keep our private life private. And Louise doesn't really care to be interviewed. But, since it's Toby . . .' He paused and then gave me his address, with a final admonition: 'Don't be late. I can give you half an hour.'

I knew that I would not achieve much in half an hour but guessed that Bentley was putting some defences in place, just in case he didn't like me or my line of questioning.

A distinct feeling of unease afflicted me as, at eleven o'clock precisely, I rang the front door bell of Ross Bentley's house, a handsome Georgian building in a quiet street a few hundred yards from Sloane Square. I knew that I was there under false pretences, that I was being paid to snoop on a man whom I thought to be wholly admirable. I felt more like asking him for his autograph than prying. But I needed the money and comforted myself with the thought that I expected my probings to prove that there was nothing in the rumours about his past.

Bentley ushered me through the door and shook hands with me. His large hand encased mine and he smiled in a friendly fashion.

'You play golf, do you, Chris?'

'A bit.'

'Give me your hand again.'

I hesitated and he smiled at me once more. 'Come on. I bet you that I can guess your handicap to within three shots. It's all in the hands.'

He took my right hand again in a gentle grip.

'Single figures,' he said tentatively. 'Five. A handicap of five.'

I was impressed and told him that my handicap was two. He laughed with pleasure and said, 'It's a good trick, eh. Come and sit down. The coffee's ready.'

Bentley led me into a room at the back of the house. It looked out over a small garden, mostly paved but with patches of bright flowers around the edges. The room was obviously Bentley's study and was kept remarkably neat. The paper on his leather-covered desk was in two squared-off piles and his books and videos were tidily displayed on shelves recessed into the walls on either side of the fireplace. An elegant glass case held an array of cups, medals and other trophies.

Bentley indicated an easy chair alongside his desk and told me to fire away. With my tape recorder on the desk and running I asked him why and how he became a professional golfer. He launched into a well-rehearsed account of his early days; there was very little which I had not already discovered in the press cuttings. His father had owned a shop in Croydon and the young Ross had attended the local grammar school where he was eventually to get several 'O' levels. He had first become interested in golf when he saw some television coverage of the Open and was soon a familiar figure at the local nine-hole public course. He helped the greenkeeper in return for free rounds of golf. At the age of fifteen, and against his parents' wishes, he became an apprentice professional. Ross Bentley's story then became a familiar one of hardship, of long hours in the golf professional's shop, with very little tangible reward, the meagre comforts of his life enhanced only by the extra pocket money given to him by his mother, who also fed him huge meals on his rare visits home.

'When I joined Fred Burgess at Brighton, I thought I was the bees knees. I was the local golf star around Croydon. I won everything worth winning at junior amateur level but at Brighton I was just another snotty-nosed assistant. I was there to clear out the shop, sell the occasional golf ball and, above all, to be polite and respectful to the members, who were the focal point of the club.'

Bentley explained how he had been put up in digs near the Brighton railway station. 'I thought my six quid a week was a small fortune, but the digs cost four and that didn't give me much leeway. Not that I minded, I can tell you. I was playing golf, even if I had to get to the local tournaments on the bus.

'Anyway, I won the Assistants' Championship a couple of times and played a few pro tournaments. I won a hundred quid at one and bought a car, a real old banger. But I really broke through at the British Masters in 1968. An eagle at the final hole won the tournament for me. I was really thinking about second place, all the money that would bring in. I hit a four-iron into the green. It was a beauty, covering the flag all the way. Two bounces and into the cup. The thing was, it was on the telly and the commentator said, "That shot has won the Masters for Ross Bentley, it will be the first of many for him, he has everything it takes to be a champion." '

Bentley smiled, the delight at his distant triumph still alive in his eyes.

'You were married the year before,' I said. 'How did you meet your wife-to-be?'

'I had a spell at Le Touquet, as a teaching pro. I had to get away from old Fred at Brighton. Looking back, he was good for me, but I wanted a change, a wider world. It's a great place, Le Touquet, a favourite for Parisians. Did you know that P G Wodehouse lived there in the thirties? He had a house which backed on to the course. Anyway, Louise turned up for some lessons and, bingo, we fell for each other. Her father was not best pleased. He was a banker in Paris and had other plans for his daughter. He whipped her away as soon as he cottoned on, but Louise is just as tough as he is and we were married a few months later.'

'How did she cope with the role of a golf professional's wife? Her privileged background, your less than privileged one; it must have been a shock for her. Lytham St Anne's hardly bears comparison with Paris, does it?'

'There were some problems early on. Especially when she used to stroll into clubhouse bars, which were then usually men only. The members used to have apoplexy.' He smiled at the memory. 'Or she'd go into the club's restaurant without the right ticket. All that nonsense. But she used to crank her French accent up and they'd soon be falling at her feet. Beautiful, of course, great style, that was Louise. Is Louise.'

'What about money?'

'What about it?'

'Well, your wife was used to a rich life-style.'

'Money was never a problem. Louise had plenty of her own.'

'How very nice,' I said with feeling.

I tried to inch nearer the subject which was the whole point of the interview. Women.

'Did Louise travel around with you all the time?'

'Oh no. Not all the time. At first she was doing up our flat in London and she also has plenty of her own interests.'

'Such as?'

'Music, books, clothes, painting.'

'A well-rounded person.'

'Absolutely.'

'And she didn't have any difficulties with your being out and about? A young man on the brink of great success. You must have been a target for lots of women.'

Few men, in my experience, can resist the temptation to talk about their conquests, or, rather, to exaggerate them. But Ross Bentley was an exception.

'Well, yes, there was a lot of crumpet about but it didn't interest me. I had Louise and I loved her as much then as I do now. I dedicated myself to practice. That was my job. I wanted to be a champion and there is only one way to get there. They say that Cotton practised more than any golfer before him and that Hogan made Cotton look like a dilettante. But I took practice on to a different plane even to those two. And I trained, lots of running and cycling to strengthen my legs. I didn't smoke, of course, and only had a glass of wine with a meal at night. What a dreadful sanctimonious old bore I must sound. But it's the truth. You can't play good golf if you're on the booze, it destroys your concentration. You must be fit. Some of the old timers used to take a nip of Scotch or brandy on the first tee, to calm the nerves, and that's acceptable. I've done it myself, but no more than that.'

'You had an agent by this time, presumably?'

'When I played in America I found that I needed one. Especially when I won the Los Angeles Open. There were all sorts of deals to be done and all sorts of con men around to roll you over. Of course I had world-wide deals on the big contracts, for clubs and clothing and so on, but there were plenty of other nice pickings. I used Mike Martinez in those early days.'

'Ah, Mr Martinez.'

'You know him, do you?'

'Yes, and it all ended in tears. He's a difficult man to deal with,' I said with feeling.*

'You can say that again. Much too greedy, too sharp for his own and his clients' good. He's run many a good golfer ragged — too many commitments, too many sponsors' days, too many exhibition matches. He was very good, Martinez, at getting big bucks up front. He did some marvellous deals for me, with Shell and Gillette, for instance.'

'I saw some of the ads, when I was doing my research for Toby.'

*See *Sudden Death*, also available from Headline.

'Well, I hope you didn't dwell on them. It was a long time ago. The one big favour Mike did for me was to show me how the big endorsements work. You don't sign yourself away to play the same clubs and balls, or wear the same clothing around the world. My British club manufacturer was no use to me in the States, he didn't even sell his product there. But the contract said I had to endorse Matchless clubs. No, Mike split the territories. One lot of manufacturers could use me in Britain and Europe, another lot in America and another lot in Australia and the Far East. And of course he tied the contracts in with tournament appearances in the different territories. It made sense and made me a lot more money.'

'So what went wrong between you and Martinez?'

'Well, he wanted me to make a pop record, for God's sake. And appear on *Top of the Pops*. No thanks. One or two deals went sour, too. A clothing company went bankrupt. That's the one thing you don't want. I couldn't afford to be associated with a failure like that. Your name and reputation can only stand so much, you've got to be careful. The final straw was some property firm he got me involved with. Blue Sky, I think it was called. The chairman was a rogue, likeable, plausible, but a villain nonetheless. It should have been called Blue Yonder because that's where he went, with all the money.

'That's when Louise took over, thank goodness. We decided only to get involved with blue-chip sponsors and only a limited number of them, so that I could give them enough of my time but not be rushing here, there and everywhere to the detriment of my golf. It worked, as you probably know, and continues to work.'

Bentley looked pointedly at his watch and I fired a few questions at him about the Ryder Cup. He answered them concisely and then walked over to the door and called out his wife's name.

As I followed him, he said, 'I've seen you at the tournaments, haven't I? With Toby?'

'Possibly. I'm a caddie as well. Jack Mason, Rollo Hardinge and Ben Massey, too.'

'Young Ben. What a disaster. I was relying on him for the Ryder Cup. Great swing, great temperament. Is there any news?'

'I'm afraid not, but I'm sure he's not implicated in the murder.'

'Let's hope not. I need him. Here's Louise.'

Louise Bentley was standing halfway up the staircase on a half landing. I couldn't help but believe that she'd chosen her position deliberately, since she was flooded with light from a window and I understood at once why Toby tended to drool when her name was mentioned. Although I had seen her occasionally from afar at golf tournaments and had studied press photographs, this had not prepared me for her remarkable beauty. That first sight of her seemed to print an indelible image on my mind of her grace and her eerie but fascinating kind of stillness.

'Mr Ludlow. Please come up to the sitting room.'

I could discern only the merest trace of a French accent in her even tones. We settled down in the first-floor sitting room, with its wide floor-to-ceiling windows. There were several watercolours on the walls which, I guessed, might have been done by Louise.

Over the fireplace there was a portrait of Ross Bentley, holding the famous old claret jug which is the Open Championship trophy. An upright piano was pushed into one corner of the room.

'What a lovely room,' I said politely. 'They're your paintings?'

'Thank you. Yes, I did the watercolours but the portrait is a Bratby. Now, how can I help you?' she asked brusquely. 'I was loath to see you, but since you are helping dear Toby Greenslade . . . The Press has hardly been kind to my husband recently, has it?'

It was a rhetorical question but I decided that I wasn't going to be browbeaten by Louise and replied, 'He's in the public eye and what he's done or is doing is a matter of public interest.'

'Maybe, but what is the relevance now of Ross's final putt at the 1972 Open? Why do those hooligans on the tabloid papers rake over long-dead ashes? Is it a peculiarly British trait, do you think, Mr Ludlow, to denigrate one's own heroes? Ross has done so much for British golf, why don't these so-called journalists remember that? I think that the British are uneasy with people of great accomplishment. Would you agree?'

I was shaken by the vehemence of her delivery and also by the scope of her questions and said inadequately: 'Up to a point, yes, we do tend to knock our great men. Very few seem to survive the public gaze, which can be very spiteful, especially when focused by journalists who are only interested in the next story, the next bit of scandal.' Yes, that's my role at the moment, I thought, and hurriedly went on, 'Perhaps we are more comfortable with second-raters.'

'Yes, the jolly good sport who comes second, stiff upper lip rigidly in place.' Louise did a passable imitation of a posh Home Counties accent and we laughed together.

'Ross was never like that,' she continued. 'I could see the steel in him, even though he was so young when we met. That's what made him so special. It was such a relief after those awful young men whom my father paraded before me as likely husbands. BCBG types.'

'Eh?'

'*Bon chic, bon genre*. Yuppies, hooray Henrys. Whatever your expression is.'

I asked Louise a few questions about their early days together and she gave some amusing accounts of their life on and off the golf circuit. It was time to try a leading question and I tried not to lead with my chin.

'Mrs Bentley, did your husband's job as a golf pro put any strains on your marriage in those early days? You were both young and in love and yet you spent quite a lot of time apart. Did you resent that?'

'Not at all. It was his job.'

'Your husband was successful and attractive, and in what was becoming a glamorous profession. It was the liberated decade, the swinging sixties, when the rules were changed, or so everybody said. Did this cause you any problems?'

'In your rather naive way, are you asking me, Mr Ludlow, if Ross was unfaithful to me?'

The friendly atmosphere had suddenly cooled alarmingly. Louise's rebuff made me feel as if I had put my hand up her skirt. But I had to battle on, partly for Toby's sake and partly because I was determined not to be put down by this tough and calculating woman. I guessed that her beauty and her money ensured that she usually got her own way without much trouble.

'I'm sorry, I don't want to pry into your private life,' I said, 'but I'm trying to get an idea of how you felt at that time. You were in a strange country, with a husband who was doing an unusual job. You had only been married a short time but were often parted from your husband. That's all.'

'Nicely done, Mr Ludlow. But it's still a question about our sex lives. Worthy of any of the tabloid scum who have been attacking Ross. I was under the impression that you were here to talk about golf.'

I began to speak and Louise lifted her hand to silence me. 'Let me answer your question. I trusted Ross absolutely and still do. That's what people do when they're in love.'

It was very plain that the interview was at an end. I thanked Louise Bentley and tried to apologise for my indiscreet questions as I headed for the door. I hoped that I had not alienated her totally. Toby would be furious if I had but I did not feel particularly well-disposed towards my journalist friend anyway. I knew that he had set me up to do the dirty work which he did not fancy.

As I went rapidly down the stairs, I was grateful that I did not meet Ross Bentley. I went through the front door and, with great relief, hurried away.

Chapter 11

Toby and I had agreed to meet at his office to compare notes that afternoon and I found him staring moodily at his computer screen.

'Any luck with the Bentleys?' he asked.

'None. All I succeeded in doing was upsetting Louise. Talk about a baptism by fire.'

'You wouldn't upset her. She's got a hide like a rhino.'

'Well, I haven't, Toby. I'm no good at this game. My sentiments are all on the side of the Bentleys. I'd say that there has been hardly a ripple of discord on the surface of their marriage. We're wasting our time.'

'Really. Ross's sister wouldn't agree with you. Mrs Hudson, as she now is, implied that Louise wasn't the only woman who warmed her brother's bed. At least, she didn't really call her Louise, she mostly referred to her as "that French woman". No love lost there.'

'Well, you should discount such nasty rumours, shouldn't you? A tainted source and all that.'

'Most of them are, in our business,' said Toby wearily.

'What about Ross's mother? Any joy there?'

'No. Just a very contented mum. And why not? He's done her proud. And she's obviously very keen on Louise. Her only regret is the lack of a grandchild from Ross's wife. Needless to say, Avril Hudson has a whole brood. Ironic, isn't it?'

'Why no children?'

'Nature. Louise couldn't have any. What a waste,' Toby said sadly. 'Right, young Chris, your next task is to go through all the golf magazines from the middle of the sixties to the middle of the next decade. Look at anything relating to Ross Bentley. Trips overseas, sponsorship deals, exhibition matches, and fix your beady, investigative eye especially firmly on any photographs you may find. Look at his business acquaintances.'

Toby told me to contact the public affairs director of the Professional Golfers' Association and arrange to use their library.

On the following day I sat at a table in the PGA's library and began to pick my way through the main British golf magazines, of which there were three in the mid-sixties. The formats, at a distance of nearly thirty years, seemed dull but the content was similar to that of present-day magazines: a mixture of tournament reports, features on players and on golf courses, and a number of instructional pieces.

I soon located the sections where news of sponsorships and endorsement deals was covered and, as the decade drew to a close, Ross Bentley's name began to feature more frequently. This was no surprise since his success in the British Masters, won in such dashing style and caught so prominently on national television, was followed by a couple of victories in the United States. Bentley seemed to be the potential Open Champion for whom British golf fans had hungered for so long, and many sponsors, rounded up by his agent Mike Martinez, were prepared to back him.

With Toby's instructions in mind, I pored over the reports and the occasional photographs and found nothing in the names or faces that seemed untoward.

The Blue Sky project was covered in a number of brief press releases.

By the end of the day my eyes felt gritty and my head fuzzy and I was only just over halfway through the stock of magazines. I thanked my stars that I didn't earn my living at a desk; working for a press-cuttings agency was definitely off my list of ambitions.

On the next day I soldiered on at a much greater pace. At lunchtime, the public affairs director, a former journalist called Lester Gibbs, took me to a nearby pub for beer and sandwiches. A tall man, with thinning black hair, an amiable manner and a wide-ranging knowledge of the sporting media, he knew Toby well and was eager to help.

Without admitting all the reasons why I was researching Ross Bentley's early career, I told Gibbs that Toby wanted to fill in the commercial background more thoroughly.

'There's one other magazine,' he said thoughtfully. 'It folded early in the seventies. I wrote for it a bit. That probably explains its lack of success. *The International Golfer*. We used to have copies in the library but we cleared a lot of stuff out a couple of years ago. I'll try and find them.'

In the middle of the afternoon, as I was about to pack up and go home, Lester Gibbs backed through the door of the library with a large and heavy box in his arms.

'*The International Golfer*, 1967 to 1972,' he said triumphantly, as he spilled six folders on to my table. 'Have fun.'

I thumbed through the first few copies of the magazine, whose owners had made a determined effort to produce a brighter product. They covered the business side of golf in much greater detail and there was some concentration on product launches, promotions and sponsorships. No doubt the editors hoped that this would bring in some extra advertising revenue.

Ross Bentley's name began to appear regularly and I smiled to myself as I turned a page and found a photograph of Ross among a group of people 'at the launch of the Blue Sky Resort Company'. Ross was in the centre of the shot with a man on his right who was identified as Mr Terry Davenport, Chairman and Managing Director of Blue Sky. On Davenport's right was my old adversary, Mike Martinez. He was thinner in the face and the stomach in those days, and looked even more dangerous than when I had encountered him twenty years later.

One or two women were scattered amongst the group, including Mrs Terry Davenport, resplendent in an off-the-shoulder dress which revealed most of her formidable breasts and with her beehive hair-do piled precipitously high.

Everyone seemed to be holding a glass and, since they were those impractical saucer-shaped ones, I assumed the drink was champagne.

My eye ran down the page and found the press release.

A reception at the High Cliffs Hotel, near Bournemouth, marked the launch of the Blue Sky Resort Company. The laudable aim of the company is to develop a series of golf courses with on-site holiday accommodation both in the United Kingdom and in Europe. Mr Davenport expects to have five resorts completed by 1973 and to have eighty in place by 1980. At the conclusion of his speech, the Blue Sky chairman said: 'It gives me particular pleasure to welcome Ross Bentley to Blue Sky as our consultant and touring professional. His expertise and enthusiasm will be invaluable as we start our programme to offer superb golf facilities at a reasonable cost to the ordinary people of Britain and Europe.'

I wrote the date of the magazine down, so that I could get a photocopy of the page before I left. I took one more look at the photograph and wondered why the girl on Ross Bentley's left was in the picture. She was not named and, in her simple dress, looked as if she were a member of the hotel staff. It puzzled me but I guessed that she might be a daughter of the Davenports.

I waded through the rest of the magazines, found nothing of interest and went in search of Lester Gibbs and a photocopy machine. He told me to take the magazine, unclipped it from the folder and gave it to me. 'I got these from our archives. In other words, the garden shed out at the back. They're no use to us now.' He looked at the page I'd marked in the magazine. 'I remember Blue Sky Resorts. What a con-man Davenport was. He disappeared with hundreds of thousands of pounds. It was all very messy and Ross Bentley didn't escape all the mud that was thrown.'

'How do you mean?'

'Guilt by association, I suppose. Davenport was last seen in Spain about a year after the launch and Ross had in the meantime resigned from his role as consultant. But you know what people are like especially when a sportsman or a show-biz personality is involved. No doubt Ross's agent was guilty of greed but Ross was too young and naive to know any better.'

I agreed with Gibbs and also remembered that, during our interview, Ross Bentley had been careful to dismiss the subject of Blue Sky as quickly as possible. Now I knew the reason.

* * *

When I returned to my flat, I called Toby at his office, and was surprised to find him still at his desk. It was nearly six o'clock and he was usually on licensed premises by that time. His reply to my inquiry about his state of health was predictably trenchant.

'Camel's Breath instructed me to do a follow-up on Ben Massey's continuing disappearance. Give me a quote, will you. Nobody knows a damn thing about him. How can a reasonably well-known golfer disappear like that?'

Camel's Breath is one of the politer names Toby gives his editor. I hardly brightened his day by telling him of my lack of success in the PGA library.

'But I've got one interesting photo. You ought to see it.'

An hour later Toby marched through my front door, asked for a whisky and took the copy of *The International Golfer* into the kitchen, where the whisky glasses were kept. He looked at the Blue Sky photograph and wandered over to the window.

'There's that bastard Martinez,' he grunted. 'Come here, Chris. Who's that?' He gestured at the middle of the photograph.

'That's Ross,' I said stupidly.

'No, no. The girl. Who is she? Look at the body language, for Christ's sake. There's only one place they're heading. Bed.'

'Come on, Toby. He's got his arm around her waist. It's just a friendly gesture. She's probably one of Davenport's kids.'

'If she was his daughter, she'd be done up to the nines – like her mother. Did they really do their hair like that in 1970?' he mused. 'Imagine the palaver at bedtime. I'd be asleep by the time that was all unpinned.'

Toby continued to study the photograph. He took a
very hearty swallow from his whisky and water and
said, 'I'll bet you she was a waitress; you've only got to
look at her dress. I'll also bet you there was some hanky
panky between her and Bentley. Ring through to the
hotel, tomorrow, Chris, and find out about her.'

'Toby, it was well over twenty years ago. They won't
know anything about her, even if there is anything
worth knowing, which I doubt.'

I took another look at the photograph and saw
something in the cast of the unknown girl's face that
jogged a remote brain cell. It was there but I couldn't
get at it, like an itch you can't reach. I was sure that I
had seen her somewhere.

Toby interrupted my thoughts: 'On second thoughts,
get down to the hotel in person. You can take my car.'

'OK, but what's the rush?'

'The rush is my editor. He wants a story and he wants
it before any of the other tabloid hacks get it. I am
under the whip, Chris, and I don't like it, especially
when it's wielded by that unprincipled globule of
poison.'

Toby looked grimly at me and I refilled his glass with
whisky. He continued, 'Use your charm and intelligence, my boy, and when that fails offer the buggers
money.'

Chapter 12

In his car Toby had succeeded in elevating untidiness to a kind of surreal art. Its interior was festooned with discarded pieces of paper, coins of various denominations, half-empty boxes of tissues, cassette tapes, newspapers, gloves (none matching that I could see) a scarf and even an odd sock and a pair of golf shoes caked with dried mud. A sizeable vehicle of dubious reliability, it carried me now to the southwest.

Located on the outskirts of Bournemouth, the High Cliffs is a two-storey hotel, built from red brick and forming a crescent around a well-maintained garden. It is aimed at the business market and boasts the statutory conference facilities and leisure centre.

The young receptionist, her neat features crowned by curly hair streaked blonde, smiled at me momentarily and then switched off. Click, click. Then she smiled again. Big click. It was obviously my lucky day.

'Good morning, sir, how may I help you?'

'I'd like to see the manager, please.'

'Have you an appointment, sir?'

'No, but it won't take a minute.'

'Mr Longman is extremely busy, sir. But I'll try for you. Your name, sir?'

She smiled at me again and talked briefly into a telephone.

'I'm sorry, Mr Ludlow, but he's tied up in a meeting. If you would like to write in for an appointment . . .'

I played my ace card. 'I'm with the *Daily News*. I'd

just like some help on a story. There could be some good publicity for the hotel,' I lied. I handed her a *Daily News* business card, which had been overprinted with my name.

Two minutes later I was being ushered into a chair in the manager's office. He offered me some coffee and, just like the receptionist, asked how he could help me. Oh, the power of the Press. I noticed that his desk was clear of all but a few sheets of paper and a copy of *Yachting Monthly* which lay open in the centre of it.

He was certainly busy. He saw the direction of my gaze, gathered up the magazine, coughed and said, 'One of our advertising outlets.'

I produced *The International Golfer* from my briefcase and handed it to him.

'The picture on page thirty-eight. Would it be possible to identify the girl on Ross Bentley's left? She was probably one of your waitresses.'

Mr Longman looked at me and then back at the photograph. He looked at the front cover of the magazine. 'February 1970. Over twenty years ago. How on earth do you expect anyone to remember her?'

'Well, I hoped there might be some records of salaries, of who was employed.'

'No chance. It was far too long ago. Anyway, she may have been casual, paid in cash. A couple of quid for the evening. Why do you want to find her?'

'Oh, it's just a feature about the con-men in sport. The ones who got away with it, and Terry Davenport of Blue Sky' — I pointed to him in the picture — 'did exactly that. He's still in Spain, as far as I know, and we wondered whether the girl really was just a waitress or part of his family.'

I hoped that Longman would not think too hard about my flimsy explanation and went quickly on: 'Is there anyone around from that time? A barman, perhaps, or a waitress?'

'God, no. They're gypsies, these people. They're on the move all the time. A strange bunch. Hold on, though, there is Janice. She's a part-timer. She must have worked here on and off since the hotel opened.'

He consulted one of the sheets of paper on his desk. 'She'll be in this lunchtime. We've got a conference lunch on. She'll be here in about half an hour. Why don't you wait in the bar? Have a drink − on the house, of course.

'You did say you were with the *News*, didn't you? Perhaps you'd like to make a small contribution to the staff fund. They're not overpaid, by any means; their tips make all the difference.'

I peered into my wallet and extracted a £20-note. 'Will that do the trick?'

'Very nicely, Mr Ludlow. I'll see that it goes into the staff's pool.'

Yeah, I'll bet you will.

When I was only halfway down my glass of cider, Janice, chubby of face and broad of beam, approached my table and said that the boss had sent her along to see me. She glanced at the barman, who was busily polishing glasses, and gestured towards the terrace which lay beyond the French windows.

As we settled at a table she said, 'He's a nosy beggar, that one. Antoine, he calls himself. Born in Portsmouth.'

She sniffed with disdain and I laughed.

'You're busy, I know, so I'll come to the point.' I showed her the photograph and asked her if she could identify the girl next to Ross Bentley. She took her glasses from her apron pocket and looked hard at the picture.

'Who wants to know?' she asked.

'I do. I'm doing a bit of research.'

'For a newspaper, so the boss said.' I nodded and she continued, 'The boss said newspapers pay for information, that there might be something for me.'

I fished in my wallet for another £20-note. As she reached for it, I whipped it away in true *film noir* style. 'Let's hear the info first, sister,' was what I wanted to say but contented myself with: 'Payment on delivery, Janice.'

'Well, I do remember her, love. She was a real laugh, a breath of fresh air. She used to moonlight from the local girls' school, Moordown Abbey, just up the road.'

'A boarding school?'

'Yeah. She mostly worked in the holidays but, if we were really busy in term time, she'd get down here. Susan, she was called. She never seemed to see her parents, poor soul, they were in the army, abroad somewhere. They billeted her out, mostly, though I remember that she went to see them one Christmas, in Singapore, I think.'

'What was her name?'

'Her surname? Oh dear, I can't remember that. But it was a double thingy name. You know, posh.'

'Double-barrelled?'

She nodded. 'Double-barrelled. She was a bit of a toff, I suppose, though you wouldn't have known it. Always laughing and joking, always up to mischief. But when she came back from that visit to her parents, she'd changed. She didn't talk about them nor about Singapore, either. She didn't even have any photos; you'd have thought she'd have had photos. And then she disappeared. A few weeks later, she left the school and nobody knew where she'd gone. In the middle of term, too, and that was it.'

That was it, indeed, I thought, as I slid the money across the table and thanked Janice for being so helpful. That seemed to be the end of that particular trail.

As I drove back to London I tried consciously to switch my mind off and let it coast. The immediate disappointment of finding myself hard against the end wall of a blind alley had diminished, to be replaced by a feeling that there might be a way forward. Would someone at the school help? I'd consult Toby. I needed some music and scrabbled about in the glove compartment of Toby's car to see what I could find. The first tape I found played a country and western number which sounded exactly the same as all other country and western numbers. Swiftly I ejected it and tried another. Eureka. It was Barber's violin concerto. You could rely on Toby to be as eclectic in his musical tastes as he was in his tastes in wine.

In the half reverie induced partly by the richly romantic sounds of Barber and partly by the undemanding state of the traffic, I drove steadily towards London. I wondered, for the umpteenth time, where Ben Massey had hidden himself; every day that he passed silent and out of sight seemed to confirm his guilt.

Thoughts of Ben led inevitably to thoughts of his mother. Suzi had been much on my mind since our first drink together and I had keen hopes that I could assume a much more important role in her life than my present one as her missing son's caddie.

I conjured up her face in my mind's eye and murmured her name. 'Suzi.' A moment later I shouted it out. '*Suzi*.' The tumblers had dropped into place. I pulled into the next lay-by and looked at the photograph again, studying the face that had struck a distant note in the recesses of my memory. It was the eyes, slightly elongated at the corners, very slightly oriental. Full of eastern promise, all right. I was pretty sure that the double-barrelled Susan was Suzi Massey.

At the next service station, I stopped to have a cup of tea but above all to try to sort out the implications of my deduction. It was all too obvious and I couldn't believe in anything quite so transparent. The sooner I talked to her the better.

Suzi answered her telephone on about the tenth ring and her voice sounded drowsy. I wondered if she'd had a long and alcoholic lunch but she told me that she was drying herself after a bath. Briefly I thought how much I'd like to do that for her. She'd heard nothing new about Ben nor had any more thoughts about his likely whereabouts.

'Can I come and see you?' I asked.

'That would be nice. When?'

'Now, if possible.'

'I'm off to play tennis in an hour. It's a match, so I won't be back until about six o'clock. How about a drink here at seven and then I'll take you to dinner?'

'Let me take you.'

'No, no. I can afford it,' Suzi said firmly.

'Is your husband away?' I asked hopefully.

'In Brussels until the end of the week. He didn't hang around for too long, he said he'd be better off working than moping around. But Chris, park your car around the corner and come to the back of the house. There are still some journalists knocking around. See you at seven. OK?'

Not half, I thought, as she gave me directions.

Chapter 13

Suzi lived in a large stockbroker Tudor house in a cul-de-sac. You could imagine the estate agent's blurb: 'an exclusive development of executive style residences in a much-sought-after corner of leafy Surrey.' There was a double garage and a large garden; I looked in vain for the repro gas lamp.

Suzi threw open the front door, waved me in and gave me a kiss on each cheek. She was dressed simply in a short dark skirt and a close-fitting pale green cashmere sweater which showed off her curves. She looked very fit, perhaps because of her enthusiasm for tennis, though her face, with its flawless features and bright eyes, looked drawn. Her efforts to continue a normal life, when one son had been murdered and the other was suspected of being the murderer, were making their mark.

'It's lovely to see you, Chris,' she said. 'I was about to ring you, anyway. I know you'd have phoned me, if you'd heard from Ben, but one lives in hope.'

The misfortune which had struck Suzi's family stilled our conversation for a moment. In the bleak silence I could hear a radio playing, probably in the kitchen, and Suzi said, 'Let's not talk about all the problems. I'm up to here with sympathy and concern. All well-meant and much appreciated by me, but I have to believe that everything will be back to normal soon. And I'd love to spend an evening talking about something else. So, it really is good to see you. Let's have a drink.'

I felt uneasy about my motives for being with her. Was I sympathetic friend, suitor or snooper? I knew I didn't want the first role, would like to pursue the second but felt that attempting to extract information for Toby and his newspaper would be complicated by the fact that I liked and fancied Suzi.

'It's good to see you too. I wanted to see you again.'

The spontaneity of the smile that flicked across her face made me feel that, in happier circumstances, her interest in me wouldn't be purely platonic. I reminded myself that she was married and that these weren't happier circumstances.

While Suzi opened a bottle of champagne I looked around the living room. It was clear that a conflict of styles, so far unresolved, was being fought. On the one hand there was the simplicity of an oak refectory table and the accompanying wooden chairs, rows of books and the starkness of a high-tech metal standard lamp; on the other hand there were some carriage lamp wall lights, a copy of the bestselling print 'The Spanish Dancer' and several editions of a magazine devoted to vintage cars. The print sat above a huge television screen which dominated one end of the room.

I looked around for photographs, especially of Suzi in her youth, in the hope that they might confirm that the waitress in *The International Golfer* picture was her. That was a lot to expect and the pictures were limited to one of Ben aged about fifteen, with a huge trophy in his arms, and one that I assumed was of Garfield Massey on his graduation day. He was arrayed in a gown and a mortar board and was flanked by two proud parents.

My eyes flicked along the rows of books; a mixture of novels, biographies, reference, keep-fit and travel books. The spine of one of them stood out because I had recently been reading it. I took it out of the shelf to confirm that it really was Ross Bentley's autobiography.

Suzi, bearing two glasses of champagne, walked in and I held the book up to show her. 'Garfield's a golf enthusiast?'

'No. That must be Ben's. Bentley is one of his heroes, he reads everything he can about him.'

We clinked glasses and sat down. Another silence descended. I gestured at the room: 'Nice place you have here,' I said facetiously.

'Oh, Chris, you don't have to make polite conversation. It's not a nice place but it's close to London and close to Ben.'

She realised what she had said and covered her distress by going in search of the champagne bottle to re-fill our glasses.

The bottle was soon empty and a knock on the front door announced the arrival of a taxi driver; it was all as well-timed as a Swiss watch. As we turned out of the driveway we saw a man on the opposite corner make a note in a book, but we couldn't decide if he was a policeman or a journalist.

The restaurant turned out to be a room at the back of a pub and the chef specialised in traditional English dishes, but with imaginative variations. The little awkwardnesses that usually exist between relative strangers were quickly dispelled and we were soon talking like old friends.

My responsibilities as Toby's untried research assistant were not entirely forgotten as we discovered the many interests we had in common. As casually as I could I asked her about her schooldays and Suzi told me that she'd been sent to a boarding school in the west country.

'Oh, which one?' I tried to appear casual. 'Was it Sherborne?'

'Nothing as grand as that. You wouldn't have heard of it,' she said, to my irritation. I didn't want to press her too hard on the subject and asked her about her parents.

'Oh, they were abroad. I didn't really see a lot of them and I don't think they wanted to see too much of me,' she said dismissively.

'I can't believe that. You make them sound pretty hard-hearted.'

'Not so much hard-hearted as self-interested. Looking back, I think it was OK when I was a baby. I was a nice fashion accessory for my mother, her pretty baby to be patted and admired. But when I got a bit older I needed more attention and didn't fit in so neatly with their plans. I got in the way, spoiled the even tenor of their social and their domestic lives. So they dumped me in a third-rate boarding school and farmed me out to anyone who would take me during the holidays.'

I was taken aback by Suzi's description of what sounded like a sad childhood and was curious to know what these unloving parents did.

'My father was in the army. A career soldier. Sandhurst and all that guff. My mother revelled in it all. Hierarchies like the army — you know how they breed snobbery. And my mother was one of the worst.'

By this time the coffee and some malt whisky had arrived and Suzi went on: 'When I had a child, I was determined to give him all the love and attention that I'd missed out on. It doesn't seem to have done much good, does it?' she said resignedly. 'If Ben did kill David, I hope he never comes back. I can't bear the thought of him rotting in gaol. What a terrible waste and all for that little swine David.'

I did my best to reassure her that it must be a dreadful mistake, that there was no chance of Ben having killed

David and tried to lead her away from the present, even if it evoked less than pleasant recollections of the past. She sipped at her whisky and I prompted her further. 'You must have been very young when you had Ben,' I said tentatively.

'A bit, I suppose. Youthful indiscretion and all that. But I wouldn't have been without him. Ben was a sweet child and he's turned into a sweet man. But David . . .'

'You haven't told me about Ben's father. He must be very proud of Ben, a rising young golf star, a Ryder Cup player, a sporting millionaire before he's much older.'

'He doesn't keep in touch.' She put down her glass and took my hand. 'I hope this doesn't shock you, Chris darling, but I'm not entirely sure who his father was. I'd just left school and was living in a commune in Wiltshire. We were up in the clouds on pot and rough cider most of the time. We shared everything, especially each other's beds. I think I know who it was, but it's probably wishful thinking.'

'Tell me about him.'

'No. Because he became quite famous. And I know what you're thinking.'

'What?'

'That I would say that. That's why I call it wishful thinking and that's how it can remain. It was a long time ago and I don't want to bore you. I'll pay the bill and we'll go home for coffee.'

On receipt of such an invitation, it's not the time to do the hawk-eyed and unyielding investigative reporter act. I decided to save my questions for a more opportune time. All I knew was that my theory that Suzi had had some kind of a liaison with Ross Bentley was yet to be disproved.

Chapter 14

Suzi insisted that I get out of the taxi some distance from her house and go to the back door in order to avoid any prying journalists. I did as she asked even though I thought that they might have the wit to cover the rear of the house as well as the front. However, I saw nobody and, when she opened the door for me, Suzi said that the watcher in the street was absent.

We stood in the kitchen while Suzi made some coffee and I considered various ways of steering the conversation back to her past life. Not that she was reticent on the subject, but she had proved elusive on the very points in which I was interested: her relationship, if any, with Ross Bentley and the identity of Ben's father. Was it fair to assume that she had something to hide, particularly about the latter, or was it a simple case of embarrassment that she was not sure of the father's identity?

'Tell me more about the boys,' I asked tentatively.

'No more ancient history,' Suzi said firmly. 'How do you like your coffee?'

I shrugged. 'It had better be strong and no more booze, thanks. I've got to drive home.'

'Do you have to? There's plenty of room here and I'd like you to stay.'

My momentary speculation about whether this was just a kind offer of hospitality or a much more enticing invitation was answered when Suzi turned to me, wrapped her arms around me and kissed me in a way

111

that left me in no doubt. As I responded several censorious thoughts flitted into my mind. She has a husband, the voice of conscience told me, and you're in his house; you're supposed to be helping Toby with a sensitive bit of investigation; she's only turning to you because she needs comfort in her distress. Then comfort her I would. She led me to the stairs, the coffee forgotten on the kitchen table. A few minutes later all judgements were suspended as our bodies joined together in comfort, pleasure, excitement and release.

Bright ribbons of sunlight woke me in the early morning. I had a dry throat, which was no surprise after the alcohol I had consumed the night before and the athletics which had followed. Suzi was as fit as she looked and I wasn't as fit as I thought. She lay beside me still asleep. I wanted her again, but didn't think I should wake her, as she'd slept so little since David's death.

I went in search of a teapot and, after scouring the kitchen cupboards in vain, settled for two mugs of tea. I remembered that Suzi didn't take sugar. She was sitting up when I returned to the bedroom. She grinned at me.

'That's the best night's sleep I've had for days. Sex is very relaxing, especially for the older woman.'

'You don't look very old to me.'

'Only a year or two to go before the dreaded four-o.'

'You don't act very old.'

'Come here and say that.' She lay back with her arms out to me. No, she didn't behave at all like an older woman.

It was still not yet seven o'clock and we chatted and drowsed, that wonderful half-sleep when you are aware of the sounds of the awakening day but only just — half dream and half reality.

I was slightly puzzled by Suzi's bedroom. Something

was awry and I realised that there was no sign in the room of the existence of her husband. I looked around the room, but there was no dressing gown nor a pair of slippers, not a stray shirt nor a sweater carelessly thrown aside. In contrast Suzi's dressing gown was hanging on the back of the door.

'Do you and, er, Garfield have separate rooms?' There was no tactful way of asking.

'Yes. Does that make you feel any better?' She was right, it did.

'When is he back?'

'At the weekend. In case you're wondering, we still do it occasionally. I wouldn't say that I'm wildly keen but I wouldn't deny him either.'

'Lie back and think of England.'

'I'll lie back and think of you from now on.'

Eventually we wandered down to the kitchen and made some toast and coffee, which this time we did get around to drinking. Although our relationship had now changed tack, I was still determined to find out as much about Suzi as I could.

I knew that Ben had been educated at a boarding school more notable for its sporting facilities than its academic excellence and I asked her where David had gone to school.

'A couple of local day schools. Garfield had a hell of a problem getting him in anywhere, even with private tuition laid on during the holidays. They were the last resort.'

'So the two boys were poles apart. Ben was intelligent and charming while David was none too bright and a bit devious.'

'Devious is hardly the word. Eysenck was right, heredity is the key factor. Poor David had an alcoholic mother . . .'

'Whereas lucky Ben had you.'

'Flatterer.'

'But it was extremely generous of Garfield to pay for Ben's boarding school, wasn't it? It's not cheap at Upton Manor, is it?'

'Christ, he didn't pay. It was hard enough to get the money out of him for Ben's clothes. No, his fees were taken care of another way . . .' Suzi hesitated and then went on: 'I don't know why I'm telling you all this, or even why you're interested, but my parents set up a trust fund for Ben's education. They paid.'

'Not so hard-hearted, then?'

'Pangs of conscience, perhaps. Ben's arrival blew up a storm, a major upheaval. Mother was devastated. A bastard in the family. What on earth will Mrs Colonel think? She was more worried about the scandal than she was about me. I was forbidden to go near them when I told them I was pregnant; after all, they had their position to consider. Pathetic, really . . .'

'Well, at least they came up trumps in the end.'

Suzi grunted non-committally. It wasn't surprising, I thought, that the boys hadn't got on well. It seemed to me that David had had a very unlucky roll of the dice. I asked Suzi how Garfield had coped with the problems posed by the two widely different boys.

'What coping? What problems? Garfield tried the heavy father role out occasionally and then conveniently spent most of his time abroad on business. It mostly devolved on me and it was bloody hard work.

'Ben was never a problem, but when he began to win things at golf and there were reports in the newspapers about him and the occasional photograph, David got worse and worse. He played truant and then there was a nasty business about some missing money. Garfield decided that it was best to take him away from the school when he was seventeen. He'd managed three 'O' levels and certainly wasn't going to register anything better than that.'

'What did he do?' I asked.

'Garfield found him a job at one of his clients' firms. A newspaper and magazine publisher. As a trainee. He actually lasted a couple of years and then was fired. For being drunk, he told us. But there were rumours that it was something more serious. Some persistent sexual harassment, which wouldn't have surprised me at all.'

'Oh. Why do you say that?'

Suzi poured us some more coffee and continued: 'I never mentioned this to Garfield because even he would have had to sit up and take notice, but his son's sexual curiosity went beyond the bounds of the normal. He made a habit of rummaging through my things, my underwear . . .'

'Perhaps he liked to wear it.'

Suzi looked sharply at me and saw me grinning. 'It wasn't funny, Chris. I was stuck on my own with the little creep for days on end. And he used to spy on me, when I was in the bathroom or changing my clothes.'

'I've heard nothing abnormal yet.'

'Well, listen to this. I began to get dirty phone calls. Nothing said, just heavy breathing and moaning.' These memories of David seemed to be upsetting her so I invited her on to my lap and asked her if we could do some heavy breathing and moaning. She relaxed then but clearly wanted to continue her story. 'It seemed pretty obvious that it was David because it never happened when he was at home. Then one day it did. I felt a bit remorseful then that I'd blamed him for something so tacky. I actually tried to be nicer to him, to give him more affection.'

'He sounds pretty hard to like.'

'Quite. Anyway, that was a mistake. He took it as a green light for a bit of fun. I woke up one night and he was in my bed, fumbling away.'

'Hell. What did you do?'

'Screamed blue murder and stuck my knee in his crotch. Hard. Then I told him that if he wasn't out of the house by the end of the week I'd report him to the police for sexual assault. I actually thought he was going to attack me, perhaps kill me, at one point. But I grabbed a lamp and yelled at him with all my strength and he backed off. God, I was frightened.'

'And he left?'

'Yes. He told Garfield that I was making his life a misery and he wanted to live on his own. So Garfield got a bed-sitter organised for him.'

'What did he do for a job? Did Garfield help him again?'

'No. Not after he'd been sacked from his previous job. He did all sorts of selling jobs. Because he was reasonably plausible. But mostly selling space for newspapers and magazines.'

'How come he ended up as Ben's caddie?'

'He was out of work again at the beginning of the year and begged Ben to give him a chance. And Ben is soft-hearted, he felt he ought to help his brother.'

I realised that it was helping Suzi to talk about David but all this information had brought me no closer to knowing whether Suzi had known Ross Bentley. Was she the unknown waitress at the High Cliffs Hotel?

The time had come to try more direct tactics. After all, I was being paid by Toby's newspaper and he had made it very clear that I must show some results if I were to continue on the payroll. I told Suzi I had something to show her, tipped her off my lap and made the journey to Toby's car via the back garden and returned with my copy of *The International Golfer.*

I put the magazine on the kitchen table and turned to the photograph of Ross Bentley. Suzi put her hand on my shoulder and leaned over me with a mild show of curiosity. Her face was close to mine and I murmured in her ear, 'Do you recognise anyone?'

'Well, Chris, the caption tells me that the main attraction is Ross Bentley,' she said impatiently.

'Quite. But the girl on his left seems to me to bear a striking resemblance to a young and beautiful Suzi Massey.'

Suzi looked more closely at the photograph. If she remembered anything at all about the occasion, she was hiding it well.

'Well, it could be me. I used to fill in as a waitress occasionally, especially during the holidays. I needed the money, as you do at that age.'

'Do you remember meeting Ross Bentley?'

'Not really. I was heavily into pop music in those days.' She looked at the date on the magazine. '1970. Let's think, I was probably in love with Mick Jagger at the time, I think I'd gone off John Lennon by then. Anyway, what is all this, Chris? I get a distinct feeling I'm being given the third degree.'

I told her some of the truth: that I was helping Toby to compile the research for a long article about Ross Bentley. I watched her reactions very carefully.

'It's Ryder Cup year,' I explained, 'and there is more interest than ever. Especially in the captain of the team because he is an inspirational figure. Until he came on the scene the Americans had only lost three matches. They more or less regarded the Ryder Cup as theirs by right. Ross changed all that.'

'So what has an old photograph to do with your article?'

117

'Oh, nothing, really. I just found it by accident and it reminded me of you. Just thought I'd check. I wondered if you remembered Ross then. You might be able to fill me in on a bit of local colour.'

Suzi narrowed her eyes at me. 'I suspect you wondered if he tried to screw me.' She waved aside my protestations. 'God almighty, Chris, I was just a child. I was still at school.'

I tried to deny her speculation, which was of course spot on, but she was still indignant. 'I know that I had Ben when I was young but I wasn't totally stupid.' Eventually, she appeared to believe my protestations that I had only been curious at finding a younger version of her in the magazine.

It was by now around nine o'clock and the London rush hour would have diminished. We made plans to meet again during the following week but, even as we kissed farewell by the back door, I sensed a distance between us that had not been there an hour before.

I trudged across the lawn towards the garden gate, recalling with pleasure the fun of the preceding night. As I turned into the alleyway behind the house I found a large man, a cigarette in one hand and what looked like the remains of a bacon sandwich in the other, leaning against the wall. He was wearing a forage jacket, jeans and trainers.

I nodded at him as I began to pass him but he jumped in front of me, dropped his cigarette on the ground, reached in one of his many jacket pockets and waved a card at me.

'*Daily Post*,' he said. I could smell the cigarette smoke on his breath, overlaid with bacon grease.

'Gardener,' I said, and tried to push past him.

'Just a minute, mate,' he said. 'Any info? There could be a fifty in it for you.'

I stuck out my hand. He struggled with his card and sandwich remains and produced not a monkey but a tenner. I kept my hand out until he'd made my bribe up to £20 and said, 'Well, all I know is that Mrs Massey's expecting her son home any minute.'

I grinned at his retreating back as he lumbered down the alleyway towards his 'scoop'.

Enmeshed in the lines of traffic, I mused on Suzi's reactions as I drove towards London. She had played down her encounter with Ross Bentley. Perhaps his name had meant nothing to her at the time, but surely Ben's hero-worship of the great golfer would have resurrected the memory for her. Perhaps, after all, she had good reason to deny that memory. Suzi had also picked up my insinuation that she and Ross had been to bed together. She was sharp, very much alive to such suggestions. I wanted to believe the best of her but wondered how the professional cynic, Toby, would view her.

Chapter 15

There were several messages from Toby on my answering machine and they had become progressively more abusive as the previous evening had worn on and the claret or champagne or brandy had taken its toll. By the sound of the last message he had not switched to mineral water. Some succinct aspersions were cast not only at my capacity for work but also on my parenthood and my general grasp of morality. In other words, he wanted to speak to me. Urgently. I'll say this for Toby, he doesn't become incoherent in his cups.

The last message on the tape was the one which transfixed me. It was Ben Massey and he promised to ring me again at midday. He gave me no inkling of where he was and there was nothing in the way of extraneous noise on the tape which gave me a clue.

My first thought was of Suzi and I rang her with the news. Could I call it good news? She seemed annoyed with me that her son had not called her first and her reaction momentarily irritated me. 'Well, at least you know he's alive.'

I stopped her from leaping into her car and coming to the flat so that she would be there when Ben telephoned. She wouldn't arrive in time, anyway, and I didn't want Toby, with his acute antennae, to get an inkling of our changed relationship. I promised Suzi that I would get Ben to contact her as soon as he called.

Toby was next on the list and he picked up his office telephone with a gruff, 'Greenslade, hack, speaking.'

'A hangover, Toby?' Serve him right.

'Gained in the service of my newspaper, you idle young layabout. Christ, I called you about a dozen times yesterday.'

'I was serving your newspaper, too. I was out there, on the job.'

'Yes, I'll bet. Who is she?'

I groaned and said, 'You probably won't believe this but I spent the evening with Suzi Massey and I'm expecting a call from Ben in just over an hour's time.'

I had the pleasure of silencing him, if only for a moment or two, and then Toby said, 'Bloody hell. I'm coming over. Don't leave that phone in case he rings earlier. Can you tape the call? No? I'll bring what's necessary.'

Within half an hour Toby had arrived at my front door. After making sure that he hadn't missed Ben's call, and thanking God that he hadn't, he produced a small tape recorder and a lead that plugged on to the telephone.

'This will record your conversation. Make sure you ask the right questions. This is scoop time.'

'Not necessarily, Toby. Not without Ben's consent. I'm going to tell him he's being recorded.'

'Fine, we don't want to harm your sensibilities, do we? You ought to be working for the royal family,' Toby said sarcastically. 'But you do recall, I hope, that you are being paid by the *Daily News* to assist me. If you take their shilling you must expect to move your moral threshold a bit. Anyway, I would have thought it in Ben's best interests to get his arse back here. Nobody believes he killed his brother. And, Chris, I need a good story and one of the reasons I need one is because of this.'

With a dramatic flourish, Toby threw that morning's

edition of the *Daily Post* on the table in front of me.
The banner headline blared out:

GOLF STAR'S WIFE IN SUICIDE BID

A slightly smaller one followed: 'Swedish golf ace,
Stefan Sandberg, denies allegations of wife's child
abuse.'

Toby tapped the newspaper emphatically and said, 'I
didn't have a sniff of this and my scrawny-brained, pot-
bellied editor wants to know why. A Ben Massey
exclusive will sedate him for a while. When I last saw
him he was acting like a chipmunk on crack.'

I read on:

Jane Sandberg, the British-born former promotions girl who married the Swedish superstar eight
years ago, was recovering in hospital last night
after a drugs overdose. The Sandbergs' nanny
found her in a coma on her bedroom floor after
she returned with the couple's two sons from a
birthday party at a nearby house.

The nanny, Mary Fielding, twenty years old,
from Blackburn, told our reporter: 'I was right
terrified when I found her. I thought she was dead
at first and young Nicholas (the Sandbergs' five-
year-old son) wanted to know why his mummy
was sleeping on the floor.'

It is understood that thirty-year-old Mrs
Sandberg has recently been under investigation by
the NSPCC after allegations that she has
subjected her children, Nicholas, five, and
Arthur, two, to physical abuse.

Stefan Sandberg returned to London Airport
late last night from a tournament in Jersey and

refuted all the claims of child abuse. He ended his statement by saying that it was a wicked and malicious rumour with no foundation and the NSPCC had exonerated his wife from all the charges. A spokesman at the NSPCC confirmed that they had investigated Mrs Sandberg's conduct and had no cause for further action. Mr Sandberg, the founder of Christian Action in Sport, finished his statement by saying that he forgave the misguided people who had started the rumours.

I looked blankly at Toby. 'Who on earth would do that to a mother? That's really sick. No wonder the poor girl flipped. Can't she do these people for slander?'

'No chance,' said Toby. 'Look, I spoke to my ex-wife about it this morning, she's something to do with the social services and they deserve each other. Anyway, she tells me that the NSPCC have to investigate any allegations of child abuse. They would have sent their people out to talk to neighbours, to other parents whose kids play with the Sandberg kids, even to the teachers at Nicholas Sandberg's nursery school.'

'And there's no comeback for the mother?'

'Apparently not. These things are treated in the strictest confidence by the NSPCC.'

'Not this time, though. Who talked?'

'The nanny, apparently, and there was a suicide note.'

'So Stefan decided to clear the air?'

'Precisely. Perhaps it's just as well that he's a God botherer. He'll need God at his right hand over the next few weeks.'

I reflected briefly on the various disasters and difficulties that seemed to be afflicting the members of

Europe's Ryder Cup team. First there was the unpleasantness between Ramon Gonzales and Nick Spencer; then the stories and rumours about Ross Bentley; above all, Ben Massey's predicament. Now, another star golfer had become the victim of some malign spirit. At this rate most of the European players would be either psychological wrecks or behind bars by the time the Ryder Cup began. It didn't occur to me then that anything other than coincidence could be at play.

I decided to agree to taping the conversation with Ben and to its use if it was in his interest. At midday precisely my telephone rang. Toby set his tape recorder going and then sped towards the bedroom to use the extension. Ben Massey's voice came down the line as clearly as if he were calling me from the next room.

'Chris, how are you?' he asked cheerfully.

'I'm fine, but where the hell are you? We've all been worried sick about you. Your mother . . .'

'Look, I'm sorry I disappeared like that. Sorry about our dinner. I needed some time to think things over, relax, read a few books. I've been playing golf solidly for seven or eight years, Chris.'

I tried to interrupt him but he talked on rapidly. 'Yes, I know lots of people would say "lucky old you" and they'd be right. I am lucky, I know that. But I had to get away, have a break, a mini-sabbatical.'

'Ben,' I shouted, 'where are you?'

'Oh, sorry, I'm in France. In the middle somewhere. Walking, drinking wine, eating anything I fancy, reading Dickens. I'm doing the student bit, I've let the beard grow and so on, but I'm still having a shower most days.'

Ben laughed. He was either crazy and had gone into a trauma sufficient to block out his memories of David's death or he knew nothing about it.

'Why did you leave so suddenly?' I asked him. 'Was it because of David?'

'Ah, you know about that. Yes, we had a set-to. He was still there when you arrived, was he? He upset me very badly. And I'd been thinking about my life a lot recently, so I just took off. Irresponsible, I know, Chris, but there you are. Anyway, it's worked. I feel fine now. So, back to work. I'll be home next week, practise a bit and then we'll take off for the States. I want to acclimatise and then play the California Classic in the week before the Ryder Cup. Really get in tune. Has the rest of the team been announced?'

'Next Sunday.'

'You can make it, can you, Chris? I'd like you there with me. You haven't gone back to stockbroking yet, I hope.'

I noticed Toby out of the corner of my eye. He was gesticulating at me from the door of the main bedroom; he was sawing his hand across his throat and grimacing. Damn, I hadn't told Ben about the tape.

'Ben, I have to tell you that this conversation is being taped.'

'What?' he laughed in disbelief. 'Why are you doing that, Chris? What's happening there?'

As gently as I could I told Ben that his stepbrother was dead. There was a long silence and then the questions started. Who? When? Where? How?

'It's all very nasty, Ben. He was shot. I found him at your house.'

'My God,' Ben cottoned on straight away. 'And I'd gone missing. Have the police put two and two together and made five?'

'A very logical five as far as they're concerned, Ben. I suggest you get yourself back here as fast as possible.

You've got some explaining to do.'

Toby was in the doorway again, the telephone still pressed to his ear, and was making another curious set of gestures which involved a turning motion with his right hand. Turn the screw? Yes, that must be it.

'Ben, tell me what happened. When did you leave the house and what did you do for the next few hours?'

'First of all, David was alive when I left. You do believe me, don't you?' I made it clear that I did. 'We'd had a hell of a bust-up. The worst ever. But I didn't kill him, I didn't touch him. I left the house at something like three o'clock. I threw a few basics into a bag, jumped in the car and headed for Portsmouth. All I know is that I got a spot on the ferry to Caen with around an hour to spare.'

'Have you still got your outward ticket?'

'It'll be in the car somewhere.'

'Don't lose it. It's proof of where you were and when. Ben, get a ferry, let me know which one and I'll meet you at Portsmouth or wherever.'

'OK.'

'And Ben, phone your mother, please.'

Chapter 16

Some hours later Toby and I heard from Ben Massey that he would be arriving in Portsmouth the following morning.

I had expected Toby to be busy writing his 'exclusive interview with Ben Massey' story but he dismissed such an idea.

'Don't be naive, Chris, my boy,' he boomed. 'If I give the game away too early, I'll only have half an exclusive. The Fleet Street marauders will be on Inspector Colley's doorstep and they'll get the story, too. I want that to myself.'

'There won't be much to tell. Ben will be interviewed and then released.'

'Maybe, but you should know by now how much those boys can make out of so little.'

Toby looked at his watch. 'It's just after seven o'clock. Let's go to the local hostelry for a livener or two. By the time we've done that the national papers will have been put to bed. Then, you will ring your friend, Inspector Colley, and tell him where to be tomorrow morning to meet young Ben. Then I'll have a story, a real story.'

As soon as Ben had put the telephone down I had wanted to contact Inspector Colley. The time of David Massey's death was obviously one of the crucial factors in establishing Ben's innocence. If it was any time after four o'clock, he would be in the clear, as long as he had booked on to the Caen ferry at the time he claimed.

But Toby made me curb my impatience and leave the call as late as possible.

After our several liveners and a take-away Chinese of dubious content, Toby motioned me towards the telephone and then took up his customary station in my bedroom, the extension phone to his ear. A call to Camberley police station established that Inspector Colley was 'at a function' but could be contacted if it were important. After some explanations, it was promised that he would return my call.

Within minutes Colley was on the line: 'You've just rescued me from one of the most tedious after-dinner speeches I've heard in a long time,' he said.

'A Masonic do, Inspector?'

'We don't all wear aprons and sashes and have funny handshakes, Mr Ludlow. It's a rugby dinner. What can I do for you?'

'You can be at Portsmouth tomorrow morning to meet Ben Massey.' I gave him the details.

'Are you sure he'll turn up? Confession in hand?'

'He'll turn up because he's not a murderer. I would guess that he was on a ferry when David was killed.'

'But Ben knew that his stepbrother was dead, did he?'

'Not until I told him.'

'Shit. God save me from interfering civilians.'

'Let me ask you a question, Inspector,' I said brusquely. 'When was David killed? Have you got a time yet?'

'Approximate. Forensic medicine is far from an exact science. We think he died two to three hours before you found him.'

'Ben couldn't have done it, then.'

'You've been reading too many detective stories, Mr Ludlow. Stick to caddying. I'll be there tomorrow.'

* * *

He was, with a colleague who was also in plain clothes and who looked like an anxious spaniel. Suzi, Toby and I were peering through one end of the customs shed in our efforts to spot Ben's Mercedes, whereas Inspector Colley was waiting amongst the customs officers, who were wearily inspecting the lines of early morning travellers, their cars laden with children, grandmothers, nannies, luggage, beer, wine and many varieties of French cheese.

Inspector Colley saw us, beckoned us over and introduced the spaniel as Detective Sergeant Smiles. Colley announced that he was only offering evens on Ben appearing. As he finished the sentence I saw Ben's dark blue car roll into the shed and he flashed his lights at us.

Suzi took off, raced towards Ben and threw her arms around him. Ben had retreated far from the image of an international golf star. His hair was longer, he had a good growth of beard and was wearing old jeans and a faded Lacoste shirt.

He smiled at us and said, 'Quite a reception committee.' Inspector Colley had been sensible enough to hang back for a moment but now took control. Ben would tavel to Camberley police station with him and his colleague. Would someone please volunteer to drive Ben's car? I volunteered quickly when Toby remarked that he'd never driven a big Mercedes before and rather fancied a try. After Ben had reassured Smiles that his insurance covered any driver, our convoy set off for Camberley.

If Ben had been surprised by the reception committee at Portsmouth, he must have been astounded at the scrum of journalists, photographers and radio reporters which awaited him at Camberley. As Colley's car went through the gates to the car park it was accompanied by the flash of cameras and shouted questions. Toby, Suzi and I were, to my surprise, also allowed into the station car park and were therefore out of reach of the media.

'How the hell did they know about Ben?' I asked Toby.

'Probably a tip-off from Portsmouth. The news agencies have an inside track with the customs boys. It came too late for any activity there but they would have passed it on.'

We all gathered in the reception area of the police station and Inspector Colley told us that Ben would be questioned on his own. It was a major concession that Toby and I were allowed to wait with Suzi inside the building. 'You should be out there with those charming colleagues of yours, Mr Greenslade, but in the circumstances . . .'

'How long will this take?' Toby asked.

'Not very long, if Mr Massey is co-operative,' said Colley, as he ushered Ben down a corridor.

Two hours later, Ben reappeared. During that time Suzi and I had become more and more nervous. How could a simple statement take so long? The facts according to Ben were cut and dried; the apparent time of David's death exonerated him. Toby, fortified by endless cups of pale coffee from a nearby vending machine, was much more patient. He kept himself busy by writing pages of notes. 'The Ben Massey exclusive, my boy. This should keep that brain-blighted buffoon of an editor off my noble back for an hour or two.'

Although Ben looked pale and tense, he smiled at us as they came through the door. I looked at him inquiringly and Suzi said quickly, 'Let's get on our way. We'll talk about everything later.'

'There's a back exit from the car park, if that's any help,' said Colley. 'I'll go out and tell the gentlemen of the Press that Ben has made a full statement and that we're satisfied that he was not implicated in his stepbrother's death. It'll give you a chance to get going.'

'They'll have someone on the back gate,' Toby said wearily. 'Look, Ben, why don't you take refuge at my place. No sense in going home, those reporters will be swarming all over the place.'

'That's very kind, but I'm going home. I've got to face this thing out. Nobody is going to make me go into hiding.'

'You don't know what bastards they are,' Toby said. 'Telescopic lenses, listening equipment, including phone taps. Some of them even use long-range video cameras and then use lip-readers to decipher your conversations. And their presence – they'll be outside your front door all the time. And your back door and on the roof, if possible.'

'They'll get fed up before I do. If they annoy me, I can be deadly with a one-iron. Break an ankle or two, no trouble.'

Suzi suggested that we all head back to Ben's house and have a late lunch. It was decided that she would drive there directly and brave the reporters while Ben and I took a more circuitous route. Toby was going back to the office to finish his story.

Off we went, each trailed by several cars. Ben took a few back roads at speed to test the mettle of his pursuers; predictably he failed to shake them off. But he had one more trick up his sleeve and he played it as we got to within a mile of his home. As we were passing his neighbouring golf club he suddenly threw his car to the right in the face of an advancing lorry, screamed through the car park and headed down a track between a line of trees. We bumped and rattled along for about a quarter of a mile and then he turned into a clearing and ran the car into an open shed which held various bits of machinery. He jumped out and yelled at me to follow. 'It's OK. The greenkeepers know my car,' he said as we ran through the undergrowth. We came out on to a fairway and startled two elderly men who were enjoying a few holes of golf after their lunch.

I was puffing hard in my efforts to keep up with Ben as we ducked and weaved our way through more heavily wooded ground and came out at the back of his house.

'There's a gap in the fence,' he panted, and we forced our way through it into his garden. As we trotted across the lawn towards the back, two men, with cameras at the ready, came down the side of the house. As we heard the click and whirr of the motorised cameras, Ben, with his keys in his hand, sprinted for the back door; I veered towards the photographers and deliberately charged into them. Taken by surprise, they both went down in a tangle of arms and legs and camera cases. The subsequent outburst would have shocked a Northern club comedian. Ben and I collapsed into kitchen chairs, and, though we were out of breath, the incident made us heave with laughter.

Suzi fixed us with a steely eye. 'I believe you two are actually enjoying this.'

'Yes, but Ben's fit enough for it. I'll have to step up my running schedule if I'm to continue as his caddie.'

Suzi had closed all the shutters, blinds and curtains and it gave us all a spurious feeling of security.

'Are those buggers allowed to do this? Surely they're trespassing?' Suzi said.

'I could phone Colley,' I volunteered, 'and get them moved. They should at least be outside the gates.'

Ben wasn't really worried by them. 'They've got a job to do, just like us. They'll get fed up soon. I don't mind.'

'Well, I do,' said his mother and strode to the telephone. Half an hour later a police car arrived and we watched from an upper window as a finger-wagging sergeant told the Fleet Street boys what was and was not permitted. They'd heard it all before but moved back beyond the gates anyway.

During our very late lunch we all shied away from the subject which was uppermost in our minds but, as she made some coffee, Suzi asked Ben what had caused the quarrel with David.

'I don't really want to talk about it. He said some unforgivable things.'

'Like what?' Suzi asked.

'They're not worth repeating. Maybe I over-reacted but I had to get away from him and then I just kept going. Why not have a break, I thought to myself. God, if only I'd known, I'd have stayed put.'

'And David might still be alive, is that what you're saying?' asked Suzi.

'Well, yes.'

'Well, I'm sorry, Ben, but he's no loss to the human race. He never contributed anything worthwhile, and never would have. He just made everyone around him uneasy at best, but mostly very unhappy. He was lazy and corrupt, all he wanted was easy money, without ever making any effort.'

'He should have been in the City in the eighties,' I said in an effort to cheer up the conversation.

Ben said thoughtfully, 'I can see how David might push someone to think of murder, but I still can't understand how they could actually screw themselves up to do it. Could you do it, mum? Did you?' Ben smiled at his mother as he asked the questions.

'No, I couldn't take someone's life. And David's murder must have been so cold-blooded. He was shot and there was no sign of a gun. So whoever did it must have planned it or at least took a gun along as insurance, and was not afraid to use it.'

'But that would imply that he mixed in criminal circles. I know you think he was a bad 'un, but surely not that bad?'

'Could be. David knew lots of dodgy people. There was always some hare-brained project, usually it was just on the edge of legality, sometimes beyond it, I'm sure. Maybe he got in too deep with someone.'

Ben continued on the same theme and explained how David had, as long as he had known him, been a dreamer, someone who concocted exotic money-making schemes and was always on the brink of achieving success and wealth. Arthur Daley without the fun, without any fun at all.

Ben and I arranged to meet a couple of days later on the practice ground so that he could start an intensive programme before we both left for America. I then faced the problem of getting home and the obvious way seemed to be by rail. Ben described the route to the station for me, which again took in the gap in his back fence and the outskirts of the golf course.

'Maybe I'll create a diversion,' he said. 'I've got lots of bottled beer in the garage. I might offer them all a drink. Might as well try to get them on my side.'

Chapter 17

Toby Greenslade's exclusive appeared in the *Daily News* on the following morning and every stop was pulled out in support of it. It took up most of the front page and made Toby appear to be a combination of Hildy Johnson and Hercule Poirot. There were several judicious quotes not only from Ben but also from Inspector Colley and from Suzi. I was happy to see that my name didn't appear; someone would have told my mother, who would have rushed over to save me from certain disgrace and incarceration.

The great investigative reporter rang me quite early to arrange a 'conference', the said conference to begin at noon in a nice little bistro he knew off Notting Hill Gate.

The place was solid with people when we finally got to our table, which, insubstantial and plastic topped, was more reminiscent of a transport caff than a fashionable bistro. The seats were nearly as uncomfortable as the prices. The owners clearly had no intention of pandering to the recession and their clientele had probably not noticed that there was one. The level of noise, as it bounced off the hard plastic surfaces in the room and echoed off the ceiling, almost breached the pain barrier. Even Toby's boom didn't carry far and I wished I had the ability to lip-read. I suppose it was a good place to have a confidential chat.

Shouting is quite hard work at the best of times and I had to convey to Toby what I had learned about Suzi

Massey and her connection, slender as it was, with Ross Bentley. I'd told him that Suzi had more or less admitted that she was the young waitress in the photograph with Bentley but only had vague recollections of the occasion; and that, although Ben had been born when she was young, she had left school by then. He said, 'If she was a bit vague about old Ross and vague about dates, Chris, she's got something to hide.'

'You're a cynic, Toby. She didn't have the happiest of times then. Perhaps the memories are painful and she doesn't want to remember them. She was more or less abandoned by her parents, in a genteel middle-class way. Oh yes, they sent her to a boarding school but she hardly ever saw them even in the holidays.'

'And she became very tough and self-sufficient, no doubt.'

'She's very bright, Toby. I don't know about tough.'

Toby smiled at me in a knowing way. 'A bit smitten, are we? You shouldn't mix pleasure with business, my boy,' he said smugly. He could talk.

I started to mention a few of the pleasures Toby had mixed with his business, but the star journalist was not to be side-tracked.

'Less of the banter,' he said. 'Now, how old is Ben and how old is Suzi?'

'Well, Ben will be twenty-three in a couple of months and Suzi is . . . I don't know.'

'Well, have a guess. You've been closer to her than I have.' Toby attempted a leer, but his wine glass got in the way.

'She did say that she was a year or two off forty,' I said tentatively.

'That could mean she's well over forty or is several years away from it. It depends on the woman,' Toby said with authority. 'Let's think about it. You said she'd left school when she had Ben. Let's say she was eighteen and Ben is twenty-two, that makes her forty. She could have left school earlier than that, of course.'

I remembered what the waitress at the High Cliffs Hotel had told me about Suzi's sudden disappearance from the school.

'Suzi went home to her parents in Singapore for Christmas but disappeared from view a couple of months later. She didn't reappear at the hotel and left the school as well.'

'Maybe because she was pregnant,' Toby said. 'And she would have been sixteen, perhaps.'

'It's not difficult to check their birth certificates, both of them. Why don't we do that?'

'Good idea. We need to know Suzi's maiden name and where she was born. Then we can do it.'

'It's simple enough, surely. A visit to St Catherine's House will do it.'

'It's not quite that simple if we haven't got the date of birth. That's exactly what we want to know. I'll get one of the lads in the office on to it. He'll know how to do it. One of the first things they do when they're digging for dirt on someone, an actress, for instance, is to check for any illegitimate children.'

'Perhaps, too, we should try and check how Ben's fees at Upton Manor were paid. Suzi said that her parents set up a trust to cover them but I wonder.'

'How can we check that?' Toby asked.

'I'll chat up the headmaster. For an in-depth profile of one of our most promising Ryder Cup players.'

Toby grinned and congratulated himself on how well I was learning under his tutelage.

Ian Crisp, the headmaster of Upton Manor, was

guarded at first; wisely, I thought, having seen a bit of how the Press operate. He had clearly liked Ben and agreed to an interview 'as long as you mention the school and stress that Ben learned his golf here'.

I gave him my assurances and a time was set for the following morning. Toby gave me permission to hire a car at the expense of the *Daily News*.

Crisp had been a prominent sportsman in his youth; he had played first-class rugby and had opened the bowling for Sussex. He had ruthlessly milked the contacts he had made in those days in order to improve and extend the facilities at his school through sponsorship and donations. Hence his concern for publicity. I expected, rightly, that I'd gain his good will by playing my sporting and City cards to their full extent.

Upton Manor was located not far from Gloucester and on this Saturday morning had a relaxed air to it. Crisp met me at the door to his office. He had a lean body with a deeply lined and tanned face and looked as if he spent most of his time out of doors rather than in the classroom. He first took me on a tour of the school and its grounds and I saw how his entrepreneurial flair had procured remarkable amenities for his school. Practically everything was sponsored, from indoor tennis courts and a full-sized swimming pool to the new theatre and concert hall; even the science laboratories were sponsored.

When I expressed my admiration, Crisp said, 'It's the way I decided to do it. You can't rely on endless appeals to the old boys and girls and you can't keep increasing the fees ad nauseam. It's a competitive world and schools have to compete for their slice of the cake just like any other organisation.'

We played the name game on the way back to his

office and I discovered that we had many City acquaintances in common, including my ex-employer, Andrew Buccleuth.

Crisp became more and more relaxed and asked me if I played golf. 'It's not a game I ever got to grips with,' he said. 'It doesn't mix too well with cricket. But I suppose you play with young Massey?'

I thought that an admission that I was his caddie might destroy the credibility I had so far built up and contented myself with a vague statement that we'd been out on several courses together. By this time we were seated in the headmaster's office, with a large cafetière of coffee and some biscuits in front of us. I told him that I was interested in gaining some insight into Ben's time as a schoolboy and Crisp gave me a very concise picture. It was rather like an end-of-term report, which was not surprising since he had done thousands of them.

'A delightful boy, honest, self-contained. Never any trouble. Despite his prowess at golf, and you could tell that he really was special, he joined in all the sports. A good footballer, passable cricketer, very quick sprinter.' Ah, that's why my chest was nearly bursting when I tried to keep up with him.

'What about his academic side?'

'Unrealised. A few passes at GCSE and one A-level, I think. Let me see.' He consulted the brown folder which lay on his desk. He gestured at it: 'It's all going on computer soon, but I still like the old files. Yes, one A-level in English. He could have gone to university, I'm sure, but it seemed pre-ordained that he would become a professional golfer.'

'What about his family? I know, of course, about his stepbrother and stepfather and I've talked to his mother. Did Ben's grandparents ever make an appearance?'

'Well, if they did, I never met them. She was a lovely lady, Mrs Massey, an absolute stunner,' Crisp said enthusiastically.

I tried to get him back to the point. 'It seems strange that the grandparents never visited, especially since they paid Ben's fees.'

'Did they? But why should that interest you?' he asked sharply.

I shrugged. 'Oh, just a detail, but it fills in Ben's background, that he came from a comfortably off family.'

'Well, I suppose so. Trusts from grandparents are quite common, as you know.' Crisp laid the file flat on the desk and flicked over a few pages. 'This doesn't tell us much. The money came via a French bank. Anyway, I shouldn't be telling you this.'

I put my hands up placatingly and asked Crisp if he had a photograph of Ben as a boy. He looked around the room at the various pictures of past school teams and wandered over to one of the corners.

This was a fleeting chance. I quickly rose halfway from my seat, leaned across the desk and looked hard at the document in the file.

One of the valuable things I had learned during my truncated City career was to read numbers upside down. I saw the heading, Banque de Paris, and a group of numbers which I guessed was the branch reference. It was easy enough to remember, but I wrote the numbers down for safety.

I showed interest in the football team photograph which the headmaster thrust in front of me and, a few minutes later, he stood and asked me to remember him to Ben and Suzi Massey and to Andrew Buccleuth. I set off back to London with another nugget of information to offer Toby.

Chapter 18

Sunday was rarely a day of rest for me, especially during the summer months when I would normally be carrying a professional golfer's bag during the final round of a tournament. If your employer is close to the leaders, there is nothing quite like the scent of a victory; the senses are heightened and the expectancy sharp.

My own adrenalin stayed at a modest level as I ploughed through the newspapers. There was some concentration on Ben's reappearance and his elimination from the inquiries by the police into his stepbrother's death. The Ryder Cup team was due to be announced at midday and one or two of the tabloids speculated that, in view of the stress caused by his stepbrother's murder, it might be in Ben's and the team's best interest if he withdrew. But Ben had already won his place and I knew that there was no question of his declining it, nor of Ross Bentley asking him to stand down.

The names of the Ryder Cup team were duly read out on the midday news. There were no surprises; nine of the players, including Ben, Stefan Sandberg and the two adversaries, Nick Spencer and Ramon Gonzales, had won their places automatically. Ross Bentley had played safe with his prerogative of picking the final three players by choosing the two who came tenth and eleventh in the Order of Merit. His one controversial decision was to exclude the man in twelfth place, a young and mercurial Irish player with a fast and

unorthodox swing, in favour of my old boss, Jack
Mason, a golfer with well-proven qualities and a sound
record in the Ryder Cup. The team was composed of
three Spaniards, one Swede, one German and seven
British players. There was no mention of Rollo
Hardinge and I wondered whether he had been
considered.

An hour later Ross Bentley was interviewed on the
radio. He was an articulate interviewee and gave a clear
explanation of his preference for Jack Mason over the
young Irishman, stressing the need to maintain the
balance between youthful fire and solid experience.

The interviewer asked him if he had any doubts about
Ben Massey's state of mind. 'None whatsoever. He's a
fine young player who has earned his place in the team.
Ben has just been through a testing experience, a time of
stress and emotion, but from my observations of him,
he'll be all the more determined to do well. And
remember I'm there to help these players, I'm a father-
figure if you like, they can turn to me.'

'While we're on the subject of stress and emotion,'
the interviewer continued, 'your players have had more
than their fair share recently, haven't they? Apart from
Ben Massey, we've had the attempted suicide of Stefan
Sandberg's wife. How do you think that will affect his
motivation in the Ryder Cup?'

'I feel very sorry for that young man and, above all,
for his wife. I hate to imagine the misery she must have
been through and we are all looking forward to seeing
her, fully recovered, at the Ryder Cup with all the other
wives and girlfriends. As for Stefan, he is blessed with a
high degree of inner strength. He's proved that time and
time again on the golf course and he will no doubt prove
it in his personal life. His faith as a committed Christian
helps him, of course.'

'Did you consider Rollo Hardinge as a wild card?'

'Yes. He was next on my list and must consider himself very unlucky not to play. I was thrilled by his win earlier this year in America. It's never easy to win over there.'

'You said that with feeling, Ross. You managed a few victories there, including the Masters, didn't you?'

'Well, I had my moments,' Bentley said modestly, 'and that's why I hope I can help these young men. But I would have liked to have seen more of Rollo in Europe. The Ryder Cup team does, after all, represent the European golf tour and he has chosen to play mostly in the States this year. That's fine while he's learning his profession, so to speak, but I would like to see him lend his support to our tour. He's a talented performer, very dashing and I look forward to seeing him over here in the future.'

The interviewer reminded Bentley of a newspaper article which had appeared after the Open Championship. 'You said then that the excellent performances of the European players were in marked contrast to those of the Americans, who had not performed well under the pressure of a major tournament.'

'Not quite true, Gary. I wrote that it was a good augury that the Europeans had done so well. I certainly did not knock any of the very fine American golfers who came over for the Open. We owe them a great debt because they, along with all the other foreign players, make the Open the best and most international of all the major tournaments. No other championship can remotely compare itself in that respect with the Open.'

The interview ended with a few conventional comments about the importance of the fixture; with pious hopes that it would be played in a sporting manner and the great traditions maintained.

And so say all of us.

The *Daily News* hire car came in handy for my journey to meet Ben for his practice session at a course near Winchester. The professional was an old friend of his and the facilities were superb.

Ben had shaved off his beard, his hair was newly trimmed and he was wearing some smart new clothing. 'Welcome back,' I said drily, as he emptied a large bag of balls on to the grass. He grinned, made a few practice swings and began to hit wedge shots down the range. The thump and crack of his shots showed that none of his timing had been lost during his short holiday from the game.

Between the salvoes, I asked Ben who coached him; virtually every professional golfer now has an adviser and some of them have been elevated to the status of gurus and have attained a greater celebrity than many of their pupils.

'I don't have a regular coach. At the moment, I don't feel I need one. Danny, the pro here, knows my game as well as anyone and I have a check-up at the start of every season with him. We just go through the basics. It's an easy game, Chris.'

'Like hell,' I replied with feeling.

'You set yourself up comfortably to the ball, grip the club nicely, take the clubhead back, turn and release the club into the ball. Your momentum takes you through to a nice balanced finish. That's all there is to it. Simple.'

Ben proceeded to demonstrate the essential simplicity of his own swing, his shots soaring straight and true into the bright sky. I couldn't see a fault in his method. Just before we broke for lunch he gave me a short lesson. By the time he had adjusted my stance and my grip, I knew I wouldn't be able to hit the ball at all, but from the first shot, it flew down the practice ground like a shell. It was a revelation; I had discovered power and timing that I didn't know I possessed.

'There you are, told you. It's an easy game,' Ben said smugly.

'Clever bugger.' I knew, and so did he, that next time I played I wouldn't be able to hit my elbow.

We sat on the terrace of the club in warm sunshine and savoured our sandwiches and beer. I asked after Suzi and added, 'She seems to have liked David even less than you did.'

Ben looked sharply at me, took a pull at his beer and said carefully, 'She bore the brunt of his nonsense. I was away at boarding school and Garfield seemed to be abroad on business most of the time and mum had to cope. It wasn't easy. David was dangerous, I'm not kidding, it was like leaving something untended on the stove. He was always on the verge of boiling over, there was always that awful feeling that something nasty was about to happen.'

'Difficult to live with.'

'Yes. Sometimes I couldn't wait to get back to school, but that meant that I'd be away from my mother and then I felt disloyal to her.'

While we were on the subject of David, I took my chance to press Ben for more information about him. I hoped that he would feel able to open up a bit more when he was away from Suzi.

'What was he up to?' I asked bluntly. 'You mentioned that he said some unforgivable things about Suzi. What was it that was so terrible?'

Ben shook his head and looked away from me out over the lush green of the golf course, over the rows of magnificent trees standing like sentinels along the fairways, and towards the distant hills. 'I can only make a guess at what he was up to and I can't tell you what he said about Mum — it made me sick. As I told you, he always had these amazing schemes to make loads of money. Well, this time, he really seemed to believe he was on to something big. He was very excited but wouldn't give me any details, which was unusual, because he loved to boast, but he kept saying that he'd soon be well on his way to his first million. I told him not to be so idiotic, but David shouted something like, "When could you make a million dollars in one hit?" '

'He said dollars?'

'Yes. He'd been fantasising about moving to America. To Florida, I think.'

'And that was all he told you?'

'More or less. Then he waded in about Mum and other things and you know the rest. I left and headed for the ferry.'

I changed the subject slightly. 'How do you get on with Garfield?'

'So so. There was always tension about David. They both resented my going to Upton and there were sometimes sly digs about who paid the fees.'

'Who did?' I asked innocently.

'Grandpa, apparently. Some sort of trust fund. It's the one thing they did for Mum, since my father was not around to help.'

'Did you see much of them?'

'I met them once, briefly. But when the old man retired from the army, they stayed out east. He got a job in Hong Kong.'

We spent an hour or so on the putting green and, as with the rest of Ben's game, I couldn't fault his action. It was slow, repetitive and as sound as the Bank of

England used to be. As I prepared to leave for London, Ben was making preparations, along with his friend, Danny, to coach a squad of junior players. If they absorbed Ben's golfing method they'd all be playing off scratch in double quick time.

Chapter 19

Full of good spirits and optimism, I headed back to my flat. Not only was my employer hitting the golf ball with unwavering power and aplomb but, even better, he had passed a little of his magic on to me. Perhaps I'd win a monthly medal again.

The light was blinking on my answering machine but I poured myself a glass of cider before attending to it, then settled down, message pad and pencil in hand, and rewound the tape. I had expected Toby's forceful delivery, perhaps with instructions to follow up some lead or other, but it was an American voice which addressed me. 'This is Lee Brandel calling Chris Ludlow. Would it be possible to arrange a meeting this Monday evening to talk about the Ryder Cup? I'm doing an in-depth article for an American magazine.'

Christ, not another one, I thought, and wondered if his in-depth interviews were as genuine as mine. I rang the number he'd left and he agreed to come round to see me an hour later. As soon as I put the telephone down it rang again and Toby arranged to visit me later that evening. 'I've got something very interesting to show you,' he said mysteriously.

Lee Brandel's dark blue blazer did nothing to conceal the massive breadth of his shoulders and, as we shook hands, I realised that we had crossed paths recently. The light brown of his moustache, in contrast to his jet-black dyed hair, gave me an instant recall of the aftermath of the fight with David Massey. Here was the

American journalist who had thrown some sarcastic remarks in Ben's direction as we thrust our way through the throng of pressmen.

As he opened a shoulder case to reveal a tape recorder I said, 'We've met before, haven't we? You were less than pleasant to my boss, Ben Massey, at the Open. Is that right?'

'Well, I really had hoped you'd forgotten that. Just doing my job, you know.'

'And what is your job?'

'Oh, I work for a group of Californian newspapers. We're doing a special issue on the Ryder Cup and I'm doing profiles of all the players.'

'So why come to me? Surely you can get enough information from the usual sources. I'm just Ben Massey's caddie and I've only recently joined him.'

Brandel shrugged his wide shoulders. 'I'm sure you know the form. I want to put some flesh on the bones, if possible. Tell me a bit about Ben's background. He's unusual, isn't he? Went to a private school?'

I didn't want to explain to an American that Ben's 'private' school is actually called a 'public' school; it would be as bad as trying to explain the rules of cricket. I nodded and said mildly that not all the British professionals came to the game these days via the caddie shed.

We discussed Ben's career for a few minutes and then Brandel returned to the subject of Ben's family. 'I guess that his father was well-off, if he paid for boarding school?'

'Presumably,' I said non-committally.

'But he's out of the picture. During all this furore over his stepbrother's murder, there's been no mention of a father. His mother, yes, and I wouldn't mind an hour in a locked room with her, but no father. So, who is this mystery man?'

Brandel grinned at me and I felt my dislike for the man increasing by the second. Before I could react to his questions he continued, 'Do you think the Massey family have something to hide?'

'I think you've got a vivid imagination, Mr Brandel,' I said brusquely.

'Well, I didn't imagine that punch-up at the British Open, did I? I didn't imagine the murder of Ben Massey's brother, did I? And I didn't imagine the disappearance, temporary though it was, of Ben Massey, did I?'

Brandel delivered the words fast and aggressively and I tried to head him off by saying in my most dismissive English tone, 'It's not the *British* Open. Ours is *the* Open. I wish you Americans would remember that.'

He brushed aside my pedantic comment with the remark that his readers in Santa Monica didn't give a shit about such niceties but would be very interested to know that a suspect in a murder case would be representing Europe in the Ryder Cup.

'Tell me,' Brandel said, 'did they really hate each other that much? I mean, trying to carve your initials on your brother is one thing, but shooting him in the eye is another.'

I was already on my feet to urge Brandel on his way out of my flat, when the doorbell rang. It was Toby. I explained who my unwelcome visitor was. 'He's asking some very pointed questions and I'm about to get rid of him.'

'Just give me a moment or two,' Toby said softly, as we went into the sitting room.

After introductions, Toby commented, 'I believe you're a west-coast journalist, Mr Brandel. *San Francisco Examiner*? *Los Angeles Times*?'

Brandel fiddled with his tape recorder and said, 'A

subsidiary of the *LA Times*, based in Tustin.'

'But you write on sport, so you'd know the sports editor, Harry Unser?'

'Can't say I do but I'm a freelance. We're the humble troopers, we don't get to meet the generals.'

'Do you have a card?' asked Toby. 'I'll give you a call when I'm in your great country for the Ryder Cup.'

Brandel packed his tape recorder away in his shoulder bag and groped in one of the outer pockets. 'I don't have an LA number but here's my office number in Florida. My assistant will pass on any messages.'

The American levered himself to his feet, thanked me — with little warmth — for my time and made for the door. As I opened it I said, 'Why don't you dye your moustache to match your rug?' and closed the door on his astonished face. That felt better.

Toby's first remark when I went back into the sitting room was that if Brandel was a journalist he was Ben Hogan. I laughed at the bizarre idea of Toby's well-rounded body and friendly face being compared to the lean frame and sharp-eyed looks of the legendary hard case from Texas.

Toby looked hurt. 'Any sports journalist who operates at all on the west coast, freelance or not, knows Harry Unser. He's a legend, the best sports editor in the business. And what's Brandel doing in California if his office is in Florida? He's a ringer, that's for sure.'

'Agreed, but what's he up to? He was after the dirt on Ben and his family. But who for? He was asking all the questions we've been asking.'

'I have a theory about that, but first things first.' Toby reached into a jacket pocket and produced an envelope. With a flourish worthy of an Italian waiter, and a triumphant grin, he handed it to me and asked me to open it. Inside there were copies of two birth certificates. The first related to the birth of a girl, Susan Meadows-Price, in the county of Kent, and the second to the birth of a boy, Benjamin Meadows-Price.

Toby was looking over my shoulder and said, 'Lovely handwriting, isn't it? What used to be called copperplate and it was once very important to have a good hand. That was in the days before those liberal boobies started to ruin the best educational system in the world with their cant about freedom of expression.'

I started to play an imaginary violin and Toby ground unwillingly to a halt. 'Anyway,' he grunted, 'you've got there already, I expect. Kindly note Miss Meadows-Price's date of birth. March 1955.'

I hadn't got there and Toby, like a schoolmaster taking a particularly dim boy through his maths tables, asked me, 'and when was Benjamin born?'

'October 12, 1970,' I replied.

'Yes. So how old was Suzi when she gave birth?'

'God almighty, no wonder she was vague about her age. She was fifteen when she . . .'

'And fourteen when Ben was conceived,' Toby said with finality. 'My case rests.'

I wandered over to the window and looked out at the patch of communal garden; parts of the lawn were well worn from the games of cricket played by the children from the top-floor flat. Their test series, England versus an England Eleven because neither boy wanted to be Australia or the West Indies, had been going on throughout the summer. I occasionally umpired through the open window when their disputes got too fierce. My memory flew back to the same games, played in my boyhood with my brother, Max, and my father; a fading snapshot of two young and very competitive boys. Innocent pleasures, simple lives. For a moment the jab of nostalgia in my chest was almost too much for me.

I swallowed hard, turned to face Toby and said, 'Are we guessing that Ross Bentley was the father?'

'Why not? You remember the photograph in the magazine. The function itself when he and Suzi met was in January of 1970. They went to bed and nine months later out popped baby Ben. That's how it's done, isn't it?'

'Well, it's not as simple as that for some people. How do we prove anything?'

'I don't know. Why don't you ask Suzi? Point blank. That should get a reaction.'

'Are you crazy? I happen to like Suzi and I like Ben and I wouldn't want to harm or embarrass them.'

'Oh yes, it's pretty obvious how much you like Suzi. But would she be embarrassed? Ross Bentley's the one who'd be embarrassed, not the Masseys.' There was certainly some truth in that and Toby continued, 'Can you imagine the headlines? "Love-child mystery in Ryder Cup captain's past. Under-age mother reveals her lonely secret." ' He smacked his lips with theatrical gusto. 'What a story.'

'And one which would blight several lives,' I added heatedly.

'I wish I could live on your lofty moral plateau, Christopher, but I'm a journalist who has to earn a living and you, in case you need reminding, have been assisting me down here in the ethical swamplands. This is a story that any journalist would shop his own mother for, let alone someone else's mother. You'd be surprised, by the way, by the average person's ability to survive such shocks. I would imagine that the temperature might be a little cool in the Bentley household for a while, the marital bed a touch icy, I wouldn't wonder. But the marriage will survive. It was, after all, a youthful indiscretion by Ross and they'll pull through.'

'That's a pretty facile point of view, Toby. It's OK because not much harm will be done? But you haven't actually got any proof that Bentley was the father. You have no evidence that he bedded Suzi. You have no story.'

'Such a minor detail as proof won't hold my deformed bug of an editor back this time. That document we had about Bentley and his illegitimate child was from an unknown source and was totally unsubstantiated, so we couldn't use it. But this time we at least have Suzi's and Ben's birth certificates, we can demonstrate that she was an under-age mother and we have a photo of Suzi with Ross at the right time. If we run that story, it might even flush Bentley out. A bit of innuendo here and there and he might even hold up his hands and admit the dirty deed, or, even better, Suzi might accuse him.'

'Why should she? It was long ago and far away. She's married, Ben is in the public eye, why should she rock the boat?'

Toby was silent and I resumed the attack. 'What you will do is wreck our chances in the Ryder Cup. Whichever way you play it you'll put Ben under intolerable strain. Apart from the fact that it's his first Ryder Cup, he's got his stepbrother's death to contend with and there will be plenty of people who will be only too happy to believe he was implicated, whatever the police have said. If you add the story of an under-age mother, you'll bury him.'

Toby began to speak, but I overrode him for once. 'And Bentley, if he is the father, will guess that he's under scrutiny too. You can't do it, Toby, you'll be playing right into the Americans' hands. Our team has got enough problems already, what with Sandberg's wife and the business between Gonzales and Spencer.'

'I'm as keen that we stuff the Americans as anybody, as you well know, Chris. But I don't want to be stuffed by my editor for sitting on one of the year's best sporting stories. And you must see that if I don't expose it, someone else might.'

The whole problem needed some analysis. All the different facts and assumptions were jumbled in my mind and I suggested to Toby that some discussion, as rational as we could make it, would benefit us both.

'Let's have a drink,' I suggested. 'It might help.'

'I thought you'd never offer,' grumbled Toby. 'Any fizz?'

'On my earnings and with my debts, you must be joking.'

Toby, generous as ever, volunteered to go to the nearest off-licence to buy 'a couple of cold ones'.

In his absence I tried to think my way through the events of the last few weeks. The only hard facts were that David Massey had been murdered and that Suzi had conceived Ben when she was fourteen years old. Although I tended to believe that Ross Bentley was the father of Ben, there was as yet no evidence to support the theory. Maybe Suzi had been to bed with several men at that time. Maybe her story of the commune was true. She had been practically abandoned by her parents, was lonely and perhaps had sought love and affection in the only way available.

Above all, I wondered what was the source of the information which was contained in the letter to the national newspapers about Bentley's illegitimate child. There was something about the letter that nagged me; something was odd.

At this point in my reverie, Toby reappeared with two bottles of champagne in one bag and several sandwiches in another. I asked him if he had a copy of the Bentley letter and he delved into his briefcase, shuffled through a file and found it. I read it through carefully and said to Toby, 'This is American. Look. "The *British* Open" and "*the* Masters". If that had been written by a Brit, it would refer to "the Open" and "the US Masters". The source must be American.'

Toby gulped at his champagne, took the document from me and nodded his agreement.

'I'm also getting the shadow of a theory about all this,' I said. 'I wonder if it's the same as yours.'

'Well, turn the shadow into substance, my boy,' Toby urged.

'That fracas between Gonzales and Spencer took place in America and was blown up out of all proportion mainly by the media over there. Second, that nonsense about Ross Bentley's winning putt in the seventy-two Open was resurrected on the basis of some film discovered in America. Third, this letter was written by an American.'

'Interesting, even though I'm not a great believer in conspiracy theory. But Brandel could well be closely involved in all this, that was the starting point for my theory.'

'And he must be working for someone, someone who has a lot to gain from an American win in the Ryder Cup.'

'He looks nasty enough to work for the CIA but I don't suppose it's gone that far,' Toby said with a smile. He sat back in his chair, a smoked-salmon sandwich in one hand and a glass of champagne in the other. 'Think on this; what about the guy who runs the American golf tour?'

'Kyle Coker?' I prompted him.

'Uhm. I can't see it. He runs a huge operation. The prize money on the various tours over there is well over a hundred million dollars and his revenue is double that. The Ryder Cup is just a sideshow to him.'

'What about Tony Bendix?'

'The American captain? Absolutely not. He's as hard as nails and he's talking up a storm on the Yanks' behalf. He's coming on like John Wayne in plus fours, but he's an honest sort of bloke. He's been on the golf scene far too long to go over the top in the way you're suggesting. Anyway, if there's a conspiracy afoot, where does David Massey fit into it all? Are you suggesting that this latter-day Machiavelli, or perhaps a latter-day Borgia would be more appropriate, knocked David off in order to implicate Ben in a murder?'

'Well, no, that is a bit far-fetched,' I agreed. 'You know, Ben told me that his brother was involved with some very unpleasant people. Could have been drugs, I suppose. Apparently David boasted that he was on his way to his first million. Made a point of saying dollars. So there is another American connection.'

'Hmm. It could be drugs. Though how he could've got involved to that extent, I can't imagine. He lived in cloud cuckoo land. But if he got out of his depth . . . say there was a mafia connection, for instance, that's just how they'd take him out. A bullet through the head.'

'All right,' I said, 'let's assume that David's death has no connection with the Ryder Cup. But the Sandberg incident could easily have been engineered to embarrass and upset Stefan, couldn't it?'

'I agree, but I bet it was done by someone close to Jane Sandberg. Some nasty piece of work who is jealous of her or her family or has imagined some slight or insult.'

'Someone who ought to head for the nearest psychiatrist's couch.'

'Ugh, what an awful pun,' Toby groaned. 'The theories are fine but we don't have much evidence.'

'As you say, Toby, let's do the story first and worry about the facts later. Anyway, we're agreed that Brandel is probably orchestrating some of these rumours. By the way, he was well to the fore at the Open after my fracas with David. And I'll bet you that he was at the Memorial Tournament when Gonzales and Spencer had their disagreement. So, given that the Bentley letter was penned by an American, perhaps it's Brandel's work. Maybe I'll ask him when we meet in the States. I don't like him and, big as he is, I might have to twist his arm a bit.'

'Before you go to the colonies, Chris, why don't you twist Suzi Massey's arm? It will be more pleasurable and perhaps more productive. Have a go at her, brandish the birth certificates before her eyes and she might spill the beans.'

'But you won't, Toby, until after the Ryder Cup? Is that a deal?'

'God help me if I'm ever found out. I'd never get a job in journalism again. But, yes, it's a deal.'

Chapter 20

The rest of that week was mostly taken up with intensive practice as Ben tried to prepare himself for the golfing battles to come: the California Classic which was to be played at a new course on the famous Monterey peninsula and then the Ryder Cup.

The hire car had been returned and to solve the problems of travelling I stayed at Ben's home for a couple of nights. To my astonishment there were still several journalists on watch outside his house, but Ben had evolved his own way of dealing with the nuisance. Whoever was there in the morning was invited in for coffee and given a full briefing on his movements; and when we returned in the evening Ben told them if we were planning to go out again.

I wanted to see him in the most relaxed state possible and deliberately kept off the subject of his family. We mostly talked about golf and books and watched television.

The one task which I had to perform on Toby's behalf was to talk again to Suzi and I arranged to see her on my return to London at the end of the week. This was no hardship since in many ways I was longing for her; it was a physical longing but there was a lot more to it than that. On the other hand I had to confront her with what I knew about her past. She had every right to tell me what to do with my knowledge and with my questions; from what I knew of her forthright character, she would probably exercise that right with alacrity. I was apprehensive of her anger and also of her rejection.

Shortly after seven o'clock Suzi Massey pressed the bell on my front door and, as I admitted her, I admired the dark suit which complemented her slim body to perfection. A creamy silk shirt and a coral necklace offset the sombre colour. I held her in my arms for a moment and kissed her; I had hoped for something more enthusiastic than a quick and formal brush of the lips, but Suzi was swift to disengage herself. The auguries for another night of passion seemed to be poor.

As I saw her to a seat on a sofa, I complimented her on how smart she looked. 'Power dressing?' I asked.

'Not really, but I've made plans to join some friends in Chelsea later, after we've eaten. I'll stay the night with them, rather than drive home.'

Well, that certainly put paid to the night of passion.

As we had our pre-dinner drinks, the conversation was desultory. It was as if we were comparative strangers rather than people who had shared the most intimate of all experiences. I wondered what I had done to make Suzi so cool and detached; I also wondered if I would get through the evening without running out of neutral topics to discuss. I had suddenly gone off the idea of waving copies of her and her son's birth certificates under her nose and interrogating her about her past. I did not fancy an unscheduled confrontation with such a self-possessed woman. Let Toby do his own dirty work.

We dined around the corner at a favourite restaurant; it was noisy and cheerful, as always, and the atmosphere lightened the moods of both of us. A few glasses of potent Italian red removed some more of my inhibitions and I decided after all to press on to some sort of conclusion with my various queries about Suzi. Her cool demeanour had already told me that my carefully hoarded plans for an affair with the elegant and lovely woman opposite me should be shelved. I had very little to lose.

We talked a little of Ben's plans and Suzi surprised me by telling me that she would be in America, too. 'I'm going to see the last day or two of the California Classic and I'll be there for the whole of the Ryder Cup.'

'With your husband?' I asked gloomily.

'He says he may come over for a few days, but I doubt it. He's still intent on blaming Ben for his son's death. Oh, he'll boast about Ben to his cronies in the golf club but that's as far as it goes. I'm going over at Ben's invitation, by the way.'

'He looks after you, doesn't he,' I said innocently. 'As he should do, because I can't conceive how difficult it must have been when he was a baby. You were so young, little more than a child yourself, really.'

I was looking into her eyes, which was a pleasure in itself, and waiting for her reaction, prepared for anger or scorn. But her eyes softened and she smiled at me, a little wearily.

'So you and Toby have ferreted out my little secret, have you? I might have guessed. You're too sharp by half, aren't you, Chris?'

I grimaced warily and wondered whether a storm was about to break over me. 'I'm sorry we've been prying,' I said swiftly, 'but Toby found out while we were researching . . .'

'. . . and he's got a job to do.'

'Yes, but there's no reason for him to use the information. There's nothing to gain unless, that is, he finds out that Ross Bentley is the father.'

Suzi burst into laughter. 'You don't give up on your

pet theories, do you? No, Ross Bentley isn't the father. If Ben wasn't involved in golf, I wouldn't have any idea who Ross Bentley is. The only reason I'm cagey about the father's identity is because he's well known and I promised a long time ago never to give him away. And I would never, never break that promise.'

Her words, said with complete conviction, came as a great relief to me. For one thing, I could get away from such a contentious subject; I believed her and Toby would have to as well.

I wanted to pacify her and nodded eagerly at her to signify my good faith. 'To go back to my question,' I said, 'how on earth did you cope? Your parents were on the other side of the world. Who helped you? Were you lonely, afraid?'

'When I knew I was pregnant, I went to Singapore — it was at Christmas — to tell my parents. I had a misguided idea that they'd take over, that they'd make me stay with them in Singapore, that I'd have the baby there. They told me to get an abortion, but to do it in England. They had their position to think about, Dad's career and so on.'

'Why didn't you have an abortion? Or have the child adopted?'

'No fear. Whatever the problems, I was going to have the child and give it all the love I could. I knew I was saying farewell to my childhood, not that I'd had a conventional one anyway. A distant relative of my mother's took pity on me and I stayed with her for nearly two years. And then I lived in a commune for a while. That wasn't a lie, I just altered the time scale a little.'

'Does Garfield know all about this?'

'Most of it, but not how young I was when Ben was born. Nobody knows that, except you and Toby.'

'I'm full of admiration but how on earth have you concealed your age? What about things like passports and insurance policies, they always ask for your birth certificate. Do you mean that your husband has never noticed?'

'No, because I've always handled that kind of thing. If you're careful it's amazing what you can get away with.'

A few minutes later we were strolling companionably back towards my flat, the earlier tensions forgotten. As we approached her car I expected her to drive off to her friends in Chelsea, but without more ado she carried on past it. 'One more coffee before I go,' she said.

I got as far as putting the kettle on but that was all. As I returned to the sitting room, Suzi asked me where the bedroom was. We forgot the coffee.

Some time later I asked her about her friends in Chelsea. 'Won't they be worried?'

'No. They're imaginary.'

'Why?'

'Partly to tease and partly because I wasn't decided about you. They were an escape if I needed it.'

'Why did you think you needed an escape?'

'Because I wasn't sure of my feelings. The first time we made love might have been a one-off. The turmoil of David's death and Ben's disappearance knocked me sideways. I wanted to try and forget it all for a while and you happened to be handy.'

'Thanks a bunch.'

'No, it's my pleasure,' Suzi said, and proved it.

Chapter 21

A journey of around ten hours in a confined space is not my idea of fun, but the flight from London to Los Angeles was made bearable by our good fortune in travelling first class. Ben's agent had made a deal with the airline and Ben insisted on it being applied to me as well. The extra space, the comfortable seats and the attentive service made me feel like a man of substance and importance. It was a rare glimpse of the good life and gave my self-esteem a boost.

We arrived in California in the late afternoon and by the time we had secured our luggage and suffered the protracted processes of customs and immigration, it was getting dark. Ben and I made a joint management decision to go no further than the nearest airport hotel, after we had collected our hire car.

Although we were on the road before seven o'clock the next morning, the perpetual lines of traffic, moving at walking pace in some instances, were already strung out along the huge freeways. With Ben in the driver's seat I paid close attention to the map and managed to call the correct route for our journey north to the Monterey peninsula. We eventually got beyond the sprawling urban jungle of the Los Angeles suburbs and enjoyed the arid landscape. Several hours later we began looking for the Harbour Dunes Golf Resort. We need have had no qualms about finding our destination since huge signs began to appear at regular intervals; they welcomed us to Harbour Dunes, the home of the

California Classic golf tournament. The Harbour
Dunes logo, a sea-otter wearing tartan plus-fours and a
golf visor, was very much in evidence: on posters and
flyers, on free-standing signs and occasionally on large
balloons. But Hector, the Harbour Dunes sea-otter,
did not have things entirely his own way since the
sponsors of the California Classic, an American car
manufacturer, had collared just as much space.

'They really go for it, don't they?' Ben said.

'Well, you've played in America, you've seen it all
before.'

'Not like this, I haven't. Remember, this is a new
venue and a new sponsor and they're pulling out quite a
few extra stops between them.'

'Whoever built Harbour Dunes has to,' I said.
'They've spent millions developing it and it all stands or
falls on how many houses, villas and condominiums
they can sell. It's quite a gamble, isn't it?'

We reached the entrance to the resort. Wide wrought-
iron gates guarded the way forward and on each side
there was a brick and timber lodge, painted a dazzling
white. Two security men, in smart light blue uniforms
with the Hector motif on the breast pocket, were on
duty. I noticed that they both wore handguns in holsters
clipped to their waists.

One of them approached Ben's window; as he
lowered it a blast of hot air mixed with the air-
conditioned coolness of the interior. The guard leaned
on the window frame, ducked his head slightly and said,
'Resident, staff, sponsor, what, sir? You should have
your sticker in view, sir.'

'Oh, yes, I'm sorry,' Ben said, as he searched in one
of his pockets. 'Here we are. Competitor.'

'Just a moment, sir.' The guard walked over to the
lodge and returned with a clipboard. 'Name, please.'

'Ben Massey.'

'Right. Are you from Australia?'

'No, England.'

The guard gave us some directions to the reception area and wished us a nice day. The hub of the resort was a huge octagonal hotel with all the accoutrements demanded by such an establishment: bars, restaurants, swimming pools, conference rooms, a gymnasium, a night club, a cinema. An array of houses and apartments stretched away from the hotel and many of them were concentrated around a huge marina. The ocean and miles of blond sand stretched away on either side. I could see why the owners of Harbour Dunes had adopted a sea-otter as their mascot, since hundreds of them were bobbing, diving and cavorting in the gently rippling sea. It was a splendid sight.

Ben had been allotted an apartment alongside one of the many swimming pools. It was on the grand scale with a kitchen, dining room, sitting room, terrace, bedroom with a king-size bed and huge bathroom with a jacuzzi.

'This is the life,' Ben said with real feeling. 'Where are you booked in, by the way?'

'At a motel down the road, with some of the other caddies.'

'Stay here. The sofa's big enough to sleep two of you.'

'No, no. It's all booked, I'll be fine.'

Ben threw the car keys at me. 'Take the car. Let's have some practice in an hour. OK?'

The Sands Motel was about three miles away from the resort, just off the main highway and some distance from the beach. It was an archetypal, two-storey motel built in a hollow square. No frills, but what could one expect for less than thirty dollars a night?

A cheerful middle-aged woman with a lined brown face and faded blonde hair gave me my key, told me to turn left out of the door and asked me if I was from England. I admitted to it and she told me that she had a cousin in Birmingham and loved London.

I dumped my small bag of belongings inside my room, which was mostly occupied by a bed and a television set. My neighbours on either side had their televisions on. It could have been stereo sound but they were tuned to different channels. The insistent canned laughter from one side indicated either a comedy or a game show. I hoped that my fellow guests were not night owls; otherwise my chances of some long and restful sleeps were poor.

There was nothing to make me linger and I drove back to meet Ben. We took up our station on the practice ground which was much like those on any of the courses on the European golf tour, except that it was much bigger. It was strange also to hear predominantly American tones. In Europe the practice ground is a hubbub of different accents and languages: Lancashire, Yorkshire, Brummie, Scots, Irish, South African and Australian mingling with Swedish, Spanish, German, Italian and French.

High seriousness was the order of the day on this practice ground. Most of the players seemed to have, in addition to a caddie, at least two advisors. It would soon be necessary to have as much back-up as a Grand Prix motor racing team and I had heard of one eminent American golfer who referred to himself as Team something or other. What with his caddie, nutritionist, golf coach, fitness coach, physiotherapist, press agent, psychologist, business manager, his wife and four children, it was no wonder that he looked prematurely aged.

Beside me, Ben Massey demonstrated once again that golf is essentially a simple game. There was a sharp smack of perfect timing to his shots and, by the time he had moved on to some of his longer irons, several of the neighbouring groups of golfers were casting interested looks in his direction.

A few minutes later one of them wandered over. With his round face, thinning fair hair and squat body, the man resembled anything but a professional golfer; he looked more like a successful insurance broker. But I knew that he had recorded over twenty wins on the American tour and was in the opposing Ryder Cup team. As he came up to Ben, he held out his hand. 'Hi, Ben, Travis Hanson, we played in the Florida Open together. I thought I recognised that swing of yours. You've come to hijack more of our money, I suppose.'

Ben smiled modestly and said he had no chance and Hanson continued, 'I read about your brother and I'm sorry, Ben. I'm going to apologise in advance for some of the muck that'll be thrown at you over here. There are some people who have forgotten that the Ryder Cup is a game of golf. They've built it up into something much more – World War III – and it's a shame.'

'Who are these people?' I asked.

'The media, son, mostly. And they've got it in for Ben. But remember that the players want no part of it. I certainly don't, you're as welcome as you've always been. As long as you don't finish ahead of me on Sunday. See you around.'

Travis Hanson ambled away and Ben said, 'Nice man. He helped me a lot in Florida, calmed me down during the final round. He's a real gent.'

Ben pronounced himself satisfied with his practice and we walked down the line of players to look at some of their swings. It is amazing how much more uniform are the styles these days than they used to be and Ben remarked on it as we watched a tall, strong young man thrashing huge shots effortlessly down the range. 'Mechanical, isn't it?' Ben said. 'Very effective. Slow take-away, huge arc, great extension. I wouldn't walk over the road to watch him, though.'

'No grace, no poetry?'

'Exactly. You remember what somebody wrote about Sam Snead? His swing was as "graceful as the spring of a cat". That guy's swing . . .' and Ben gestured at the nearby golfer '. . . is as graceful as a pneumatic drill.'

'Would you walk over the road to watch Stefan Sandberg?'

'Oh, sure. He's in a different class.'

'Well, he's down there. Let's go and have a word.'

Sandberg was in the last position on the side of the practice ground. He was a lean man, all sinew and concentration on the golf course, a fighter who was deadly in a tight finish. His caddie and his coach, alongside, were studying his swing with great intensity. The Swede looked up as we approached and greeted Ben with as near a smile as he could manage.

'Ben. It's good to see you. My condolences about your stepbrother. I've been praying for you.'

Ben thanked him and asked after his wife. 'Jane is recovering. She'll be OK, we'll all be OK, with the Lord's help. Which reminds me that we'll be having our weekly prayer meeting on Wednesday evening. It'll be in my suite. You will come, won't you, Ben, and you, Chris? We all need God's help and perhaps you and I, Ben, need his love more than most.'

Ben promised to do his best to be there and I mumbled something incomprehensible in reply.

As we strolled away Ben said, 'Maybe he's got something, who knows?'

'He's got a great putting action,' I said nastily. 'Did you know that the captain of the British Ryder Cup team in 1947 called his team together for prayers on the eve of the match.'

'No, I didn't. What happened?'

'We lost, eleven matches to one.'

'You're a profoundly cynical person, aren't you?'

Chapter 22

Ben and I had an early breakfast together in the hotel on the following morning. Neither of us made any pretence of trying to resist the vast choice of food which was laid out on the buffet tables. We piled our plates high and tucked in with a will. After all, we had a long day ahead of us. We were on the practice ground soon after seven o'clock and Ben went through his rigorous routine. Once he was satisfied that his timing was in order he went through a full repertoire: high and low shots, hooks and fades, drawn shots and cut shots, running shots and stopping shots. It was an impressive demonstration of power and finesse.

I remembered how, a few years back, an American golfer, who was leading the Open Championship after the first round, had entertained a press conference with his thoughts about the swing. He had explained to the disbelieving cynics that he had twenty-seven different check-points in his swing. It surprised nobody that his opening score of 65 was followed by one which was fifteen shots worse; he sank without trace on the wild Scottish shore where the Open was held that year and I hadn't seen his name since.

During a pause in his routine, I asked Ben what he thought about when he played a shot.

'Nothing.'

'Nothing?'

'All my thinking about the swing is done here, on the practice ground. And of course, during a tournament I

177

decide what type of shot I'm trying to play in advance. I want to get my ball on the correct side of the fairway or on to the safe side of the green. So that dictates the shape of the shot. But once I've worked that out I try to clear my mind totally. Any mental clutter, any reservations must go. You've got to commit yourself utterly to the shot, trust your swing, let your muscle memory do the job; let nature take its course, you might say.'

To demonstrate this, Ben set himself up for a shot, shut his eyes and swung his club. The ball soared away down the range.

'Ordinary club golfers should try and free their minds,' Ben continued. 'All this tightness and anxiety is what messes their swings up. Take putting, for instance. Once you can see the line and how far away the hole is, relax and hit the ball. Your muscle memory will take over, there is inherent natural judgement in every golfer.'

'Make your mind up what you're going to do and then go ahead and do it.'

'Exactly. Here endeth the lesson.'

Ben had booked himself a practice round that morning and we were joined on the tee by Nick Spencer. Though short of stature, his stocky frame made him one of the most powerful golfers in the game and I was looking forward to seeing him at close quarters. It was a puzzle to see where all his power came from, but it was based on a deceptively simple style, a model of the uncluttered philosophy about which Ben had been talking. Spencer walked up to the ball, put his clubhead behind it and bashed it on its way.

His approach to virtually every other aspect of life was just as simple and was expressed forcibly in his flat

Midlands accent. The only problems he seemed to have were the non-availability of Bass bitter in America and his putting, the game within a game.

'I can't hole a bloody thing,' he complained. 'Nothing wrong with my stroke, but I can't buy a putt. I just hope it comes right this week or I'll be on my bike after two rounds. It's all about holing the putts over here.'

The designer of the Harbour Dunes course had moved mountains in his efforts to create an archetypal American stadium course. The fairways ran between a series of mounds and hillocks where the spectators could perch and view the play with ease. The propensity for American golf architects to introduce water hazards at every opportunity had also been thoroughly indulged and lakes and streams encroached on virtually every hole. Vast bunkers, formed into bizarre configurations, added to the golfers' problems. It added up to a long and arduous course which demanded great power and accuracy and, as is usual in America, the greens were frighteningly fast and slippery. I hesitated to speculate how the ordinary holiday golfer would cope with such a monster. I also shuddered to think how much the whole creation had cost; it looked as though the designer had been granted an unlimited budget − and had probably exceeded it.

The so-called signature hole, where the architect tries to stamp his own distinctive mark on the course, was probably the fifteenth where the players had to drive across a lake to a narrow ribbon of fairway, bounded on one side by the sea and on the other by an enormous elongated bunker, and then hit their second shots to a green which was completely surrounded by water. A footbridge was the only access to the green.

Both Ben and Spencer hit their balls successfully on to

the putting surface and the Midlander remarked, 'I'd like to have the golf ball concession here. There'll be hundreds of balls in the drink every week. And I'd like to employ that Spanish bastard, Gonzales, to fish them out. One by one.'

'Haven't you two kissed and made up yet?' asked Ben playfully.

'If he comes anywhere near me, he'll get a right-hander.' Spencer gestured pugnaciously with his huge fist.

'Come on,' said Ben, 'you shouldn't bear a grudge. You beat him in the play-off and you'll be team mates next week. We've all got to pull together. Anyway, what caused the problems between you and Gonzales?'

'The bastard more or less accused me of cheating. He said I was coughing deliberately on his backswing.'

'Were you?'

'No, I bloody wasn't. I was up to here with a cold and I was coughing and sneezing all week but I kept well away from him, for that reason.'

'Well, why don't you just explain? After all, you might be foursomes partners next week.'

'Sod him,' said Spencer as he crouched over his putt and sent it sweetly on its way. It hit the back of the hole and screwed out sideways.

'Sod him and sod it,' he said. 'That's the way my putting's been for weeks.'

'Perhaps you should attend Sandberg's prayer meeting,' I said. 'Some divine help might do the trick.'

'He's driving me mad, as well,' said Spencer. 'Every time I see him he tells me about this meeting or that meeting. And he keeps trying to give me pamphlets to read. I keep telling him that I'm happy with *Golf World* and *Penthouse* but he won't take the hint.'

'Has anybody got to the bottom of that business with his wife and the NSPCC?' I asked.

'No,' said Spencer. 'But if I ever find out who did it, they can look out. She's a lovely girl, is Jane. I've always fancied her. God's will, Stefan calls it; I'd call it something different to that.' He teed his ball up and turned towards Ben. 'Talking of fanciable women, is your mum coming over for the Ryder Cup?' He grinned and hit his drive a prodigious distance down the fairway.

Ben smiled back and said, 'She's not your type, Nick, and anyway she's married and relatively content with her lot. But, yes, she'll be over in a day or two.'

I kept my own counsel on the question of Suzi's marital contentment and, as we walked down the fairway, reflected that what you saw and heard was exactly what you got with Nick Spencer. 'A simple man of immense strength'; there were no hidden depths. No hidden shallows either. He hit a towering one-iron on to the green of the par-five hole and, as we went in pursuit, I asked him if he and Gonzales had actually come to blows.

'No bloody fear,' Spencer replied. 'I don't want to end up in front of the PGA Committee again. I told the bugger what I thought of him, but there were no fisticuffs. Some bloody newspaperman made that up.'

'Who in particular, do you know?'

'No. But I collared friend Ramon in the locker room and told him in no uncertain terms that I'd ram his teeth down his throat if he ever accused me of gamesmanship again. There was nobody much around because, remember, we'd had a play-off over three holes for the Memorial title. The rest of the players had cleared off. But there was one geezer who might have heard what I said.'

'A big bloke, was he?' I hazarded. 'A bandido moustache, black hair?'

'You've got him. A mate of yours?'

'Not really.'

After a couple of beers for lunch the two players had a second practice round. By the end of it we were all worn down by the heat of the sun and the extreme length of the course. At its full stretch of nearly 7,500 yards it was a real tiger. But at least Nick Spencer sorted his putting out, or rather Ben did it for him. He suggested a change in his alignment and suddenly the putts started to drop from all over the greens. 'I'll probably live to regret giving him that bit of advice,' Ben said cheerfully. 'Probably on Sunday night.'

It's surprising how often a tiny adjustment in a player's grip or his stance can make all the difference. For the moment, Spencer had, with Ben's help, found something that had solved his problems.

Neither of the British golfers was playing in the pro-am tournament on the following day. Only about forty professionals, usually the ones at the top of the American order of merit, were selected for this curtain raiser which gives the sponsors the opportunity to press large quantities of food and drink upon their receptive clients; and, above all, to reward them with a round of golf in the company of a leading professional.

After our exertions Ben and I settled down on the terrace with a jug of iced tea while Nick Spencer went off in search of a copy of the draw for the opening day of the tournament proper on Thursday.

Within minutes he came bouncing back with a sheet of paper in his hand. 'Look at this,' he said angrily. 'They're not going to do us any favours, are they? I'm off first at sparrow-fart seven o'bloody clock and you're next, Ben. They've put Gonzales and Sandberg out last.'

'And that means that we'll be out last on the second

day, doesn't it.' The draw is usually reversed at professional tournaments during the first two rounds, the premise being that this will even out any differences in the conditions.

'Never mind,' Ben continued, 'we'll give them a run for their money. We must make sure we qualify for the final two rounds, that's the first thing. I don't want to disappoint my mother. She's travelling a long way to watch me play.'

'Well, she's welcome to watch me, any time,' Spencer said.

Ben and I made plans to meet on the practice ground in the morning and my young boss surprised me by saying, 'Just a short session, then we'll drive down to Big Sur for lunch.'

'Big Sur? Why Big Sur?'

'Because I've always wanted to see it, it's beautiful down there. Remember *One-eyed Jacks*? Well, some of that was filmed down there. And Henry Miller used to live there.'

'Was he on the tour?' Nick Spencer asked innocently. 'Brother of Johnny?'

Ben smiled at me and said, 'No, Nick, but he used to write a bit about your favourite pastime.'

Chapter 23

Ben had not exaggerated the beauty of Big Sur and we both stood and looked in awe at the wide sweep of the bay and listened to the insistent pulse of the ocean as it foamed against the rocks. In the distance, the blues of the sky and the water merged into one deep colour. No words were necessary as we absorbed the extraordinary tranquillity of the scene; the ebb and swell of the water was hypnotic. The traffic was so far away that we only heard its slight hum.

A few hundred yards away from our vantage point there was a picnic area in the trees. Wooden tables and chairs were scattered about and a small shop provided us with a few cans of cold beer, some sandwiches and fruit. A few families had stopped to enjoy an al fresco lunch and we meandered over to a table which gave us a view over the sea.

With our shirts off to take advantage of the sun, we ate and drank and enjoyed one of those rare periods of total relaxation. Our conversation muted, we were both in a semi-comatose state of contentment.

'Golf tournaments, the Ryder Cup, David, they all seem a long way away at the moment,' Ben said, his eyes half-closed and his arms drooping at his side. 'This puts it all in perspective, doesn't it?'

I grunted my agreement and we relapsed into silence. I was in a gentle doze when the spell was broken by an alien voice. 'Great heavens to Betsy, if I didn't know my son was in Denver, I'd swear that it was him, right before my eyes.'

The words were uttered by a small, wizened man with a lined, sun-beaten face and wire-rimmed glasses. He was wearing jeans, a faded plaid shirt and a white cap. He was beaming at Ben; in one swift movement he drew up a chair and sat down with us.

What can you do in a situation like that? It would have been churlish to have walked away and Ben politely offered the old man a can of beer and asked him what his son did in Denver.

'Oh, he's in public sanitation and has a wonderful job and a fine young wife and two beautiful children. But, my goodness to Betsy, I thought I was seeing double when I saw you, young man.'

He patted Ben on the arm and continued, 'And what are you doing here? On holiday, are you?'

I gave Ben a warning look and he agreed that we were on holiday, just for a few days. I feared the conversational consequence of Ben admitting that he was a professional golfer.

After a few more minutes of question and answer, we said we had to make tracks and so we did, with the old man's parting admonitions to 'look after yourselves, you young fellas' wafted in on the sea-borne breeze.

'Well, those moments of peace didn't last so long, did they?' I said.

'Oh well, let's be grateful. I'll never forget this place, it's something to remember all my life.'

'I thought he was the ghost of Henry Miller for a moment.'

'Yes, he did resemble him, didn't he? Just a lonely old man, he wanted some company.'

'I wonder if he's really got a son in Denver,' I said. 'I wonder.'

The buzz of my alarm woke me at five o'clock the

following morning. The sky was just beginning to lighten as I drove Ben's car towards the hotel. We were due on the practice ground at around six o'clock in order that Ben should be fully in tune for his tee-off time at ten minutes after seven. Considering the hour Ben's swing looked as well-grooved as ever and, after a good session on the practice putting green, we accompanied Nick Spencer to the first tee to give him some moral support.

Spencer had been teamed with two young American golfers who seemed to have come off the same college production line. They were both well over six feet in height, broad-shouldered and had the inevitable visors shading their eyes. In contrast, Spencer looked out of place, as if he had wandered, unbidden, on to the course. The first hole was a relatively straightforward par four of just less than 400 yards; its only problems were posed by bunkers left and right at around 250 yards. The American golfers played conservative shots short of them with iron clubs; they both looked with interest as Spencer swished his driver to and fro by the side of the tee. He winked at both of us and launched himself into his opening shot; helped by his natural right to left draw, Spencer's ball soared over the bunkers and on down the fairway and left him with a simple pitch to the green.

'I think I'm going to shoot the lights out today,' he said and hurried busily down the fairway.

'Ten out of ten for confidence,' said Ben and we watched as Spencer casually flicked his second shot close to the hole for a certain birdie.

Ben's partners were a young amateur who had been specially invited by the sponsors after coming second in the US Amateur Championship, and a professional who had spent over twenty years on the American tour. Tom

Donald was a journeyman golfer who had only won one
tournament but invariably finished in the top thirty in
the money list. His was a familiar name to me from the
golf magazines but I had never seen him in the flesh; he
had never played in the Open Championship in Britain.
He cut a lean figure, neatly dressed in dark blue trousers
and a white shirt. He looked like a bank clerk on his day
off and I knew that his golf would be as anonymous as
his dress. He had earned nearly five million dollars on
the American golf circuit without ever seeming to break
sweat.

The announcer on the first tee introduced Ben as
'Macey' and the game was on. He started with a birdie,
just like Nick Spencer, and I reflected that the two
Britons were already at the head of the leader board.
But there were very few people about to notice; the
crowds would arrive later.

After nine holes Ben was three under par and his
swing never wavered in its metronomic regularity.
Neither did that of Tom Donald, who was one shot
behind Ben; but the amateur was in disarray, after
finding the water on several occasions. Ben gained
another stroke against the course on the twelfth when he
sank a putt of around twenty-five feet for a birdie and
our first alarm did not come until the difficult fifteenth
hole when his tee shot ended up in the huge bunker on
the left of the fairway.

Since the hole was judged to be one of the most
testing on the course it had attracted a large gathering of
spectators. They had collected on the mounds which
lined one side of the fairway and, with their collapsible
chairs, cardboard periscopes, cans of beer, burgers,
sandwiches and all their other accoutrements, were
looking forward to some fun. There is nothing a
spectator likes more than witnessing a professional

golfer in trouble; and, with sand and water in abundance, there was trouble a-plenty on the fifteenth hole.

Ben and I studied the lie of his ball in the sand and I computed the exact distance to the pin. I was helped by a book which contained diagrams of every hole on the course with the various distances marked. An enterprising caddie had produced this and, during the practice rounds, I had checked the measurements and added some of my own. A tournament golfer needs to know, more or less to the yard, how far a specific shot must carry. Unlike a club golfer he knows how far he will hit a specific club. The final element in the calculation was the position of the hole on the green; a chart had that morning been issued by the tournament organisers which gave us that information. Ben put his trust in me to give him the precise distance he needed to hit any given shot. It meant that he could concentrate wholly on playing the stroke.

'It's one hundred and forty-two yards to the front edge of the green. A hundred and sixty to the flag. Slight breeze from right to left,' I said and suggested a seven-iron.

Ben shaded his eyes and looked again at the pin. A voice from the crowd above shouted, 'Get on with it, Massey.' I looked up sharply, could not identify the source of the advice among the brightly dressed spectators and saw that Ben was unmoved. He probably had not even registered the noise.

'Fine,' he said, 'seven-iron.'

Ben shuffled his feet firmly in the sand, looked up once and prepared to hit his shot. I saw the slight forward press of his right knee as he began his swing and heard the same voice: 'Miss it, you limey freak.'

Even during a friendly Sunday morning fourball an

unexpected noise can be disconcerting, but it can be devastating to a tournament golfer who takes the good manners of the average crowd of fans for granted. With a small miracle of muscle control Ben was able to stop at the top of his swing and abort his shot. He gazed up at the crowd, shook his head sadly and settled in his stance once again. The crowd murmured their disapproval and someone shouted, 'Hey cool it, man.' A marshal had dashed into the crowd to try and find the person who had so rudely interrupted Ben, who was now faced with a further problem. Would the man try to put him off again?

It did not surprise me that Ben made a less than perfect contact with the ball which ended up just short of the green. But a deft pitch and run shot enabled him to make his par.

The marshal apologised to Ben on the next tee but I could see that Ben's concentration was impaired. Ben was probably waiting for the next yell. He dropped a shot on the long seventeenth hole but retrieved it at the final hole. His tee shot had been pushed out into the semi-rough to the right of the fairway. I expected him to punch a medium iron short of all the bunkers which surrounded the plateau green, and then try to pitch close enough to secure his par. But Ben seized his three-iron and hit a shot of withering power and accuracy; it hurtled high over all the trouble and dropped like a feather alongside the flag.

Ben's final score was 68, four under par, with Donald a stroke behind; Nick Spencer had finished at level par.

'Two balls in the sodding drink,' Spencer told us in the bar. 'The putter's working like a dream, thanks to you, Ben. Never mind, I'll take the course apart tomorrow.'

Spencer kept his promise with an adventurous round

of 66 which raised him up the leader board to within four shots of the leader. 'Only one visit to the briny,' he said proudly. My boss continued on his relatively serene way with another score of 68. There was no sign of the heckler, to the relief of both of us and of the officials who were assigned to our match. The young amateur failed to qualify for the final two days by around ten shots but Tom Donald, a model of quiet efficiency, was on the same mark as Nick Spencer. The other two European representatives, Stefan Sandberg and Ramon Gonzales, just managed to qualify for the final two rounds.

In the vital third round when a player must, at the very worst, maintain his position in the field if he is to have a realistic chance of winning, Ben was paired with a talkative Californian, who had been born not far away from Harbour Dunes. Jerry Farrell had won a professional tournament while still a student at the University of Southern California and had so far won around twenty events, including the PGA Championship. Chunkily built, brisk of movement and super-confident, Farrell was very much a local favourite and had qualified as a member of the American Ryder Cup team.

As we walked towards the tee Toby's ample figure materialised through the crowd and he wished Ben a hearty good luck. To my surprise I saw that Toby was clutching a can of beer in his hand.

'What's up, Toby?' I asked. 'Have they run out of fizz?'

'I cannot find a bottle on the entire course, dear boy,' he said, with a great show of disgust. 'I've spent the last two days looking for a champagne tent, but no luck. It's all beer, coke, hot dogs and hamburgers. The withdrawal symptoms are already severe, I can tell you.

And have you seen one end of the clubhouse? The ballroom is a hill of Mexican fast food and they're playing rock videos in there. What is golf coming to?' he exclaimed.

I laughed but realised that Toby was correct; there was none of the variety of food and drink on offer that is found at European events. The interior of the clubhouse had certainly been taken over by fast food and beer stalls, with just a small bar and dining room reserved for the members. The objective of the organisers was clearly to make as much money as possible during the course of the tournament.

Since it was Saturday the crowds were out in force, although in no greater numbers than at a British tournament. If I noticed a slightly greater degree of ebullience amongst the fans, it was only marginal and their clothes differed very little. Fashion has become international and I spotted most of the brand names I would normally see in Europe, even if the colours were generally more vivid; we were in California, after all. Unfortunately there were just as many shell suits to be seen as at a European tournament and as usual they were worn by overweight people. But I liked the brightly coloured satin-look bomber jackets which were occasionally to be seen, perhaps because they were mostly worn by shapely young women.

The crowd gave full rein to their support for Farrell when he was announced on the first tee and the cheers rolled out for the local boy, abetted by yells of 'Go get him, Jerry.'

The master of ceremonies next itemised the American player's impressive list of victories and really whipped up the fans' fervour by wishing luck to 'our local champion and great sportsman'. The MC followed this by announcing Ben 'Macey' of England. After Ben had hit his opening drive crisply to the centre of the fairway, I decided to put the announcer right. I shouldered the heavy golf bag and strode towards the MC's hut at the back of the tee.

He was obviously a local celebrity, a man who was a couple of stones overweight, had obviously had a face-lift and had dyed his hair an incongruous shade of chestnut. Despite the cosmetic surgery, or perhaps because of it, his face looked like wax which had changed shape under the influence of too much heat.

'Excuse me,' I said. 'You should get the players' names right. It's Massey, double S, not Macey. And you might do him the courtesy of mentioning one or two of his victories. He is the French Open champion, for example, and he won the Greater Jacksonville Open over here earlier this year. Am I coming over loud and clear?'

'Very loud, for a caddie. Should I mention that he killed his brother, too?' he said with a smile that didn't reach his eyes.

I glanced down the fairway and saw that Ben was already halfway to his ball. The MC put his face close to mine and I could smell something sweet on his breath. Softly he said, 'I should move on, you bum, that murdering sonofabitch needs you.' With another tight smile he wheeled about and disappeared inside his hut.

I knew that I would have to move on and I would hardly endear myself to anybody by rearranging the announcer's facial characteristics, much as that might have benefited him. He could wait, whereas Ben could not. Judging by the distance he had hit his opening drive he needed a short iron for his next shot; I hastened down the fairway to provide it.

'What's the problem?' Ben asked as I arrived, slightly out of breath. 'You look annoyed.'

'That prat of an announcer. I told him to get your name right.'

'Don't worry. They'll know my name well enough by the end of next week.'

That's my boy.

Chapter 24

After nine holes of the third round, Ben, by dint of four birdies and an eagle, was leading the California Classic by two shots. Jerry Farrell, grimly determined to hang on, was three shots adrift but it seemed to me that Ben was playing with such serene confidence that no one would catch him. Even Farrell's natural bounce and swagger were becoming rather forced.

Ben had only one hiccup, at the infamous fifteenth hole, when he took three putts from the back edge of the green. When he fired his subsequent shot from the sixteenth tee into a huge bunker which was splashed on the right side of the fairway, I feared that he might drop another shot. The hole is a very long par five and the green is out of reach in two shots even for a long hitter like Ben.

His cause was not helped when a knot of spectators, stationed by the offending bunker, cheered and clapped when Ben's ball dropped into the sand. He glowered in their direction and, as we walked down the fairway, I urged him to be calm.

'Just play it out on to the fairway and it's a middle iron on to the green. No heroics, we can still make par easily.'

When he asked for his three-wood I realised that I might as well have been talking Swahili. I handed it to him without a word since I could see from the set of his face that any counsels of caution from me would be ignored. The people who had applauded Ben's misfortune were hushed by other fairer-minded fans and two marshals stood nearby in order to prevent any disturbance.

Ben's ball was lying well in the sand but, despite its being a fairway bunker and therefore less punitive than a greenside bunker, there was quite a pronounced lip at its far end. I had an unpleasantly vivid image of Ben catching the ball thin and ramming it under the overhanging turf.

I almost shut my eyes as Ben shuffled himself into a comfortable position, checked his angle of shot once more and swung his three-wood. It looked as easy and rhythmic as any shot he had hit on the practice ground. With a resonant crack the ball rushed on its way to some yells of 'Good shot, man'. There were some moments of silence as we all focused on the ball as it climbed into the solid azure of the sky. Ben was muttering some encouragement: 'Go on, ball, go on.' Then the applause and cheers rang out as the ball hit the middle of the green. Ben acknowledged the plaudits with a modest wave but he was grinning all over his face.

'God almighty, what a shot,' I said with immense relief.

'What they call a career shot,' Ben said with a laugh.

Ben's birdie was a formality and his final score of 65 put him two shots in the lead from Farrell and Donald.

Nick Spencer had climbed into the top ten and Stefan Sandberg had also erupted out of his mediocre spell of form with a score of 64. He was lying in fifteenth position.

After Ben had carefully checked his card and handed it in to the officials, we were debating where to go for a small celebration of an outstanding round of golf when Ben was collared by a large man, resplendent in his MCC tie and a panama hat with MCC band, and his equally substantial companion, who turned out to be his wife. Such was their physical presence that, although there were only two of them, I felt surrounded.

In broad Lancastrian tones they both showered their congratulations on Ben, who introduced them as Lionel and Daisy Blackstock.

'Lionel runs a pro-am every year,' explained Ben, 'and knows my parents.'

'And very sorry to hear about David,' Lionel said. 'But enough said on that subject, I'm sure, lad. Now, Ben, you're staying with us tonight, we've hired a villa down the road. Six bedrooms, plenty of room, we'll leave you in peace. Sorry we couldn't get to watch before but I had some business to do in LA.'

'Well . . .' Ben began but was waved into silence by the expansive Lionel.

'No arguments. We'll pick you up in an hour in the clubhouse. Daisy's doing roast beef, aren't you, love. And Suzi arrives tomorrow, as you know. She'll be staying with us, too.'

'What line of business is he in?' I asked as they strode off.

'All sorts. Supermarkets, property, you name it. He runs the best pro-am of the lot, very generous.'

Ben and I strolled through the crowds towards his suite. One or two people recognised him and congratulated him on his round but, in contrast to Britain where he would have been inundated with fans who wanted autographs or just a few words, he was largely ignored.

Ben gathered a few oddments together for his overnight stay with the Blackstocks and we made arrangements to meet on the practice putting green at midday on the morrow. Ben handed me the keys to the suite. 'Stay here, make yourself at home, it's a bit more comfortable than your motel, I expect.'

The first step in making myself at home was to take a long shower in the lavishly equipped bathroom. Every conceivable type of soap and unguent had been provided and I availed myself of them. Swathed in a towelling dressing gown, the Harbour Dunes logo displayed grandly on its breast pocket, I sat at my ease on the terrace. With the late afternoon sun striking across the gardens in front of me and a cold beer at my side, I felt at peace with myself.

I had several more beers and, as the evening grew cooler, went indoors and tried to find a television channel to watch among the dozens which were available. I swiftly abandoned the idea and wandered across to one of the hotel restaurants for dinner.

The maitre d' found me a corner table despite the crowded state of the place and the waitress told me how much she loved my English accent. All seemed right with the world and I battled my way through a huge salad and a gargantuan plate of grilled sole, accompanied by a few glasses of Mountain House Chardonnay.

Having toyed with the idea of trying to lure the attentive and statuesque waitress back to the suite for a late drink, I decided that discretion was the safer course. After all, tomorrow was going to be a tough and tense day when I would need my wits and energies about me. A victory for Ben would earn him nearly $200,000 and my share would not only get my bank manager off my back but would also enable me to put my old Porsche back on the road. Although it was too late to embrace abstemiousness where alcohol was concerned, I recommended an early night and pure thoughts to myself and headed, alone, for my borrowed suite.

The unaccustomed comfort of the king-size bed soon

had me chasing dreams and I had no idea what woke me up. A glance at the luminous face of my alarm clock told me it was after four o'clock in the morning. My throat was dry and I decided to fetch some water from the kitchen. Without switching on a light I padded across the marble floor towards the door.

Then I heard an alien sound, a light scuffing noise from the adjoining room. The hairs on my body prickled and I felt the blood rushing to my face. I began to ease the bedroom door open and, just as I had pushed it ajar and was putting my head gingerly out through the gap, I was momentarily transfixed by a blaze of light. I tried to jump back into the bedroom but the intruder was too quick for me; he locked my right arm painfully behind my back and put a stranglehold on me as well. Since the beam of light, obviously from a powerful torch, did not waver, I knew that there must be at least two intruders.

I tried to move, to see if I could get some purchase to dislodge my unknown and unseen assailant. He merely tightened his grip. He knew what he was about.

It was shock enough to be hijacked in the middle of the night by an unknown number of intruders but I felt even more defenceless because I was clad only in a pair of underpants. All sorts of primeval fears ran into my head.

I was pushed into the sitting room and a table lamp was switched on. I was not the slightest bit reassured when I saw that the two men were not only large but wore Mickey Mouse masks as well. That sight chilled me even more.

'What do you want?' I gasped. 'Money? I've got about a hundred dollars in my wallet. Take it.'

Neither man said a word. The one who had been holding the torch walked over to me and grabbed my left wrist. It was all over in a moment but that didn't mean it hurt any the less. He stuck my hand against the door frame and slammed the heavy door against it. Once, twice. The pain was indescribable and, just for luck, he hit me powerfully in the stomach. Winded, I couldn't even scream with pain. I lay on the floor trying to overcome the nausea caused by the agony that burned my hand. I heard the front door of the suite close quietly as the two men made their exit. Eventually I crawled across the floor towards a sofa and lay against it. My first and second fingers had taken the brunt of the blows and they had already swollen to what seemed like twice their normal size. I remembered Toby Greenslade's tip about using a packet of frozen peas as a makeshift icebag and moaned and groaned my way over to the refrigerator. There were no frozen peas, but a tea towel packed with ice did just as well.

I found some painkillers and swallowed several of them, then lay in the huge bed, waiting for my brain to recover from the shock.

The improvised ice pack kept the pain under control and I began to wonder why I had been attacked. It had all been so professionally done. How could I justify such attention, such careful planning?

The answer was so obvious that it failed to register with my brain, fuddled as it was by the after-effects of the violence. I dozed a bit, packed more cubes of ice around my damaged hand and waited for the dawn. As I struggled to put on some clothing, I suddenly realised that it had been a simple case of mistaken identity. The nocturnal brutality had been intended for Ben, not for me.

I sat on the bed again as I realised the implications. Someone had decided to make sure that Ben was unable to make it to the first tee for the final round, that there should be no chance of his winning the California Classic. Was this part of a vendetta against Ben himself, a vendetta which had already encompassed a clumsy attempt to implicate him in the murder of his stepbrother, or was it part of a wider campaign against the European Ryder Cup players? If it was the latter, and I was inclined to that view, the people behind the campaign presumably wanted to ensure that the Europeans did not benefit from the encouragement that a victory by Ben would give them. Judging by the state of my hand, they would also have ensured that Ben did not make it to the starting line in the Ryder Cup.

It didn't need the deductive powers of Sherlock Holmes to link this latest incident with all the other misfortunes which had befallen various members of Europe's team. Whether or not Nick Spencer and Gonzales had come to blows, it had been a heaven-sent opportunity for whoever was behind the campaign. Ross Bentley had been attacked on two fronts; with the resurrected accusation that he had cheated in winning the 1972 Open Championship and that he had disowned a bastard child. There was also the miserable business of Jane Sandberg and the rumours of her maltreatment of her children. The one strand that did not yet fit the overall pattern was the murder of David Massey.

But I couldn't begin to think of anyone who would be crazy enough to undertake such a campaign of lies, violence and possibly murder in order to influence the result of a golf match. It made no sense at all, even in the context of such a potent fixture as the Ryder Cup which has so often kept millions of golf fans around the world in thrall to their television screens.

I forced my mind back to the present. Whatever had

happened I was determined to carry Ben's bag during his final round; whatever the pain it would be worth it if he won the tournament.

I hoped my attackers hadn't meted out the same treatment to Nick Spencer and Stefan Sandberg. They were still in with good chances of winning the event. And Ramon Gonzales? He was way down the field but might also have suffered the same violent ministrations.

I decided to seek some medical help from the hotel and headed for the reception area. Should I inform the police of the attack? Would the assailants make another attempt to injure Ben when they realised they had nobbled the wrong man?

I knew that Ben would not withdraw from the tournament. There was a highly pugnacious side to his character and he would scoff at such a suggestion; he would slug it out to the end. Neither did I relish the thought of a police escort for him during his round. That would probably ensure that he scored several shots over par; we both believed that he needed to record a 68 to win. I decided to keep the incident quiet.

The receptionist greeted me with a good-morning smile of jaw-cracking proportions. Her teeth were flawless as were those of virtually everyone under thirty whom I had encountered in California. But her smile definitely wavered when I told her that I'd had an accident and asked her where I could find a doctor.

'An accident, sir? In the hotel? Are you claiming the hotel has a liability? I'd better call the duty manager.'

I restrained her. 'No. It was my own fault. I caught my hand in the car door. I just need some treatment, an X-ray, that sort of thing.'

'We have a doctor nearby, sir. You are insured, are you? He can't treat you unless you can show him some insurance.'

I reassured her yet again and within minutes I was being driven in a Harbour Dunes courtesy car to the clinic. A young black doctor ushered me into his office, checked that my insurance cover was valid and looked at my hand.

'Very nasty,' he said as he inspected my fingers. 'If you're here for the golf, I'm afraid you won't be playing for a week or two. Broken, perhaps, but if you're lucky, only cracked. Let's do the X-ray.'

A small machine rather like those used by dentists produced the pictures quickly and Dr Michaels showed me two cracks in my first finger and one in the second.

'A good job you weren't wearing a ring. They can cause real trouble with a swelling like that.' He strapped the fingers up, told me to take it easy and gave me two tubes of tablets.

'Painkillers, no more than six a day, and pills to reduce the swelling. Come and see me on Monday.'

'I can't. I'll be down the coast at the Ryder Cup.'

'Not playing, I hope, because you won't be.'

'No, I'm a caddie. Watch me this afternoon, I'll be bringing in the winner, Ben Massey. I'll give you a wave.'

Dr Michaels shook his head resignedly. 'Mr Ludlow, no unnecessary physical activity, please. Let the hand settle down. And see another doctor on Monday.'

As he showed me out of his office, the doctor said, 'I have to confess that I prefer tennis. More girls.' He grinned at me. 'But I'll look out for you. Who's your man?'

'Ben Massey.'

He asked me to spell it for him and wished me luck in the tourney.

Chapter 25

The strapping reduced the pain in my fingers to an insistent throb and back in Ben's suite I experimented with a few lifts of his golf bag. It would be awkward but I could manage; it's remarkable how much you miss the use of one hand. But I was able to hold a telephone and I called Nick Spencer first.

'Yah,' he said grumpily.

'Chris Ludlow. Are you all right?'

'Why shouldn't I be?' he asked, cheerful now that he knew the identity of his caller. 'I'll be after your man, I'm only four shots behind.'

I wished him luck and rang Stefan Sandberg. He announced himself in his slow monotonous tones and I asked him how he was.

'Extremely well, Chris, and looking forward to the round. I wondered if you and Ben would like to join me in an hour for a little bible reading and some prayers.'

I made my excuses and Stefan said that he would pray for both of us. As I put the telephone back I thought ruefully that I could have used some divine help, or any kind of help, a few hours earlier.

At least two other European players had been left unharmed. I was thankful for that and didn't bother to check on Ramon Gonzales. His English was difficult to understand anyway and my Spanish was worse. I made my way over to the hotel for breakfast.

As soon as I went through the doors of the restaurant I heard the voice of Toby Greenslade in full boom. He saw me and waved me over to join his table of fellow journalists but I excused myself and headed for a table in the far corner of the room. About five minutes later he joined me and commented on my strapped-up hand. 'Not more fisticuffs, Chris,' he groaned. 'Honestly, I can't leave you alone for a second.'

Briefly I described what had happened to me and he offered to take over my caddie's duties that afternoon. 'For the usual win bonus, of course, Chris. But seriously, if you find you can't cope I'll be following Ben's game and I can always step in and help. What a wonderful story it would make for the *News*. "Golf writer coaxes British golfer to victory in America," I can see the headline now.'

'Over my dead body. Anyway, you've never walked all eighteen holes in your life. You'd never make it, especially carrying a tournament bag.'

Toby ignored my insult and snapped, 'It's not your dead body I'm imagining, it's Ben's. There's a maniac about and I wonder what he'll try next. He might try taking a pot at Ben with a high-powered rifle. Do the police know what's going on?'

'No, nor Ben. I don't want him put off in any way. As far as he's concerned I had a stupid accident.'

We talked a little more about the people who might have instigated the attack but Toby was as short of ideas as I was. The motivation seemed clear enough, nothing else did.

Ben and I converged on the practice green at roughly the same time and, despite my efforts to conceal my injured hand, he noticed it. To my relief he didn't question my story of an accident with a car door. Although he was even quieter than usual, Ben showed little sign of strain and we went through his practice routine without any problems.

Ten minutes before his starting time we made our way towards the first tee. Lionel and Daisy Blackstock saw us approaching and waved effusively but our eyes were on Suzi, who ran towards her son and hugged him with real pleasure. I wondered lasciviously when I would next get a hug from her; my hand twanged with pain as if to punish me for such thoughts.

We took our position on the tee after the preceding pair, which included Tom Donald, had driven off. I could see the unpleasant Master of Ceremonies standing outside his hut and chatting to the crowd. I beckoned him over and, unwillingly, he walked towards me. I met him halfway and as he stopped, splay-footed, in front of me I deliberately dropped Ben's golf bag on his foot which was encased in a casual moccasin-style white shoe. A tournament bag weighs around forty pounds and, as he grimaced, I leaned on the bag and applied as much weight as I could.

'It's Ben Massey,' I said in his ear, 'M-A-S-S-E-Y, pronounced Massey. French Open champion, Greater Jacksonville winner, Ryder Cup player. Have you got that?'

He said nothing and I pushed down even harder on the bag until he nodded. I smiled and patted him on the shoulder as if we were the best of friends. I felt so much better. Even my hand seemed to have stopped throbbing but I took another painkiller just in case.

The announcer got Ben's name right for the first time and, after Jerry Farrell had put his ball in the bunker on the left side of the fairway, Ben hit a conservative one-iron down the middle. A quiet mid-iron and two putts gave him a satisfying par, whereas Farrell dropped a shot. It was a relief to start so well but we both knew that there was a very long way to go. It is the accepted wisdom among professional golfers that the real tournament takes place over the final nine holes.

At the halfway point in the round it seemed to me that Ben had the tournament in his pocket. His swing was as smooth and rhythmic as I had ever seen it and his putting, on treacherously fast greens, was faultless. He was four shots ahead of both Farrell and Donald; a further bonus for European golf fans was the appearance of Stefan Sandberg on the leader board for the first time. He was now level with Spencer.

The sands began to shift under Ben on the eleventh hole, which is a difficult par three of over 200 yards. The architect had made it the more severe by building a lake to the right of the green; to the left there was a wilderness of scrub and sand and several deep bunkers. To make par is a tall order for a professional golfer who usually has enough power and accuracy to hit a long iron to such a small and intimidating target; I imagined that such a hole would have a shattering effect on the technique and morale of an ordinary club golfer.

With a slight breeze against him, Ben elected to hit a three-iron and I knew that he would aim to hit a safe left to right shot, as he had done on the previous three days. At the top of his backswing, which was long and steady, the heckler made his presence felt again. A loud yell of 'You're the man' hit the heavens. Ben was fully committed to his shot and tried valiantly to keep his balance, but the sudden noise was too much for his concentration and the intended faded shot to the heart of the green became the weak slice, which is familiar to all high-handicap golfers. Ben's ball plummeted into the water to the right of the green.

With a rare demonstration of anger, Ben slammed his clubhead into the turf and looked around angrily. I had an idea of where the shout had originated and looked hard at the crowd for any unusual activity, such as a man moving quickly away or ducking behind another spectator. I thought I saw one suspicious movement but it was difficult to tell amongst a large and shifting crowd, many of whom were craning their necks to see who had broken the golden rule of crowd behaviour. I pinpointed a man with a white shirt with bright red epaulettes on it.

A section of the crowd had cheered loudly when Ben's ball hit the water and Jerry Farrell had shaken his head in distaste. Like the tough professional he was, however, he put his ball on the green about ten feet from the hole. It was the signal for some ecstatic applause and renewed shouts of 'Go get 'em, Jerry'.

As we walked down the slope towards the lake I asked two of the marshals to keep their eyes open for the heckler. One of them apologised and used his mobile phone to call for some security men, while the other shrugged and told me unsympathetically that it was a big crowd and that people liked to join in.

Meanwhile, Ben had to drop a second ball on the edge of the lake and, with a penalty of one stroke, pitch on to the green. It was, understandably, a poor shot and he registered a five for the hole. It seemed inevitable that Farrell would get his birdie; he was now only one shot behind Ben and the crowd, muted up to that point, were urging the local boy on with great fervour.

A couple of security men had now joined us to watch the crowd. I knew that the next hour was crucial to Ben's cause; he must settle down and wrest at least one birdie from the next three holes. Farrell was renowned as a fierce scrapper, as a man who relished a tight finish to a tournament. The American hit a beautiful drive down the next fairway and I prayed that Ben would follow him. His shot was no more than respectable, rather short and in the light rough on the right of the fairway.

Ben had 200 yards to go to the green and elected to hit his four-iron. As he studied his shot I studied the crowd. A couple of rows back in the knot of spectators facing Ben I saw the white shirt with the red epaulettes. Instead of watching Ben's shot, I concentrated solely on the spectator; fortunately he was reasonably tall and I also registered his square jaw and closely cut hair.

Out of the corner of my eye I saw Ben begin his swing and, more important, I saw red epaulettes yell out, 'Miss it, limey.'

Without seeing the result of Ben's shot, I dropped the golf bag, jumped over the rope which guarded the fairway and plunged through the first line of spectators. My injured hand forgotten, I grabbed the man by the front of his shirt and dragged him back across the rope. 'You bastard,' I said furiously. Taken by surprise, one foot tangled in the rope, he fell on his back and I dropped hard on to his chest, my right knee leading. My right fist was raised but, before it descended to exact some revenge on the heckler, it was grabbed and restrained in a powerful grip. It was one of the security men.

'OK, fella, you've made your point, we'll take it from here. You get on with the game.'

The heckler scrambled to his feet and shouted, 'This man assaulted me. I want the police.'

'You'll get the hell outa here,' said the security man, as he bundled him away through the crowd, 'or we'll think up enough violations to put you away for years.'

Ben was waiting for me in the middle of the fairway. 'Thanks, Chris,' he said quietly. 'Exciting life, a caddie's, isn't it?'

'Where's our ball?'

'Bunker left. No problem. I'm not going to let the buggers beat me.'

It wasn't a problem. Ben splashed his ball out to less than a foot and got his par, as did Farrell, who apologised to Ben for the heckler.

The incident seemed to upset Farrell whereas it renewed Ben. Over the next five holes he recorded three birdies and an eagle to go four shots clear of the field. Just to emphasise his class he birdied the eighteenth hole.

It was a triumphant walk up the long slope to the final green. Although I had never brought in the winner of a major championship, I understood, during those moments, some of the emotions. When Ben had holed out to win the California Classic by five clear shots, we hugged each other like kids and were soon joined by Suzi, who hugged us both, and the Blackstocks who were hugging everybody within reach.

In the scrum of reporters and officials, Toby had forced his way to the front and bellowed at Ben, 'A word for our readers, Ben, about your wonderful victory. A good omen for the Ryder Cup?'

'Relief, Toby, relief,' Ben said. 'I never doubted I could win but it was very tough out there, especially with Jerry Farrell hanging on. He's a hard man to shake off.'

'What about the crowd disturbances? Did that get to you?'

'Well, I dropped two shots at the eleventh.'

'Are you worried that the crowd will spoil the Ryder Cup?' an American voice asked.

'No. The American fans are mostly very decent, very sporting. There won't be a problem. Today's upset was caused by one man, and my minder here,' he grinned at me, 'dealt with him.'

With a few more diplomatic remarks, Ben took refuge in the PGA trailer and checked his score. Toby nodded towards the scoreboard. 'The Europeans have done well. Mason and Sandberg in fourth and sixth places and even Gonzales got into the top twenty. The Yanks won't like it.'

'No, and there are obviously some who are prepared to try and stop us,' I said meaningfully.

Toby grunted and nudged me towards the presentation platform which had been set up in front of the clubhouse.

'Look who's here,' he said. 'Ross Bentley and the divine Louise. I'll bet he's pleased with the result.'

'Who's that they're talking to?'

'The big brass from the American PGA. That's the commissioner, Kyle Coker, in the blazer. I'll bet Ross is rubbing it in. Coker was never much of a player, a journeyman, but he had one big chance in the Masters and you know who beat him, don't you?'

'Ross Bentley.'

'Precisely.'

I looked across at the tall and solid figure of Kyle Coker. His hair was thick and white and wavy; bearing in mind the male American's obsession with his hair I wondered if it was all his.

'Who's the guy with him?' I pointed out to Toby a tall and very thin man who was wearing a cream suit. With his suntanned face, and his blond hair swept back from his forehead, he could have been a photographic model living on borrowed time.

'That's Coker's assistant, Neils Rutter. Harvard Business School and then an account exec in a major New York agency. He's said to be the financial wizard behind the PGA.'

A few minutes later the main prizes were presented in reverse order. Ben found himself in possession of a huge silver cup, which looked about four times the size of the

FA Cup, and the winner's cheque for $190,000 which was written on the obligatory three-feet-long piece of cardboard. After making some polite noises about the golf course and his American opponents, Ben escaped towards the clubhouse. Suzi waved at Toby and me to join them. Off we went in pursuit and the drinks were soon set up at a large table in the bar. Nick Spencer joined us, in addition to one or two of the American players, including Travis Hanson, who congratulated Ben fulsomely.

'My goodness,' he said, 'I hope you're not going to play like that in the Ryder Cup.'

'He'll play even better,' the voice of Ross Bentley interrupted from the edge of the circle. 'Well done, Ben, you did my heart good, I can tell you. And you, Nick, well played. I'll order some more champagne.'

Suzi Massey was standing to one side, chatting to Travis Hanson and Stefan Sandberg, and I watched as Ben introduced his mother to Ross Bentley. Suzi was as animated as any proud mother would be who had watched her son's triumph and there was little to be learned from her demeanour. Neither was there the remotest flicker of recognition on Bentley's face. He shook Suzi by the hand, saying, 'I'm immensely proud of Ben, so you must be ecstatic.'

At this point Toby dug me in the ribs as Louise Bentley arrived at our noisy group. She made her rather queenly way among us, with a nod here and a handshake there. Toby and I received the merest inclination of her head and a glacial look. Ross Bentley grabbed his wife by the hand and said, 'Darling, you already know Ben and I'm sure you'd like to meet his delightful mother. This is Suzi Massey.'

Did I imagine a slight pause before Louise put out her hand to shake Suzi's? Did I notice an almost imperceptible nervous flutter in Suzi's eyes? Or was it all in my imagination?

Later I asked Toby if he had registered anything unusual but he hadn't. 'You know what these attractive women are like,' he said bluffly. 'They don't like competition, that's all it was.'

Some psychologist he turned out to be.

Chapter 26

Ben drove his mother, Toby and me to the Ryder Cup course which was about a hundred miles south of Harbour Dunes. It was another recently developed golf resort and very much a mirror image of Harbour Dunes; it was no surprise to learn that both resorts were owned by the same corporation. There were three golf courses at the Eagle Cliffs resort, including a short or 'executive' one, and the championship course turned out to be a familiar and daunting melange of holes threatened by vast tracts of water and by huge and forbidding bunkers.

Toby pronounced it huffily as 'typically American, no subtlety' and Ben pointed out that they would naturally select a course which would suit the home team.

'I realise that it's all a matter of money,' Toby replied, 'of who puts in the highest bid for the privilege of having the Ryder Cup, but nevertheless I think it should be played on a great course. What's the matter with Pebble Beach or Pinehurst, for God's sake?'

'As you say, it's money, Toby,' I told him. 'Eagle Cliffs needs all the publicity it can get, in order to sell its villas and condominiums. Pebble Beach doesn't have that sort of marketing imperative.'

'Well, it's all wrong,' he grumbled. 'The course is like Harbour Dunes. It's in a wonderful spot by the sea, where without much trouble you could build a classic links course and what have they done?' Toby paused dramatically. 'They've moved mountains to create a totally unsuitable course, it's an inland course by the sea.'

The European players, who all arrived during the course of the day, had been allocated villas alongside the ninth fairway. The accommodation varied in size according to the requirements of each player. Nick Spencer, for example, had brought his wife, three children, a nanny and his parents. Consequently he had been allotted a villa with five bedrooms; Ben and Suzi had been given a much smaller house to share. Toby, along with many of the journalists, was to be accommodated in the hotel and all the caddies were given tiny one-bedroomed apartments.

Eagle Cliffs was awash with the stars and stripes; they were everywhere and I had noticed, during our drive down to the resort, that almost every shop, bar, hotel and apartment building was sporting the American flag in some form or other. The only sign that there was another team involved in the match was the European Community flag which was flying, in tandem with the stars and stripes, at the entrance to the resort.

'Look at that ridiculous flag,' Toby said, when he spotted it. 'Looks like the flag of a hotel group. A triumph of pallid design. Where's the good old Union Jack?'

'Well, I don't know that Gonzales and Sandberg would identify all that well with it, Toby,' Ben said. Toby grunted in disgust.

The first routine matter which had to be accomplished was the allocation of all the official Ryder Cup clothing. Each player was given half a dozen of everything: trousers, shirts, socks and sweaters plus the official blazer, a suit for more formal occasions such as the welcoming dinner which was scheduled for the Wednesday evening, a golf bag, two pairs of golf shoes, a set of rainwear and so on. Even we humble caddies were supplied with trousers, shirts and sweaters. It was an acceptable and unaccustomed bonus.

Late on Monday afternoon, Ben and I walked over together to the hotel suite which had been set aside as the European team's offices, in order to collect our various items of clothing.

The clothing had been donated, free of charge, by a number of manufacturers; in return they would be able to exploit the prestige and publicity derived from their association with the Ryder Cup. Apart from their logos being seen on television screens around the world, they could advertise their wares as official Ryder Cup products.

When Ben and I entered the suite, it was obvious that a considerable disagreement was under way in one corner. Apart from the raised voices, the body language told the story. Chins were thrust forward and fingers stabbed the air as Ross Bentley, Nick Spencer, an official with the European team called Hugh Gregg and Tony Swan argued away. Swan was one of the most accomplished golfers on either side, a man who had already won the Open twice and the US Masters. He was clearly speaking on behalf of Nick Spencer as well as himself. Tall and powerfully built, Swan seemed to tower over the rest of the group. 'Nick and I both have contracts to wear Castle clothing in all tournaments,' he said. 'There are no exceptions. Castle have been on to our agent, we can't be seen with any other logo on our stuff.'

'You've got to wear the team uniform,' Hugh Gregg said abruptly. 'These firms have supplied their kit in

generous quantities. Not only that but they've paid
money to be official Ryder Cup suppliers. There's no
way out of that.'

'There's no way out of my contract with Castle,
either,' Nick Spencer protested, 'except that they'll tear
it up if they see me in something else. They're paying me
a lot of money to push their shirts and sweaters.'

As a former winner of the US Masters, whose
powerful hitting and combative style made him a
popular figure in golf, I guessed that Nick Spencer was
guaranteed well over £100,000 a year to wear Castle
clothing; Tony Swan's contract would be worth a great
deal more.

Ross Bentley had not so far contributed much to the
debate but now said, 'There is a way out of this. Nick
and Tony, you must wear the regulation clothing. What
if we blank off the logos? You'll still be seen wearing the
same kit as the rest of the team, but you won't be
violating your contracts with Castle. How's that?'

Swan acted as the spokesman and said that he would
contact their agent to see if the compromise would
work.

'It's got to work,' was Hugh Gregg's parting shot.

As Ben finished collecting his gear two more players
walked in. They were Mike Dolby and Dave Curran,
who were both around Ben's age and had qualified in
eighth and ninth position in the Ryder Cup points table.

They were wearing tattered blue jeans and T-shirts,
and Curran had the headphones of a personal stereo
fixed to his ears. They nodded at Ben, and another
official began to put their bundles of clothing together.

'God alive, what's this?' Dolby asked, as he held up
his blazer for inspection by Curran.

'Not something I'd be seen dead in,' his friend said.
Ross Bentley walked over, greeted the two players

and asked if they had any problems.

'Well, only this,' Curran said, holding up the blazer.

'Wrong size?' asked Bentley. 'You were all measured up several weeks ago, weren't you?'

'Wrong style,' Dolby said.

'Wrong century,' his friend Curran drawled disdainfully. 'This jamboree is going to turn over more than ten million dollars, or so I hear, and you can't even provide us with some good gear to wear. I'd rather have the money, in fact I'd rather have a small percentage of turnover.'

'None of the players gets a penny to play in the Ryder Cup, as you well know,' Bentley said patiently. 'That's what makes it different; you're playing for the game itself.'

'Yeah, yeah,' Dolby muttered.

The two players were often referred to as 'independent spirits' on the European golf circuit. Their general irreverence and refusal to conform was regarded in some quarters as refreshing, just as that of my old boss, Jack Mason, was seen as the mark of a man with a mind of his own.

In the context of the Ryder Cup, however, when a group of disparate individuals, from different backgrounds and cultures, must unite in the common cause, such attitudes might prove to be unhelpful. We could see that Bentley thought so, despite his avuncular admonition to Curran and Dolby to wear the blazers with pride.

'They're for semi-formal occasions,' Bentley said, 'such as the press conference tomorrow. Wear your blazers, boys, we must look smart, we must look like winners.'

'Yes, Captain Bentley, sir,' Dolby threw up an exaggerated salute. Bentley smiled tightly and said to the retreating backs of the two players, 'Don't forget the team meeting tonight. My villa, seven-thirty.'

He turned to Ben and me, shook his head irritably and said, 'I know a few pros who would've killed for a Ryder Cup blazer. Ah well, I mustn't be an old fogey. See you later, Ben.'

Later that evening, as I was lying on my bed and debating the relative merits of dinner in the various restaurants in the hotel, there was a tap on the door of my apartment. It could not be Ben, since he was due at the team meeting at around that time, but was probably Toby, in search of a companion for drinks and an evening meal.

To my surprise it was not the bulky figure of the golf scribe which greeted me but the much more slender and infinitely more attractive one of Suzi Massey. Dressed in white cotton trousers and a dark blue polo shirt, she looked as irresistible as ever; especially when she produced, from behind her back, something that looked suspiciously like a bottle of champagne. I hadn't hoped to spend any time alone with her during this trip.

After kissing me on the lips she said, 'Schramsberg. It's the best I could do. Let's drink it in bed.'

We enjoyed the champagne almost as much as we enjoyed each other. What a way to start a quiet evening. As we finished the last of the bottle, Suzi said that she had to get on her way. 'Dinner with the Blackstocks. With Ben, too, of course. At least that means that it needn't go on too long.'

'Why, does the old man fancy you?'

'Old Lionel? Maybe, but it's not that, they're both a bit overpowering. All that self-made man act, the jovial and unsophisticated Lancashire lad made good, can get a bit wearing. And of course it's golf, golf, golf. Ben's not so keen on that, either. He does have other interests, as you know.'

'Why don't you have dinner with me instead?'

'That wouldn't be wise and you know why, Chris. It wouldn't do to let Ben know what we're up to, would it?'

'Not at the moment, no.' I smiled at her and continued, 'It's role reversal time, isn't it? He's more like a parent than you are.'

Suzi shrugged and, without any hint of subtlety, I asked, 'Had you ever met Louise Bentley before?'

'No,' Suzi said with an emphatic shake of her head. 'I'd seen her but only at a distance. Why?'

'Oh, nothing. I just wondered.'

'If you were observing me, Chris darling,' she said with asperity, 'you will have noted that Ross Bentley didn't know me from Adam and neither did Louise.'

Part of the statement seemed to be accurate but overall I reserved judgement.

Chapter 27

Caddies are not usually invited to team meetings and
press conferences, however informal they might be, but
I knew I could rely on a full and well-embellished
account of the latter from Toby.

I was not disappointed. On the following morning he
found me, as arranged, in one of the coffee bars and, to
the waitress's surprise, called for a large malt whisky
and a cup of tea. 'Absolutely bloody shambles,' he
announced, as much of the first drink of the day
disappeared in one eager gulp. 'Nice idea, an informal
get-together, to meet the Press. But all the American
media descended on just two or three of our boys. Tony
Swan, of course, and Nick Spencer. Sandberg, but he
soon burnt them off. Every time anyone spoke to him,
he tried to inveigle him into his bible class tonight.'

Toby grinned at the memory and told me that Ross
Bentley had spotted the problem within minutes and
had asked that the conference became more formal. He
had gathered the players around him at one end of the
room and insisted that all the questions were channelled
through him.

'Ross was furious anyway. He hates disorder and to
make matters worse he then realised that there were two
notable absentees from the European team.'

'Don't tell me,' I said, 'Curran and Dolby.'

'Yup. They did turn up, about half an hour late.
Improperly dressed, no blazers, jeans. If looks could've
killed. I would say that Ross would not be averse to

223

sending them home. Whenever a photographer tried to take a shot of the team the two of them put their hands in front of their faces, all that nonsense. And apparently they missed most of the team meeting last night.'

'You can't go into the Ryder Cup two men short,' I protested. 'There are twelve singles to play on the final day.'

'No, of course not, but Ross is allowed replacements. Rollo Hardinge is here in America and he could fly another player out. The Irish lad. It's not too late.'

'It wouldn't do much for morale, would it? So, how did it all turn out?'

'Those two aren't doing much for morale, anyway. Well, Ross doled some of the questions out to the players,' Toby reported, 'but answered most of them himself. There were no microphones, it was chaos and Ross didn't bother to hide his irritation. The American press officer got the bollocking of his life afterwards.'

'Hmm. As you say, a nice idea that didn't work in practice. Did Ben have anything to say?'

'Oh yes. He had quite a bit of attention, mostly because of his win on Sunday, and spoke up well. By the way, I noticed that the American who interviewed you was there.'

'Brandel?'

'Yes, he collared Ben at the end. I wasn't close enough to join in but Ben didn't seem too pleased with the questions.'

'I'll find out what happened,' I promised.

'Please do. I'm under pressure from Weasel-Dirt, as usual, to deliver. Especially on Bentley and his mysterious past. This story about Curran and Dolby, and Ben's victory, of course, will just about save my bacon for the time being. Remember, Chris, you're still on the payroll.'

'Am I? Then you owe me for last week?'
'I suppose so,' he said grudgingly.

I knew that Ben had been scheduled to play a foursomes with Stefan Sandberg against Nick Spencer and one of the Spaniards, Luis Moreno. Over the three days of practice it was Ross Bentley's difficult task to analyse how his various pairs of players should be disposed. On each of the first two days of the Ryder Cup four foursomes matches are played in the morning and four fourballs in the afternoon. It would be a vital part of the captain's tactics to put compatible players together in the two-man teams, especially in the foursomes, when the golfers play alternate shots with the same ball. Bentley's assessment of each player's style and his temperament would be crucial. I liked the idea of Ben's pairing with Sandberg; they were both calm golfers, long hitters and admirable putters. Whether the quiet and methodical manner of Moreno would be compatible with the sometimes erratic, do-or-die approach of Nick Spencer was debatable. Bentley was, of course, hoping to answer the same question.

As we made our way to the first tee I counted a sizable crowd along its edges and up in the stand behind it. Judging by the accents and the predominance of stars and stripes, the majority was American but there was also a good smattering of European fans. There were even a few Union Jacks – that should please Toby.

The other three players were already on the tee and, as I gazed down the fairway, I saw the unmistakable figure, and then the flowing swing, of Ross Bentley.

Nick Spencer gestured towards him. 'The boss has taken Curran and Dolby out on his own. He said he wants to advise them about the course. But I reckon it's final warning time.'

We watched the two young miscreants trudging towards the distant green, with the captain between them, and I reckoned that Spencer was probably right.

Some small bets were struck between the two pairs and we followed the threesome down the fairway. Ben had driven first to the right of the fairway and had left Sandberg an easy mid-iron to the green. We walked on and it gave me an opportunity to ask Ben about Lee Brandel and his questions.

'Do you know him?' he asked sharply, and I reminded him that Brandel was among the crowd of reporters at the Open.

'After you'd duffed up David?'

'That's right. And he arranged an interview with me a couple of weeks ago.'

'Well, you will know that he's a very hard-nosed journalist. He wasn't interested in my golf, all he wanted to talk about was David, whether anyone had been arrested. Was I under suspicion? I asked him if he thought I'd be here, if I were.'

Ben putted his and Sandberg's ball alongside the hole, which was halved in four shots and, since it was now Sandberg's turn to drive, we headed off down the fairway.

'And then he asked me a very odd question,' Ben said. 'He asked me if my father was here for the Ryder Cup. When I told him that Garfield wouldn't be able to make it, he said, "Not your stepfather, your real father." That's when I told him to get lost.'

The thought of the conversation clearly unsettled Ben because his next shot, with a one-iron, was uncharacteristically skinny and only crept on to the fringe of the green. I resolved to press him to tell me what David had said to upset him so thoroughly that day; but to do so later, because the serious business of

226

Ryder Cup practice was now well under way.

As we followed the challenging expanses of the Eagle Cliffs course, we were able to watch the progress of Ross Bentley and his two young charges. It seemed to me that the captain was doing most of the talking. Neither could I help noticing that he seldom deviated from the middle of the fairways, so his game was obviously in supremely good order. Perhaps he should play the match instead of Curran or Dolby; he certainly wouldn't let the side down.

Our first complete round of the championship course had enabled us caddies to check its measurements. We already had charts with the main distances marked, but we all wanted to confirm those and make many subsidiary checks. We had been promised measuring wheels by the American officials but they had mysteriously failed to materialise. I would be no adherent to the 'dirty tricks' theory – as long as the wheels turned up on the following day.

Our foursomes match finished level and, as we vacated the eighteenth green, Ross Bentley waved Nick Spencer over to him. Ben and I headed for the practice ground to join the other players; we were due to play nine holes as a fourball with the same opponents in about an hour's time.

About ten minutes later Spencer joined the ranks of practising golfers but not before he took Ben to one side. I sat down on the edge of Ben's golf bag and pretended to be interested in the various golf swings, some of the best in the world, around me. Nick Spencer had never been renowned either for his diplomacy, as witness his feud with Ramon Gonzales, or his discretion. I wondered why Bentley had chosen to confide in him, if he had done so; presumably because the Midlander was one of the more experienced Ryder

Cup players. I could just hear the flat drone of
Spencer's voice: ' . . . thought he should let me
know . . . one of the senior pros . . . that they're on the
next plane . . . if they don't mend their ways . . .
conform . . . dignity of the Ryder Cup . . . and make
sure they never play representative golf again.'

The timbre of Spencer's voice was ideal for
eavesdropping and I'd got the drift quite easily. If the
captain had taken Curran and Dolby to task in such a
manner, he had made some potent threats. Apart from
the disgrace of being sent home from the Ryder Cup and
the hefty fine which would surely follow, any ban from
playing team golf in the future would be extremely
costly, since there are many team events, with
substantial prize money, at the end of each season.

I wondered how much it would be morally
appropriate to tell Toby and decided to make that
decision later.

Chapter 28

Our nine holes of fourball play went smoothly enough until the fifth hole, a long par five where the second shot must be played blind over a ridge. A big bang with a wood or a one-iron can put a good golfer on or near the tightly bunkered green. Nick Spencer was about to play out of a bunker on the right when we all heard the splash of a ball as it landed in the sand next to him.

'What the hell . . .' Spencer shouted. 'That bloody ball missed me by inches.' He climbed out of the bunker and looked angrily back up the fairway. I was hoping that the misdirected ball had come from the club of someone Spencer liked: Tony Swan, for example. But Sod's Law dictated that the figure which appeared on the crest of the ridge was the purposeful one of Ramon Gonzales.

I knew that the volatile Midlander would accept no excuses from his recent adversary and, as Spencer set off up the fairway towards the Spaniard with a growled threat of what he was going to do to 'that bloody Spick', I feared the worst. A punch-up during a practice round would neither enhance the European team's reputation nor its chances of victory; I could imagine all too well the capital the American media, and there were plenty of them about, would make of such an incident.

Stefan Sandberg reacted quicker than anyone. He sprinted across the fairway and put his wiry body between Spencer and the approaching Gonzales. I saw the brawny Spencer push hard against the Swede, who did not give an inch and kept talking at speed. Fortunately, Christian counsel prevailed and Spencer descended once again into the sand and flew his ball out on to the green. Ben nudged me and we saw Spencer stamp Gonzales's ball firmly into the sand.

'I hope they're not playing for a lot of money back there,' Ben said.

'With Tony Swan in the group they probably are,' I replied.

As we paused on the next tee, we watched Gonzales fail to remove his ball from the bunker and Nick Spencer shouted, 'Nasty lie, was it, you dull Spick?' Gonzales gave the traditional insult with the second finger of his right hand.

'That's team spirit,' muttered Ben with a rueful shake of his head.

I was hoping to get Ben on one side some time that evening. I still wanted to know precisely what David had said to him on the afternoon of his murder, but Ben was due to attend a barbecue together with the rest of the team, at the Bentleys' villa. I casually suggested that we met for breakfast on the following morning and Ben asked me round to his house.

That didn't suit me at all and I said, 'Will your mother be there? We don't want to bore her to death with golf.'

'No problem. She's leaving very early for a boat trip with the Blackstocks.'

As a result, I passed the evening with Toby in a seafood restaurant just along the coast from Eagle Cliffs. As was usual in Toby's company, it was a convivial evening, insidiously so, since I woke up the next morning at around six o'clock and regretted my last glass or two of Chalk Hill Sauvignon. My injured hand, inspected and strapped up again by the team doctor, seemed to be aching a little more than usual.

After a shower in the cramped little cabinet which took up most of the tiny bathroom, I decided to have a walk in the early sunshine. It was another sparkling day and a great variety of wildlife, especially seabirds wheeling and swooping over the sea, welcomed it with gusto. I walked briskly along the edge of several fairways and then struck across the course towards the hotel. I was in search of a newspaper and bought several, including the *Los Angeles Times*.

It was a column in that paper which caught my eye. I couldn't miss the headline in the sports section, which read:

BRITISH RYDER CUPPER IN MURDER PUZZLE

The report was the familiar account of the circumstances of David Massey's death and ended with the statement that Ben Massey was still 'under suspicion of being implicated in the tragedy'. This was a lie and would certainly do nothing for Ben's morale during the week of the Ryder Cup.

I was sure that the story came from the same source as all the other rumours and disinformation about the European team, but Toby and I were no further forward in identifying the prime source even though we were convinced that Brandel was implicated.

It was after seven o'clock and I turned my steps towards Ben's house. As he opened the front door an enticing smell of fresh coffee assailed my nostrils; close behind came that of newly toasted bread.

'You're just in time,' Ben said cheerfully. 'Scrambled egg with smoked salmon, bacon and toast on the side, coffee.' He waved me towards the back of the house.

'Let's eat on the terrace. My goodness, I could take to the American way of life in a big way.'

'It's fine if you're rich.' I made sure that a smile took any sourness out of my remark.

We settled down with our plates loaded and Ben asked, 'What's the problem? I know it's not golf, so it's probably to do with David.'

Without speaking, I showed Ben my copy of the *Los Angeles Times*. He merely nodded, went into the house and returned with a tabloid-style newspaper of his own. 'The *San Simeon Examiner*. Some kind person put this in our mailbox this morning. It's the same story, isn't it?'

'Yes, and it's all a part of a campaign to embarrass and upset our team. Your problems, the stories about Ross Bentley, my busted fingers, maybe even that dreadful business over Stefan's children. But you, Ben . . .'

'Hang on,' Ben interrupted. 'What've your fingers got to do with all this? I thought you caught them in a car door.'

'Not quite, but I'll tell you later.'

But Ben insisted that I told him the full story and it didn't take him very long to realise that he himself had probably been the assailants' real target.

While he pondered that, I pressed home my advantage. 'What I'm trying to say, Ben, is that part of the solution to the problem may be buried among the debris of your relationship with David. He may have been involved in this conspiracy, if I can call it that. You've tried to forget your last meeting and for good reason, but you must tell me as much as you can. I assure you I'm not asking out of vulgar curiosity.'

For some time Ben gazed past me at the rolling fairways of the Eagle Cliffs golf course. I thought for a while that I had lost him, that the gates had closed with finality to exclude the distasteful memories and emotions which the spectre of his stepbrother raised. At last, he drained his cup of coffee and spoke. 'I told you that he said some unforgivable things about my mother. I don't have to tell you how much I love her; she's been the one constant in my life. Strong, ever reliable, loving, the sort of mum every boy should have, I suppose. I've been very lucky.'

I didn't want to interrupt him even when he paused for what seemed like minutes. He continued: 'On that day, David called in at about midday. He'd already been drinking and he was in his usual boastful mood. I tried to make him welcome, take an interest in him, but he was worse than ever.

'He said he was about to make a lot of money; I told you that. The last piece of the jigsaw was about to drop into place, he said; it was the sort of tripe he always talked. Well, I humoured him as best I could but then he started slagging my mother off and I wasn't going to have that. I told him she was worth ten of him and that Garfield had been bloody lucky that she'd put up with him.

'Now comes the unforgivable bit,' Ben said as he toyed with yet another cup of coffee. He stopped again and then the words tumbled out in a rush. 'David said that when Garfield was away, and I was at boarding school, he used to fuck my mother. That was the way he said it. She couldn't get enough of him, he said . . .'

'But you didn't believe him?'

'No, but David followed up with the ace in his pack. He told me that mum had always been a goer, since the age of fourteen when I was conceived. I didn't believe him, of course. But he showed me a copy of her birth certificate. Simple arithmetic said that he was right.

'Though I hadn't believed a word of what he said about mum up to then, this threw me. And then he asked me if my mother had ever spoken to me about my real father. This was David's moment of real triumph. I can still remember the look on his face, gloating, sneering. "No, she wouldn't talk about him, because he was a criminal. And those are your parents, Ben, a criminal and a tart." '

Some tears started in Ben's eyes and he looked away as he wiped them. He went on: 'At that point I wanted to kill the fat slug and I knew I was capable of doing it too. So I ran upstairs, out of his way. I knew the best thing to do was get the hell out of there, try to sort my mind out, have some solitude. So I threw a few things into a bag, passport included, well, it's second nature to pack my passport, and it seemed that a few minutes later I was on the ferry for Caen.'

'There's only one grain of truth in what David told you,' I said firmly. 'That was about Suzi being fifteen when you were born. The rest is lies, Ben, I promise you.'

I had spoken too confidently and Ben at once questioned me, 'How come you know so much about it, Chris? You're a good friend but—'

I interrupted him. 'It's only what Toby's told me. He's had to keep tabs on it all.'

'I see,' Ben grunted without much conviction. 'Well, anyway, it was the birth certificate that did it for me. I thought if he'd got that right, the rest must be true. I was stupid, really strung out. I should've talked to someone, you perhaps.'

'Your mother?'

'I couldn't bring myself even to utter the things David had said, I wanted to shut my mind down. So I ran away.'

'Look, Ben, I don't have to tell you what a marvellous woman your mother is. As for your father . . . didn't Suzi ever talk to you about him?'

'When I was very small she told me that my dad was a very famous man but she had promised never to tell anyone his name. It was a secret. So I used to imagine all kinds of things. Mostly that I was a prince, like all little boys, I suppose. When I got older and the story stayed the same I just let mum have her way. I put it down to wishful thinking. It didn't bother me.'

'If it bothers you now, I may be able to help. I think I have an idea who your father was.'

'Who?'

'More later, Ben. My educated guess could be wrong but as soon as I know more I'll tell you.'

I was certain now that I knew who had fathered Ben and it seemed that David had not only made the same deductions but had found the evidence to prove it. Along with the birth certificates that showed Suzi had been a mother at fifteen, this added up to a potent bit of scandal which David, with his contacts in the media, knew he could exploit. But it was bonanza time for him when Brandel came on the scene. I was more and more convinced that Brandel had been sent to Britain by Kyle Coker with a brief to investigate any material, however insubstantial the source, which could be used to discredit the European team. It was all part of the commissioner's campaign to destroy their morale. Thousands of pounds, in David's unscrupulous eyes, had miraculously been transformed into hundreds of thousands of dollars.

But if David Massey had been part of the plot, why had he been murdered and where was the rest of the evidence? I guessed that he had got carried away by his sudden glimpse of easy street, become too greedy and had suffered the consequences.

I looked at my watch. 'Come on, you're on the tee in twenty minutes. You've got work to do and you can leave the other problems to me.'

Chapter 29

If the implications of what I had been told by Ben had sent my mind into overdrive, Ben himself looked almost serene. His golf swing was so relaxed and rhythmic that he seemed to have the ball on a piece of string. Teamed up with the German, Ernst Tillman, in a fourball against the two Spaniards, Miguel and Moreno, Ben beat them on his own and went round the course in an approximate 64 shots. Like all golfers, he is superstitious and did not want to count the shots accurately, in case the gods turned against him for his presumption.

At last we caddies got our measuring wheels and, during the morning round, I checked a number of distances: from this bunker to the edge of that green, from the edge of this lake to the centre of another green. This is all part of a caddie's routine and I also checked the first short hole, from the back of the tee to the centre of the green. I was glad that I did, because my measuring wheel showed a discrepancy; the official distance on my chart was 195 yards but my wheel measured the hole as 210 yards. That is why caddies are so meticulous in measuring courses; a professional golfer knows to within a few yards how far he will hit with a given club and the necessary adjustments for a breeze, or rain, or his own adrenalin levels are second nature to him. A difference of fifteen yards was nearly the equivalent of an extra club, for Ben the difference between taking a three-iron as opposed to a four-iron.

In the heat of a Ryder Cup battle, it could well be a crucial difference.

We all grabbed a rapid lunch and then set out to play a round of foursomes. Ben was teamed with Nick Spencer on this occasion against the young rebels, Mike Dolby and Dave Curran.

On the first tee, Nick's caddie, who was known as Scotch Willie, said that he had found one or two odd measurements during the morning round and I told him about my findings on the short hole, which is the fourth on the course.

During the first three holes I noticed that the players were too long with their second shots into the green, but I put it down to their becoming increasingly aggressive as the start of the Ryder Cup approached. It was a good sign from the European point of view.

It was at the short fourth hole that I began to wonder. Both Ben and Nick Spencer put their shots through the back of the green and I asked Ben to hit another ball.

'Aim for the back right of the green,' I said, 'because that's where the pin is bound to be at some stage. Take one club less, your four-iron.'

Ben hit his ball perfectly into the back right corner of the green. As we looked at each other in some confusion, I heard a loud, 'How ya doin', Ben?' from the right. It was Travis Hanson. The American team had begun their afternoon practice an hour or so ahead of us and he was playing down the eighth fairway.

'Call him over, Ben,' I said. The amiable American responded to Ben's wave and ambled through the intervening sand and scrub to say hello.

'Would you do me a favour, Mr Hanson?' I asked.
'If I can, son. Ask away.'
'Could I borrow your measuring wheel for a couple of minutes?'

He waved his caddie over and, from the back of the tee, I set out towards the green. I stopped in the middle of it and checked the counter. Well, well, 195 yards. An error of between five and ten per cent compared to my own wheel.

We thanked Travis Hanson, restored the wheel to his caddie and Scotch Willie and the other two caddies made the same journey from the back of the tee to the middle of the fourth green. At worst the error was just over ten per cent and at best just under five.

'The conniving bastards,' was Scotch Willie's summary of the incident and he spat generously on the turf. The other two caddies suggested some interesting places to put the sabotaged wheels and Nick Spencer, as impetuous as ever, wanted to walk in and confront the American officials immediately.

'It won't be the officials,' I said quietly. 'They're reputable people, they wouldn't countenance such behaviour. No, someone else is behind this.'

'Who?' Ben asked.

'I'm not sure yet,' I replied, 'but let's get hold of Ross Bentley. Let's not give anything away.'

'The laddie's right,' said Scotch Willie. 'Don't give the buggers the satisfaction.'

We waved one of the European officials over and he contacted Ross Bentley by radio. Within minutes, the captain was on the scene and we told him of our problems with the measuring wheels. He looked at us in disbelief until we demonstrated their inaccuracies to his satisfaction. Off he went at speed on his buggy to check with the other players, eventually to reappear about half an hour later.

'The bastards,' he exclaimed simply. 'All the wheels are out, the other lads have been all over the shop because of it.'

Scotch Willie spoke up and reaffirmed his view that
we should keep the tampering secret. 'Me and Jimmy
Wilson, we'll sort the calibrations out before tomorrow,
boss. Simple enough. We know what we're doing.'

So it was agreed but, despite the secrecy, the
Thursday edition of the *Daily Post* was to carry a huge
banner headline:

THOSE CHEATING YANKS

The Ryder Cup had been conceived in 1927 as a
competition which would foster the friendship between
golfers on both sides of the Atlantic. Several decades
later it seemed to have been hijacked by people with
much baser motives.

The Ryder Cup dinner, traditionally held on the
Wednesday evening, is another occasion designed to
encourage those tenuous ties of friendship between the
American and European golfing fraternity. Apart from
all the players and the officials, and their wives and
girlfriends, the net was cast widely and many of the
journalists, as well as local politicians and dignitaries,
were invited to join the fun. A limited number of tickets
had been made available to supporters of the two teams
and I had noticed that the Blackstocks were on the guest
list.

It was not thought politic to invite the caddies but we
were not forgotten; we were to be entertained in a small
dining room which adjoined the banqueting hall. A
loudspeaker system had been installed so that we could
hear the speeches and the presence of a giant television
screen indicated that some other form of entertainment
would be provided.

The other guests could not hear us, which was

fortunate since the talk, as is usual when caddies gather, was ribald, irreverent and, occasionally, extremely vulgar.

The seating plan had been arranged so that the American and European caddies alternated and I found Travis Hanson's man on my right. Ed Templeton, I learned, was a psychology graduate and had given up a career as a rock musician to follow the sun as a caddie. We were soon swapping stories about our respective golf tours, until we were interrupted by the master of ceremonies who called for silence while grace was said by the President of the United States Professional Golfers' Association.

The conventional words of thanks for life's blessings did not demand any comment from anyone but, to the surprise of all of us, the President concluded by asking God, in his infinite wisdom and kindness, to favour the American team with victory in the Ryder Cup. There are many committed Christians in sport, Stefan Sandberg, for example, but I think that they would judge that God probably has more pressing problems to address than the result of a golf match. It seemed to us a singularly tactless and undiplomatic request at the best of times, but especially in front of the opposing team, whose members must be afforded the status of guests on such an occasion.

Even Scotch Willie, who was opposite me at our table, was momentarily silent; but he recovered quickly and said loudly, 'You Yanks must be really worried if you need the help of the big fella.'

The meal was pleasant enough, helped along by generous quantities of California wine, which included a special Ryder Cup vintage. The marketing boys hadn't missed a trick.

As the debris was cleared away the godly President

announced that a short film would then be shown 'to celebrate the tradition and friendship of this unique golfing occasion, the Ryder Cup.'

The lights were dimmed and the name and logo of the Univision Corporation, the producers of the film, filled the screen. We were shown footage of the early years of the Ryder Cup and, as always, it was fascinating to see action sequences of those giants of the golfing past: Hagen and Sarazen, Duncan and Compston, Cotton and Rees, Hogan and Snead. The film rattled through the sixties and seventies, when the American golfers had been paramount, and there was hardly a British golfer to be seen; it was a succession of brilliantly executed strokes and winning putts by American players.

Several of the European caddies were becoming restive, especially Scotch Willie; but I was looking forward to the coverage of the eighties when, under Ross Bentley's guidance, the Europeans had imposed their own dominance. Several minutes were accorded the match in 1983, the occasion of the last American victory, and then it was a fade-out over a shot of the victorious American team. Loud music and a caption told us, again, that the film was a Univision production and that was it.

'That was a somewhat prejudiced view of the Ryder Cup,' said Ed Templeton from my right.

'Prejudiced — it was a sodding disgrace,' Scotch Willie said. 'We're not here just to make up the numbers for you bloody Yanks, you know.'

'No, that was way over the top. Chauvinist America at its worst. Merv Sorenson seems to be running the PGA these days, not Kyle Coker.'

Before I could pursue the matter with Templeton, the master of ceremonies announced that Ross Bentley would say a few words on behalf of the European team.

His image appeared on the screen and I settled back, wine glass full, to listen.

After saying how delighted he was to be the captain of the team for the fifth time, Bentley said, 'I think it is pertinent at this point to quote the wise words of the man who donated this illustrious trophy and was the founder of the fixture. Dear old Sam Ryder said this in a radio broadcast before the last World War.'

Bentley paused, drank from his glass and continued. ' "I trust that the effect of this match will be to influence a cordial, friendly and peaceful feeling throughout the whole civilised world. I look upon the Royal and Ancient game as being a powerful moral force that influences the best things in humanity." '

'Let us dwell for a moment on some of the words Sam Ryder used. Cordial, friendly, peaceful, civilised, moral force, humanity. These ideas should be in the forefront as these two fine teams of golfers prepare for the match. I nearly said "prepare to do battle" but this is not a battle, it's not war, whatever the media in their constant search for more sensation and hyperbole might say and write. There is no need for posturing and confrontation.'

I looked around the table of twenty-four caddies and saw that every one was concentrating on what Bentley was saying. That was unusual in itself, and there was hardly a sound from the main dining room, beyond the occasional cough or scraping of a chair. Everyone could sense the depth of feeling in Ross Bentley's words.

'In all my encounters in the Ryder Cup,' Bentley said, 'I never had anything but a high-spirited match. Though, judging by the film we have just seen, it seems that my forty-odd games have gone unrecorded, just like the recent victories of the European team.' Bentley paused as the sound of laughter rippled through both rooms. 'I think I spotted myself in the distance at Muirfield in 1973 but it wasn't clear what I was doing there.'

The camera panned away from Bentley and focused on a small man who was sitting alongside Kyle Coker. He was wearing a light grey suit and had rather delicate features except for a prominent, slightly curved nose. The camera caught him as he spoke emphatically to Coker.

I nudged Ed Templeton and asked him who the man was. 'That's the man himself, Merv Sorenson, owner of Univision,' he rumbled.

Bentley carried on speaking: 'I couldn't help but notice that the film was produced by Univision and, although I was never a classical scholar, I suppose an approximate translation of that company's name would be one-eyed.'

Amid more laughter and some applause which obviously emanated from the Europeans, the camera again switched to Sorenson, who was talking furiously at Coker, with much wagging of his finger.

'It's time I sat down,' Ross Bentley said, 'but let me conclude with my hopes for a great and exciting Ryder Cup. I hope we see many brilliant shots, from both teams, and that we all respect the tradition and dignity of this illustrious event.'

The applause rang out, loud and long and, I hoped, genuine. It was now the turn of Tony Bendix, the American captain, a tough character from New York, whose golfing career had been founded on a supreme short game and an unquenchable spirit.

With a face that might have belonged to a veteran of several hundred fights at Madison Square Garden, Bendix looked tough and talked tough.

'I won't try to equal the fine words of Ross Bentley.

I'm here to tell you that the American team will win the Ryder Cup. No ifs or buts. We've got the most successful team in golfing history. The American tour offers the most prize money and as a result we have the best and the toughest players in the world.'

There was a startling burst of applause from the main room and the camera cut again to Sorenson and Coker who were both smiling and nodding in approval.

In his flat and unmelodious New York tones Tony Bendix talked on. 'Thank you. Your American team have won sixteen major championships between them, they have won nearly two hundred tournaments and their total prize money earnings amount to over fifty million dollars. I don't know about dignity and humanity but I find a lot of moral force in those statistics.'

Bendix raised his hands to silence the applause. 'I count myself lucky to belong to this great nation of ours. I know we have the strength to achieve whatever we want, just as we showed recently in the Gulf. We did what we had to do.'

'With a bit of help from us, prat,' shouted Scotch Willie, who had procured a bottle of whisky by this time.

'So let us raise our glasses to another American victory in the Ryder Cup.' Tony Bendix concluded his address by raising his glass and the camera panned back to see half the dining room on their feet and the other, European, half firmly in their seats.

Travis Hanson was one of two or three American players who had stayed firmly in their seats; he was surveying the scene before him with a weary despair.

Ed Templeton did not get to his feet either but shook his head gloomily and said, 'So much for dignity and friendship, eh. How can that Bronx turnip get it so wrong? I thought we'd got over all that xenophobic shit after Vietnam.'

As everyone resumed their seats we saw a group of people on one side of the dining room rise to their feet. There were around twenty of them and as the cameraman reacted by going in close, I identified the solid figure of Lionel Blackstock. He had clambered on to his chair and had his arms raised as if he were about to conduct the Manchester Philharmonic. Although he did not have the musical skills of that orchestra at his command, the makeshift choir at his disposal made a very respectable job of the opening phrases of 'Land of Hope and Glory'. Within seconds Blackstock's choral volunteers were augmented by many more voices and the camera, panning back again, showed virtually every European supporter on his feet and bellowing. If the words were indistinct the famous tune came over loud and clear. Even the players were joining in and I saw Stefan Sandberg up on his feet and singing away lustily. I wondered what words he was using. Not far from him I spotted Toby; he was standing up as straight as a guardsman and roaring out the words. It was quite a sight. Ben and Suzi had linked arms and were also singing lustily.

Although a group of American supporters were attempting a choral counter-attack, and I assumed that they were singing the 'Star Spangled Banner', they made little headway against the formidable sound of the British supporters. By this time all the European caddies were singing and even Scotch Willie, a dyed-in-the-wool Scottish Nationalist, was waving his arms about and giving his all. I suspected that he was singing 'Flower of Scotland' but I couldn't hear amid all the din.

The noise slowly began to diminish and the Americans on the main tables, bemused by the very effective and vocal reaction of the Europeans, began to head for the exits.

As I moved towards the doors, in the hope of seeing Toby before the evening ended, I saw that Scotch Willie and his friend, Jimmy Wilson, were dancing a Scottish jig around a bottle of whisky. They were no doubt only at the beginning of their evening. I wondered when they were going to fix the measuring wheels – and how reliable they'd make them.

I paused in the entrance hall and was nearly bowled over by a phalanx of men moving speedily away from the main dining room. Merv Sorenson was easy to identify, yet again in the middle of another harangue directed at the US Tour Commissioner, as was Neils Rutter, who was close alongside Kyle Coker. Lee Brandel, the so-called journalist, was at Sorenson's elbow and several dark-suited men, brawny, with the watchful eyes of professional bodyguards, brought up the rear. Maybe one of them had done for my left hand last week in Monterey.

Close on their heels came Toby, who was grinning all over his face. His voice was more resonant than ever as he bellowed at me, 'First blood to the Brits, my boy. How did you enjoy the concert? It brought tears to my eyes. A spontaneous assertion of British self-confidence, just as Elgar intended.'

'It certainly startled our American cousins. Judging by the looks on some of their faces it hasn't done a lot for the spirit of friendship between the two countries. By the way, what do you make of Sorenson? He's certainly in cahoots with Coker, isn't he?'

'Well, he's a tour sponsor. A sour-looking bugger, isn't he? But they had it coming. That film. My God, you'd think the Americans were the only team in the Ryder Cup.'

'Did you notice our friend Brandel at the dinner?' I asked. 'He's very close to Kyle Coker, isn't he? I'm convinced that Coker is behind this conspiracy and that Brandel is his fixer.'

'No, Chris, I can't see a motive for Coker. He's in charge of the most prosperous golf tour in the world. Why should he be bothered about the Ryder Cup? I can't see it. Anyway, let's discuss it tomorrow. In the meantime, let's go to the bar and purchase a bottle of their best fizz.'

I declined Toby's invitation more sharply than I should have done, but I was annoyed by his dismissal of my theory about Kyle Coker. I went off to bed in an irritable and rather sanctimonious frame of mind.

Chapter 30

It was no surprise that as soon as my back touched the mattress I fell into one of those wonderful deep sleeps that comes after hard physical exertions. Carrying a tournament bag for around ten miles in over 80 degrees of heat tends to tire you out.

It was with a shock, and a feeling of injustice, that I woke up at around two o'clock in the morning. Oh well, roll over and go back to sleep. Half an hour later I was still awake and decided to capitulate and read myself back to sleep. I still had about twenty pages to go on the thriller I was reading and read steadily to the end.

Still wide awake, I decided to embark on another novel. What other novel? I realised, with some irritation, that I had read all the books I had with me and had failed to replenish the stock. I was reduced to shuffling through the various newspapers and magazines I'd acquired over the last few days in search of something of interest.

The best bet seemed to be an American golf magazine and I slowly thumbed through the early pages, whose articles promised to transform all aspects of the reader's golf game. In my head I checked my grip on the club, especially the position of my left thumb, my set-up and posture, my take-away, my initial shift of the legs at the start of the downswing, my action in the hitting area and my follow-through. Perfect — so why wasn't I a perfect golfer? A few waves of sleep began to wash over me and I flicked over a few more pages out of idle curiosity.

What I thought was to be the last page before I turned off the light brought me sharply out of my near slumber. A full-page photograph of Kyle Coker stared out at me with a caption which read, 'Can Coker survive?'

My sleep forgotten, I read the two-page article with close attention. The writer didn't pull any punches as he described the tour commissioner as a man under siege to an array of business problems. He pointed out that the American golf circuit was almost devoid of the personalities whose charismatic appeal and outstanding skills had fuelled its extraordinary growth during the previous three decades. 'The college-educated clones, indistinguishable from each other in their visors and sponsored clothing, with computer-generated golf swings and identikit personalities have about as much appeal as an annual tax return. They go to public relations courses, courtesy of the PGA, and then make it clear that a reporter is persecuting them if he asks them anything more difficult than "how are you?" '

The journalist pointed out that these grey golfing men could not even win the major championships, which were now, with an occasional exception, the preserve of the leading European and Australian golfers. The result was that the television ratings were dropping and the corporations which poured vast amounts of their money into golf were beginning to question their own wisdom in doing so.

There were other clouds on Coker's business horizons, too, including the threat of litigation over the siting of a golf complex which was being developed by the American Tour and rumours of disquiet over some of the deals he had done in the recent past. The journalist speculated that Coker would be lucky to retain his job beyond the following season and promised to reveal more in the next edition of the magazine.

A full day of practice awaited me but I knew that I must talk to Toby. It seemed obvious that my theory about Kyle Coker was correct. He would go to desperate lengths to ensure an American victory in the Ryder Cup. It would bolster the reputation of his tour and help to revive the sagging interest of his sponsors and of his public.

Toby was not renowned for his early rising, so I left a message for him to meet me in one of the hotel bars at one o'clock that afternoon. I calculated that I would be able to spend half an hour with him between the foursomes and fourball practice.

At the appointed time I found Toby on a high stool by a corner of the bar. He was talking to a square-framed man with a wrinkled, suntanned face; he wore a black beret on top of his head. His age could have been anything from forty to seventy.

'Meet Mal Tomas,' Toby said. 'One of the best golf photographers in the business.' I had seen Tomas's photographs in books and magazines and agreed wholeheartedly with Toby's assessment. He had an unusual knack of capturing the different aspects of the sport, from the ridiculous to the sublime. Nevertheless, I was wary of being lured into a conversation with Tomas when I didn't have long to talk to Toby about Kyle Coker.

'Can you spare a minute, Toby?' I asked. 'It's about Coker, I need your help.'

'Fire away, my boy. Mal knows as much about Coker as anyone.' Toby waved at the bartender and two more bloody marys appeared in record time; I settled for a beer.

I told them what I had read about Coker's problems and Tomas nodded. 'It's pretty much true. The faceless

251

automata that play pro golf these days are killing off the interest of the public and the sponsors. They want the same things; colour, excitement, personalities, and they're in real short supply. Where are the Hagens and the Sneads? They sure as hell aren't on the American tour.'

'This article I've read referred to some bad business deals done by Coker. What are they?'

'There are several points to make here,' Tomas replied. 'First, he was determined to get the Tour involved in building golf courses, these piss-awful stadium courses, where he could hold his official pro tournaments. And of course he reckoned to make a killing by selling the real estate all around them.'

'A good idea,' said Toby, 'as long as the economy holds up and people can afford expensive retirement homes and second homes.'

'Yeah,' continued Tomas, 'and as long as there are no problems. One of Coker's biggest investments was in Clearwater Bay in Florida. A huge project; four golf courses, you name it. He put all the money up, started building the courses, and then the environmentalists stepped in. A group of them are opposing his plans on the grounds that they will destroy the wildlife, pollute the sea and generally foul up the whole of the surrounding neighbourhood.'

'Didn't he clear all those questions at the planning stage?' I asked.

'He thought he had, but the environment has become a very hot issue over here in the last few years and this particular group wanted to focus on golf. And who best to attack but the American Professional Tour; very high profile, lots of publicity guaranteed. And of course Coker played into their hands; he tried to cut corners over wildlife protection.'

'So he's committed a lot of money to a project that's at a standstill?'

'Yes,' Tomas continued, 'and he's getting no revenue in the way of deposits on the houses and apartments, the interest payments are colossal, and he may end up paying millions in damages because a group of environmentalists are suing him for failing to conserve the wildlife of the area.'

'And the players are no doubt peeved because they can see their old-age pensions going up in smoke,' said Toby.

'Exactly, and there's no love lost anyway. Coker comes on very strong, he rules the Tour like an absolute dictator. He's the judge, jury and executioner. Of course, he loves his power over these players because he was only a moderate performer at his best. He resents their popularity, their earning power, even, although he is the man who has brought so much more money into pro golf.'

'But he must get his fair share?' I said.

'Oh yes,' Tomas agreed with a smile, 'he has a great lifestyle. A salary of nearly a million dollars, a bonus last year of nearly half a million, he's got the use of a corporate jet and of a condominium in Florida. That also bugs the players, they say he's doing better than most of them.'

'Well, they're right,' Toby said. 'He's got his nose well into the trough. Not that he doesn't deserve his rewards, because he's built the Tour up over the last few years, hasn't he? But perhaps he should be more discreet.'

'He doesn't know what the word means, Toby,' replied the photographer. 'Coker has expensive tastes. He has a wife, a couple of ex-wives, and a mistress, for a start.'

'God help him,' Toby murmured with feeling.

'And he loves the trappings of success, too, fast cars, the best wines, exotic holidays, grand houses.'

'So, falling attendances, lower TV ratings and disappointed sponsors are exactly what he doesn't need,' I summarised.

'Exactly, and if he's not careful the Clearwater Bay project could be the last straw. He's already had a lot of stick for some of his business deals,' Tomas continued. 'The players have criticised him for being too close to Sorenson at Univision. Apart from selling him TV and video rights they're in bed together on too many other deals, including Clearwater Bay.'

Mal Tomas had given me a lot to think about but I was due on the tee with Ben Massey in under ten minutes. I thanked him and headed for the door, with Toby in my wake. Out of Tomas's earshot, I whispered, 'This confirms what I was trying to tell you last night. Coker needs a Ryder Cup win, he must be behind this campaign against our players.'

'Yes, well, after due consideration, I think you may be on the right lines,' Toby pronounced airily.

'The theory has your backing, has it?' I asked drily.

'It'll make a great story. But how does David Massey's murder fit in?'

'David found out that Ben is the son of Ross Bentley and he must have found some evidence. So, under-age mother and famous father. It's big bucks time when he sells the info to Brandel.'

'And a mighty scandal which would probably force Bentley to resign as captain and wreck the morale of the Ryder Cup team.'

'Well done, Toby,' I said nastily.

'But why should they kill him? Why not just do the trade and pay him off?'

'No doubt he got too greedy and they ran out of patience with him. But you and I, Toby, have got some digging to do. With Brandel and with the Bentleys, and no holds barred this time.'

'And with your friend, Suzi, too. No holds barred there either, eh Chris?'

With a revolting leer, Toby turned back into the bar and I headed at speed for the first tee in order to resume my duties as a caddie.

Chapter 31

During the afternoon practice session Ben was paired with Tony Swan. Tony is one of the most accomplished players in the game, but Ben didn't suffer by comparison. The British golfers demolished the Spanish pair of Jose Miguel and Luis Moreno. We were all glad that the final practice was over; the real battle would begin in just over twelve hours. Like most of the European players, my confidence was high and I was sure that Ben would give an excellent account of himself.

The opening ceremony for the Ryder Cup always takes place on the day before the match actually begins. With four foursomes and four fourball matches to play there is no time available on the opening day.

At six o'clock we all gathered in front of the clubhouse and the teams, dressed in their respective Ryder Cup uniforms, lined up on either side of the dais. Also gathered there were friends and relations of the players. The American wives would have been grossly overdressed for Ascot or even for the Academy Awards. The brightly coloured, figure-hugging, cleavage-revealing collection of dresses, enlivened with feathers and flounces, frills and sequins, made me wonder whether they'd come as lampshades or Christmas trees.

Just before the start Tony arrived alongside, with Mal Tomas in his wake.

'Have you spotted the wives?' he asked super-fluously.

'Trophy wives,' grunted Tomas.

'What?' Toby and I said in unison.

'They're the second or third wives of pro golfers. Morgan-Jane Farrell for a start. She's empty-headed, drop-dead beautiful and has no desire to breed. She's all Jerry's, she's his trophy.'

'There are one or two first wives, too,' Toby whispered. 'They've had so many face lifts you'd bruise your lips kissing them.'

'If they have any more, they'll be sporting beards,' Mal Tomas muttered.

We had to stifle our laughter as the speeches began. There was no repetition of the nationalistic sentiments which had marred the dinner, and a series of displays marked the opening of the fixture. A girls' pipe band whirled and twirled its way across the grass and was followed by a marching display by a detachment of the US Marines. They looked very fit and fierce to me but Toby deemed them 'just passable'.

The finale was a fly-past by veterans of the Gulf war; everybody ducked as they hurtled seemingly only a few feet above our heads.

The fighter aircraft peeled off high into the heavens, their vapour trails leaving their marks on the flawless blue of the sky. Toby punctured the moment by shouting in my ear, 'I think I'll go back to my room and play my cassette of Winston Churchill's war speeches.'

I pretended to believe him. 'What about the press conference? They're announcing the pairings for tomorrow morning, aren't they?'

'Yes, do you want to join me?'

Toby ushered me past the security guards into the press room; his brusque statement that I was his assistant brooked no challenge and we grabbed a couple of chairs near the front.

With a handshake and a smile the two captains, Ross Bentley and Tony Bendix, handed sealed envelopes to Charlie Rensburg, the press officer for the Ryder Cup.

'It's like the Eurovision song contest, isn't it,' Toby said in an attempt at a whisper which only carried twenty yards or so.

Rensburg spoke up. 'The matches in the first series of Ryder Cup foursomes are as follows: Ben Massey and Stefan Sandberg against Jerry Farrell and Marvin Gull.'

'That's a tough one,' I whispered to Toby.

'They're all tough,' was his predictable reply. But I already knew the sterling qualities of Farrell, and his partner was a very experienced golfer from Texas who had played in four previous Ryder Cups and had a brilliant record.

I hardly registered the rest of the draw as I tried to assess the chances of success of Ben and his partner. I learned later that Nick Spencer was to partner his friend, Tony Swan, the two erstwhile rebels, Dolby and Curran, were together and two of the Spaniards, Jose Miguel and Ramon Gonzales, were the anchormen.

While Toby scribbled down the pairings, which had been projected on a screen for the benefit of the journalists, I eyed up the crowd, a gaggle of world-weary wordsmiths who had adopted the international golf uniform of brightly coloured, branded golf shirts, accompanied by storm-proof cotton golf jackets. Toby was one of the few journalists who was different; he was wearing a tie, the distinctive one worn by members of the Lords Taverners.

As Toby finished his notes we were both surprised to see several American and British officials, accompanied by the two captains, reappear in the press room. Many of the journalists had by now departed, in search of food and drink and other pleasures.

'What's all this?' asked Toby as the group paused by the dais. I didn't need the services of Desmond Morris or a copy of his *Man Watching* to tell me that a severe disagreement was in progress. The arm-waving and raised voices told me that, as did the pronouncement by Hugh Gregg, one of the British officials, that 'the whole business is a disgrace'.

By this time, Toby had led a charge of the remaining journalists towards the group of dissenters. Amid the shouting I saw that Ross Bentley remained the calmest person present. He jumped up on the dais and said: 'Gentlemen, please be quiet.'

It did not have any effect and, in exasperation and splendid voice, he roared into the microphone, 'Will you shut up and listen.'

Everyone did and the captain continued, 'It has been brought to our attention by American officials that some members of the European team are suspected of using illegal clubs.'

There were a few shouts of surprise from the journalists and then a volley of shouted questions. Above them all, Ross Bentley said, 'No questions. Just a statement, gentlemen. May I go on? American observers have suggested that the European players are imparting so much spin on the ball with their irons that the grooves cannot conform to the rules. In other words, the grooves are either too wide or too deep. In my opinion the imparting of such spin has everything to do with a golfer's skill and very little to do with the design of the clubs.'

'Hear, hear!' shouted Toby in concert with several other British journalists.

Bentley smiled and held up his hands for silence. 'We have agreed, nevertheless, that American officials can inspect the clubs of all our players. That's all, gentlemen. Mr Neils Rutter would like to make a statement on behalf of the American Ryder Cup Committee.'

Rutter jumped athletically on to the dais. Clad in a beautifully cut dark green blazer, with a light primrose shirt and a striped tie, he looked more than ever like a model in an ad for one of those stores which sells clothes for the up-and-coming executive.

'I would like to thank Ross Bentley for explaining the situation. It's one which we deeply regret but, in the interests of the European team as well as ourselves, we feel we have to act on the recommendations of our officials.'

'Smooth bastard, isn't he?' muttered Toby.

'We all feel, and I'm sure the European players and officials feel the same way, that it's better that the matter is resolved now, rather than tomorrow when the matches start. Thank you.'

Bentley, Rutter and most of the officials made a quick exit but Hugh Gregg threw a few words over his shoulder. I heard 'unnecessary', 'dirty tricks brigade' and 'disgraceful insult' and the pursuing journalists dutifully wrote them down.

Toby grabbed me by the arm and urged me towards the hotel and one of its welcoming bars.

'Rydergate,' he said smugly as we tackled a bottle of Schramsberg's best sparkling wine. I groaned and he said, 'Twelve players with ten or eleven irons apiece. That'll take the officials well into the early hours. It's Coker again, isn't it? Dirty tricks time, as Gregg said.'

'A nasty bit of psychological warfare. Our players must be wondering whether they'll get their own clubs back for tomorrow. That's not conducive to a good night's sleep. And Rutter, impartial demeanour and all, is enjoying every minute.'

'Yes, I've taken a distinct dislike to that young man. Too clever by half.'

'And not so young, either.'

We finished the bottle and parted company. Toby had an extra article to write for the *News* about the 'illegal' clubs and I wanted to follow a snack with a good night's sleep. Ben was due off the first tee at eight o'clock and we therefore had to meet on the practice ground one hour before that. I hoped that he wouldn't be using borrowed clubs.

Once again I was standing in a deep bunker by the eighteenth green at some championship course or other. The leader board showed C Ludlow leading the Open Championship by one shot. But my arms were paralysed; I couldn't move; I couldn't play my shot out of the bunker. Thank God for alarm clocks. Six o'clock.

As I stepped out of the shower there was a knock on the door. To my amazement, a dishevelled Toby stood there, two cartons of coffee balanced in one hand and a large bag in the other.

'What on earth . . .' I began.

' . . . are you doing up at this hour?' Toby finished the question for me. 'Coffee, breakfast and this.' He juggled two bacon rolls on to a small table and handed me a copy of *The San Simeon Examiner Ryder Cup Supplement*. 'Take a look at the profile of Ben,' he ordered.

Apart from a list of Ben's few tournament victories, it described him as a promising, though lightweight, player. The final sentence read: 'Massey is here at the Ryder Cup with the permission of the British police, who have yet to solve the murder of his stepbrother, David Massey.'

'Is it libellous?' I asked.

'Not at all. Now take a look at Bentley's profile.'

The sting was in the tail again, as the writer mentioned the controversy over Bentley's final putt in the 1972 Open Championship and referred to accusations in the British press of an illegitimate child. My eye went to the bottom of the page and it was no surprise to see that the piece was written by Lee Brandel.

'He doesn't give up, does he?' I said bitterly. 'I will interview him, Toby, on my own.'

'How's your hand?'

'Improving by the second.'

A few minutes later I was tapping on the door of Ben's villa and it was opened by Suzi, who looked so fresh and sexy that I wished we were somewhere else, alone.

'Stranger,' she said, as she kissed me on the cheek. Ben walked towards the door and I thought he looked paler than usual. Well, that was hardly surprising, since he was about to make his first appearance in the Ryder Cup.

'You OK?' I asked.

'In the circumstances, not bad. I didn't get my clubs back until nearly midnight and somebody delivered a message through the door at about four this morning. And it wasn't a good luck message, either.'

'They bashed on the door and woke us up,' Suzi said, as she handed me a sheet of paper. Scrawled on it was one word: 'MURDERER'.

Chapter 32

Ben and I took a buggy to the practice ground and the warm air put the colour back into Ben's face. As he limbered up, along with all his team-mates, Ross Bentley went along the line with words of advice and encouragement for everyone.

'How are you feeling, Ben?'

'Not so bad. Though I've thrown up twice already this morning.'

'Nothing wrong with that,' Bentley said, with a smile. 'I used to do exactly the same, every Ryder Cup match. Don't worry about it. You'll probably get over it in twenty years or so. I suppose you got your early morning wake-up call, did you?'

'Yes, how did you know?'

'Every player got something, a knock on the door or a telephone call. Poor Stefan had a particularly charming note. It had the words "child molester" scrawled on it.' Ben shook his head but said nothing about his own message. 'They even woke me up, the miserable buggers,' Bentley continued. 'Never mind, on with your practice, I'll see you on the first tee.'

I was delighted to see that Ben's swing was as fluid and unhurried as ever, a lovely movement, full of rhythm and power. He and his partner, Stefan Sandberg, walked to the first tee together and I asked them who was going to hit the first shot.

'Not me,' said Sandberg, 'I won't be able to take the club back, let alone hit the ball.'

265

Ben smiled and said, 'I'd better go first then, hadn't I?'

The stewards made a gangway for us through the milling crowds and all I could see at first were little American flags being waved and a great array of T-shirts with the slogan: 'Europe has it, USA wants it.' But, once we had stepped on to the tee, we found a sizable British contingent in position and there was a great cheer and shouts of 'Good luck, Ben' and 'Good luck, Stef'. It cheered me to hear their voices and even Sandberg's tense features relaxed into a small smile as he waved his acknowledgement.

Etiquette dictated that the visiting Europeans had the honour on the first tee. I had no idea how Ben was now feeling but my mouth was dry, my stomach queasy and I fumbled around in Ben's bag for his driver. My fingers wouldn't work properly. I finally managed to remove the club and handed it to him.

'Good luck,' I croaked.

In what seemed like a terminal silence, Ben lazily swung his club up and down, addressed his ball and, with a sharp crack of metal on balata, sent the white sphere soaring and spinning majestically down the right centre of the fairway. There seemed to be a communal intake of breath, a sigh of relief and then a huge cheer. The Ryder Cup was on its way. To his great credit, Jerry Farrell hit a similarly fine shot and the balls ended almost side by side.

Sandberg, perhaps buoyed up by his partner's confident start, hit an unwaveringly accurate mid-iron shot to within ten feet of the hole. The Americans were perhaps twice that distance away and missed their putt. Ben didn't and the European pair immediately went one hole up.

It was an encouraging start and by the end of the first

half the Europeans were three holes up, which was not surprising since they had taken only thirty-three strokes for the nine holes.

Although the crowd which was accompanying our game was large and composed predominantly of American fans, it was well-ordered and I noticed that there were at least a dozen stewards to keep the peace. I had a real dread that a heckler might reappear and direct his malevolent attentions towards Ben. The 'murderer' taunt which had been delivered made me think that there were strong odds that something unpleasant was still to come.

By the tenth tee I studied the big scoreboard and saw that the rest of the European pairs were struggling; two were in arrears to the Americans and the Spaniards were on level terms. In the circumstances, it was especially important that Ben and Stefan registered a point.

As I turned away I saw Suzi arrive with Toby. They both grinned and gave me the thumbs up. I smiled back and wondered whether my journalist friend was making a play for Suzi; it wouldn't have surprised me.

A crack appeared in the facade of the Europeans' superiority over the next few holes. Helped by an eagle at the long thirteenth hole and a birdie at the next the American pair reduced the deficit to one hole. At the fifteenth, Jerry Farrell hit a mighty hook that seemed to be sailing a long way left into a no man's land of scrub and sand. Marvin Gull was already reaching into his bag for a ball in order to play a provisional shot when we saw Farrell's ball reappear, as if by magic, and bounce back on the fairway.

'Did it hit somebody?' asked Gull.

'Act of God,' Ben said drily and we all knew that some misguided American spectator had thrown the ball out of the rough back on to the fairway.

Any golfer will tell you that such incidents can often alter the course of a match. Having fought back from three holes down to only one, the American pair probably felt that the tide had turned in their favour; this piece of extra luck would have convinced them. On the other hand the anxiety of the European pair would have been considerably increased. If they lost this hole, they would be in big trouble. It was imperative that Ben hit a respectable drive. As he stood in the address position and prepared to swing, the crowd pressed forward in their eagerness and he had to step away and begin his drill all over again. 'You're the man,' came a shout from some idiot or other and I was relieved when Ben hit a steady, if unspectacular drive down the middle of the fairway. Stefan, almost rigid with tension, managed to hit an iron on to the front edge of the green and Ben putted up to less than a foot. Jerry Farrell missed his putt for a win. A half. Crisis over.

It certainly was when Stefan put his tee shot at the short sixteenth hole to within two feet of the hole and Ben sent the ball solidly into the cup for a winning birdie. A half at the seventeenth meant a win for Ben and Stefan and first blood to the European team.

No more blood was spilt by the Americans, who had won the other three matches. Although Nick Spencer and Tony Swan took their game to the final hole, the other two European pairs lost heavily; and so the Europeans were trailing by three points to one at lunchtime on the opening day.

Ross Bentley had decreed that the caddies should join the players at lunchtime and we all gathered in the captain's villa. A huge buffet was laid out but I noticed that it remained largely untouched. Even my old boss, Jack Mason, a renowned trencherman, confined himself to fruit.

After a few minutes of desultory chat, Bentley called for silence and said, with a wry smile on his face, 'I hope that we've got our one bad session out of our system. Because we can't afford another. I don't understand why we are so bloody useless at foursomes. It's supposed to be the traditional British game and yet we always seem to be upstaged by the Americans.'

Bentley went on to ask if any of the players had anything to say about their performances that morning and the ex-rebels, Curran and Dolby, said that they were definitely out of kilter and would prefer to stand down for the afternoon fourballs. Miguel and Gonzales said nothing, although they had suffered the worst defeat, and Bentley announced that the Massey/ Sandberg and Spencer/Swan partnerships would remain together for the afternoon; in addition Jack Mason would team up with Ernst Tillman and Luis Moreno with the young English player, Dan Appleby.

'At least you'll all have had a game by the end of the day,' Bentley said grimly. 'Now, I know that your motivation is not in doubt, but just to increase it, you'll be aware that someone or other in the American camp is trying to unsettle us. As well as the tampering with our measuring wheels the other day and the wake-up calls, we had that bloody nonsense over our clubs. They all turned out to be entirely within the rules of golf, as I expected.

'Well, there's one more trick I should tell you about. As you know, I keep in touch with all my helpers on the course by short-wave radio and I was promised a secure line by the Americans. Well, it isn't. I heard an American voice on the line at one stage. They've been listening in.

'They want to win this match very badly, so let's make sure they're disappointed. As usual. Good luck, boys.'

When the pairings were exchanged, we saw that our opponents would be the amiable Travis Hanson and a young golfer called Larry Sussman, who was reputed to hit the ball immense distances.

On the way to the first tee we were intercepted by Toby, who wished Ben the best of luck, and then took me on one side. 'What about the Bentleys? Can we get at them tonight?'

'Well, it's open house at their villa,' I said and then, with a smirk, 'even for journalists.' With an airy wave I set off after Ben and left Toby doing a theatrical splutter of rage.

Larry Sussman, with his remarkable power, was an ideal partner for Travis Hanson, a steady and meticulous golfer who looked incapable of going round any course in more than three under par. But, despite a couple of eagles from Sussman, the Europeans were never in arrears in the match and eventually won it on the sixteenth green.

Hanson, ever the gentleman, congratulated Ben and Stefan on their victory and said, 'You're playing far too well, Ben, I'm praying that I don't meet you again. If the rest of your boys were as hot we'd be in big trouble.'

The scoreboard told us they weren't in any sort of trouble as the rest of the Europeans were far from hot. Jack Mason and his partner were in the best position and they were only on level terms; it looked like being a very disappointing day.

As Toby said an hour or so later, when all the matches had been concluded, 'It could have been much worse.' At one stage the Americans were ahead in all of the three other matches but some typically determined play by Jack Mason won him a half and the youngster, Dan Appleby, in concert with Luis Moreno, produced some dazzling golf over the closing holes. They were two holes in arrears with only three to play but managed to salvage an unlikely half from a dire situation.

At the end of the opening day the American team had five points to Europe's three, two of which had been won by Ben Massey and Stefan Sandberg.

I could see that Ben was drained of energy and emotion and he told everyone that, as soon as the team meeting was over, he would head for his bed. I saw my chance to get Suzi on my own and arranged to take her to dinner.

But first Toby and I had to grasp the nettle and confront Ross and Louise Bentley. A convenient time would be after the team meeting when the captain had decreed open house at his villa. But first I guided Toby to a quiet corner of the bar and summarised what I knew about Suzi Massey's past and what I surmised about the Bentleys' roles in it.

Chapter 33

The Bentley's villa was built in a style grandiloquent enough to house royalty; there was a fountain in the hall, several pieces of fine antique furniture and some impressive oil paintings on walls which climbed up to a semi-circular gallery. A magnificent chandelier hung portentously down from the dome ceiling. As Toby and I walked into the hallway that evening, Nick Spencer, head down, came out of the sitting room and made for the front door.

'Who are you playing with tomorrow, Nick?' I asked.

'No bugger. The skipper may keep me fresh for the singles, he says. Not that I blame him. I played like a dog today. I'm going to get pissed, no point in holding back now, is there?'

Off he went, as busy as ever, and I guessed that Spencer would bustle his way through about twenty bottles of American beer as a matter of principle.

Ben was next out of the sitting room and told us that he had been paired with Dan Appleby in the morning foursomes. 'The boss has split Stefan and me up. He says we're both playing well enough to bring him the points he needs with different partners.' Ben shrugged and headed for the front door. 'See you in the morning.'

'That's a brave decision,' Toby said, 'to split up your best pair. It's a gamble but you have to gamble when you're down.'

Ross Bentley saw us and waved us into a huge room,

273

its tables laden with food and drink.

Toby grabbed gratefully at a bottle of cold beer, gargled most of it down in one and said, 'How are you going to approach this rather delicate subject, dear boy?'

'Hang on, Toby, you're the experienced journalist, the man of the world, the erstwhile friend of the Bentleys, you do it.'

'Not on your life,' he replied, as he put his empty bottle down and helped himself to a glass of wine. 'I've got my future in journalism to protect. I need Ross's good will, you'll have to do the dirty work this time.'

'This time,' I said in disgust, but the argument was cut short by Ross Bentley's appearance at Toby's side.

'Help yourself,' he said, 'though I needn't encourage you in that area, Toby. Well done today, Chris, thank God for young Ben. We'd be up the creek without him and Stefan.'

Oh well, I thought, I might as well jump in with both bovver boots. 'Mr Bentley,' I said quietly, 'may I talk to you about Ben? In private.' I gestured towards the French windows which led out to a large terrace and a garden which stretched away for several acres. I noticed that Toby was looking vaguely over Bentley's shoulder, as if to dissociate himself from whatever was about to happen.

'What's the problem? Is he in trouble again?'

'It depends, but you could certainly help with one problem.' I steered him with my undamaged right hand through the French windows and to a table on the terrace. Toby was close behind us.

I paused for a moment and tried to slow everything down; I had an overwhelming temptation to blurt out all the questions and assumptions that were in my mind.

'You'll remember all the unpleasant rumours,' I

began, 'about the murder of David Massey and the attempts to implicate Ben. Then the rumours about you, when you were a young man, that you'd had an illegitimate child.'

'Absolute bloody nonsense,' he said aggressively. 'Why the hell are you raising that again?'

'I'm raising it again because I think there's a connection between the two, Mr Bentley,' I said coldly. 'You're the connection. Don't you remember Susan Meadows-Price? Don't you remember going to bed with a young girl back in 1970? Don't you know that she became pregnant?'

Bentley stood up, his face red with anger, and turned to Toby, who had stayed silent up to this point. 'Toby, is he off his head? Am I imagining all this crap, or what?'

'Well, Ross . . .' Toby began, but I interrupted.

'The result of your bit on the side,' I said, 'was Ben Massey. Suzi Massey was once Susan Meadows-Price. Am I getting through loud and clear?'

If I was, the response was very slow in coming. Ross Bentley just stared at me, opened his mouth to speak without producing a sound and turned helplessly to Toby. For the first time, I believed that he really had no knowledge of what had happened to Suzi. Eventually some words were uttered. 'Toby, I promise you on my honour that I did not father an illegitimate child. I think you know me well enough to understand that I would have met my obligations.' Bentley sat down heavily in a chair. 'I met Suzi Massey for the first time less than a week ago, at the California Classic, for God's sake.'

'Okay, but let's go back. You had been married a couple of years, you knew that Louise could not have children, and like many young men at that time, you had the occasional fling. Is that fair?'

Bentley looked around nervously, to ensure that no one else, and particularly his wife, was within earshot. 'Sure, girls were easy. I was randy as the next man and, remember, I was being talked about as a future star of golf. I had more offers than I could cope with and of course I went astray. I'm not very proud of myself, I was married, but you know what it's like when you're young; you can't get enough of it. Well, you probably know what it's like, Chris.'

'Thanks very much,' Toby muttered.

'All this has sod all to do with you two,' Bentley continued. 'But I put my hand on my heart and tell you that I did not have an illegitimate child.'

As he finished, Louise walked on to the terrace and called out, 'Ross, you're neglecting the guests, don't let these two gentlemen monopolise you.' The way she said 'gentlemen' made me feel anything but.

When her husband did not respond, Louise looked at him sharply and said, 'What's going on, Ross?' She addressed herself to me. 'Are you bothering him with your questions again? We're in the middle of the Ryder Cup, in case you hadn't noticed. Toby, you should know better. And you, Mr Ludlow, should be ashamed of yourself.'

I knew well enough how protective Louise was of her husband but such vehemence was unnecessary and probably fuelled by her suspicions that we had uncovered something which was potentially damaging.

I stood up, as if about to leave, but wanted to be on my feet the better to challenge the formidable Mrs Bentley. Toby was looking as uneasy as I had ever seen him but I was determined to press the matter to a final conclusion.

'It may not suit you, Mrs Bentley,' I said, with as much calm as I could muster, 'but we want to resolve several matters and they all seem to be connected. First, there are the rumours that your husband fathered an illegitimate child. He denies all knowledge of this and his denials ring true, but our evidence suggests something different. Perhaps you can throw some light on it all.'

Not the remotest tremor in Louise Bentley's poise was discernible to me; all I saw was a glance at her husband, who looked back at her with total confidence. In that moment, I saw the secret of their long, happy and successful marriage. She walked round the table and stood with her hand on her husband's shoulder and said, 'I'll talk to you for one reason and one reason alone, to clear the air. I think I know how these disgusting rumours started and it's time to scotch them. There is a condition, too, that this talk is off the record. If a word of it appears in your newspaper, Toby Greenslade, I'll sue. I mean it.'

Toby nodded his agreement and Louise continued, 'A long time ago, something happened which almost ruined my marriage for me. Ross was away in America, so it must have been early in the year. A girl contacted me and said she had to see me. It concerned my husband. Well, I put her off at first, she persisted and eventually ended up on my doorstep. She said that she had been sexually assaulted by my husband and that, unless I paid her five thousand pounds, she would go to the newspapers with her story.'

Ross Bentley intervened, 'God almighty, Louise, how could you believe it of me? Sexual assault? I simply wouldn't be capable of it, you must have known that.'

'I know, I know.' Louise patted her husband's shoulder placatingly. 'Of course I didn't believe it and I was tempted to call her bluff. But others might have believed it and five thousand was no great sum to pay to shut her up. So I gave her the money.'

'How did you know she'd shut up?' I asked. 'These people usually come back for more.'

'Because I made her sign a letter. It looked very legal and official, but it was mumbo-jumbo really. She wasn't very bright, I fear, and that was the end of the matter.'

'She was bright enough to con five grand out of you,' I said nastily. 'Do you still have a copy of the letter?'

'No, I don't.'

Before I could pursue that point, Louise spoke up strongly again. 'Whatever the truth was, Ross, I was determined to protect you, to protect your career. I knew you would achieve great things in golf. Above all, it was my duty to keep our marriage going. Things were difficult, we knew I couldn't have children. I assumed that, on your travels, you might have sought the comfort of other women. I am French and I understand these things.' She bent down and kissed her husband on the cheek and finished fiercely, 'Whatever happened I was going to make sure that our marriage survived.'

I was full of admiration for the way in which Louise had manoeuvred the situation in her favour. She was unnervingly clever in the way she had changed the facts so plausibly, but I couldn't let her get away with her sleight of hand.

'So that's the story,' she said, 'are you satisfied, gentlemen?'

Not on your life, I thought, as she smiled at Ross and went to pull him to his feet. Toby looked inquiringly at me, one eyebrow raised and I said, 'It's an interesting story, Mrs Bentley, and I know that you paid out five thousand pounds. But it was for a different reason. I know it and now let's have the truth.'

Louise Bentley gave me a look in which hatred and

disdain only just triumphed over uncertainty and addressed her husband: 'Ross, darling, I suggest that we remove this lunatic from our midst. I'll call the security people.'

I had to go all the way now and took a gamble with the slip of paper which I had seen in Ben Massey's file when I had sat in his former headmaster's office.

'Why did you make regular payments from your personal account to Upton Manor School for nearly seven years? Banque de Paris, account number 0225 9559.'

I watched, without any satisfaction, as Louise Bentley's face paled. Her husband jumped out of his chair and lowered her gently into it, at the same time waving a dismissive hand at Tony Swan who had appeared at the French windows to the terrace.

'What the hell are you two doing?' Bentley shouted angrily. 'What is all this about?'

'Sit down, darling,' Louise said quietly and then spoke to us. 'You must give me the courtesy of a few minutes alone with my husband. I think I owe him an explanation.' She looked directly at me. 'Either you're a very clever young man or Suzi has told you all this.'

'Suzi has told us nothing,' Toby stated firmly.

'No, she gave me her word all those years ago,' Louise said thoughtfully.

I could see Ross fretting alongside his wife and I led Toby away to the far side of the garden. I saw Louise take Ross's hand and talk earnestly to him. Several minutes later, she beckoned us over.

'It was Susan Meadows-Price who appeared on my doorstep all those years ago,' Louise began. 'Ross was in America at the time. It was March 1970, and the girl had no one to turn to. She was pregnant and Ross was the father. In the end, I believed her story. Although I had reason to hate her, I took her to my heart. So young, trying to be so brave and carrying in her body something that should have been mine.'

'Why didn't you arrange to adopt the child? It would have been easy,' Toby said.

'Because Susan wouldn't hear of it. I begged of her . . . I fought with the problem for days. In the end I agreed to help her, to do all the things that Mr Ludlow has discovered. I gave her five thousand pounds for the expenses of the birth; I paid her so much a month and I agreed to pay Ben's fees at boarding school. At least he would have a proper education. But I made one very important condition, that Suzi would never tell Ben who his father really was and that she would never attempt to contact me or my husband.'

Tony Swan appeared at the French windows again and Toby moved quickly to meet him; I heard him explain that Louise was feeling a little unwell and would he keep everyone away from the terrace for the moment.

Louise continued, 'Of course, when Ben appeared on the golfing scene, I knew there would be trouble. So, when he was eighteen and our financial arrangements came to an end, I warned Susan, Suzi, once again to keep well clear of me and of Ross. When we were introduced at the tournament last week, it was a shock. And you noticed, didn't you, Mr Ludlow?'

I nodded and she smiled at me for the first time.

'Why didn't you tell me?' Bentley asked, his voice heavy with sorrow.

'Because the girl was fourteen and you could have gone to gaol. Your career would certainly have been ruined. But there was another reason too. I wanted to keep you. You'd have supported Suzi, you'd have kept in touch with the child. And I might have lost you. I wasn't going to allow that to happen.'

'I thank God for that, anyway,' Ross said quietly.

'It wasn't all altruism, darling. I was bloody determined that you would never know that you were a father. I could hardly contain my anger; it was just as well that you were away in the States at the time. It gave me time to think, stopped me doing anything decisive and possibly foolish.'

'Ross, what are you going to do?' Toby asked.

'Nothing, until the Ryder Cup is over. What are *you* going to do?'

'Well, this talk is off the record . . .'

'When has that ever meant anything?' Louise muttered.

'This is a remarkable story,' Toby continued, without quite hiding his journalist's enthusiasm for it. 'Maybe we can play around with it, bend the truth here and there, omit embarrassing facts. As long as I can have the exclusive, that is.'

'Aren't you forgetting something?' I said. 'Ben, and above all, Suzi. They might not want their story splashed all over the *News*. Presumably you will consult them?'

'Well, yes . . .'

'And respect their wishes.'

'I suppose so, Chris. There's no need to make a meal of your moral idealism.'

'Chris is right,' Louise said. 'Ben Massey may have no wish to acknowledge Ross as his father. On the contrary.'

Ross Bentley looked indignant for a moment and said, 'It isn't as if I abandoned him, I didn't know he existed. And I'd be proud to have him as a son.'

'Let's wait and see,' I said. 'I'll talk to Suzi. In fact I'll be late for dinner with her if I'm not careful. In the meantime, let's all keep this under our hats.'

Bentley waved us goodbye while Louise walked us across the lawn. Near the French windows, she paused and said, 'I'm proud of Ben, too, you know. How different he is to that loathsome stepbrother of his.'

As I headed quickly for my rendezvous with Suzi, I wondered how Louise had come to know David Massey.

Chapter 34

Suzi was celebrating her son's success with the Blackstocks and some other European team supporters. I was greeted with many a congratulatory pat on the back and greatly enjoyed the praise, vicarious though it was.

After a while I managed to pilot Suzi away to a table in the hotel's seafood restaurant and, after we had ordered, I gave her a rapid resumé of my recent encounter with the Bentleys. She showed little surprise. 'I often wondered when it would all come out. So, Louise has spilled the beans. We had a pact of silence and I'd never have broken it. You'd worked it all out pretty well, Chris, hadn't you?'

I smiled modestly and she continued, 'It won't do Ross Bentley's image much good, will it? And I suppose the intrepid Toby will make sure that it is all exposed for the titillation of the great British public.'

'Not necessarily. Only in a form acceptable to everyone.'

'None of it may be acceptable to Ben.'

'That's what Louise said.'

'Ben's grown used to his past, if I can put it that way. He may not want to accommodate a father like Ross Bentley. He may not want the responsibility. His only real problems have centred on David and even he is out of the way now.'

It was a valid point and an intelligent one which I wanted to return to later. In the meantime, I asked Suzi whether David had had any inkling of the truth about his stepbrother. 'For instance, in an unguarded moment, did you ever mention how Ben's school fees were paid?'

'I never had any unguarded moments,' Suzi said crisply.

'Okay, but did you leave anything lying around? Like a passport. Because David knew that you were under age when Ben was born. That was one of the facts that he used to upset Ben so much.'

'I think I know the answer to that, Chris. The house was burgled about a year ago. Not a lot was taken, just some cash, a bit of jewellery, the usual stuff. The police put it down to an opportunist, someone who needed ready money. I didn't think any more about it.

'But, a few months later, I was looking for various bits and pieces. Personal things, such as my birth certificate and Ben's. I thought I ought to put them in a really safe place, perhaps in the bank.'

Suzi paused while the waitress refilled our wine glasses. 'Well, they'd gone, along with my bank statements stretching back many years and the letter from Louise Bentley when Ben turned eighteen. I was in a flat panic, I hunted all over the house. When I calmed down I realised that there were only two people, apart from Ben, who would have understood the significance of those documents. Garfield, and he would've tackled me straight away, and David. So it seemed pretty obvious that David was responsible for the break-in.'

'And he struck gold. But weren't you worried that the police would find the material, amongst David's belongings?'

'Yes. But they returned them to me without comment. Strangely enough, Louise rang me a few days after she heard the news of David's death and Ben's disappearance. And she asked me similar questions to yours; had David known anything about Ben's past, had he got his hands on any documents?'

'And she was relieved when you told her nothing was missing any more?'

'I told her that David had pinched a few bits and pieces but that they were safely back with me.'

'OK, but when those rumours began about Ross Bentley and his illegitimate child, did you put David down as the source?'

'Yes, it was the kind of nasty scam he'd enjoy.'

'So you killed him to put a stop to it?'

'No, I didn't kill him, Chris. But whoever did deserves a medal.'

By now I thought I had a very good idea of who had killed David Massey and it certainly wasn't Suzi. But there was one thing bothering me; it was the relationship between David and Louise Bentley, if any.

'Did Louise have any contact with David?'

'Not to my knowledge. Why should she? He wasn't exactly her type, was he?'

'He doesn't seem to have been anybody's type.' I asked Suzi to excuse me while I made a telephone call. From the hotel lobby I got through to Louise. She sounded tired and, when I announced myself, distinctly frosty. I apologised for disturbing her and said, 'Just one more question, Mrs Bentley. How well did you know David Massey?'

'I didn't.'

'But earlier this evening you referred to him as the "loathsome David" or something like that.'

'Hearsay. I knew of him and I had heard that he had information to sell about the Ryder Cup players.'

'And you guessed that might include the facts about Ben Massey's father.'

'I was worried at first but, as Suzi will confirm, we had an agreement. Neither of us would have dreamed of breaking our silence. And I wouldn't have done, if outside pressures — you, Toby Greenslade, the Press — hadn't forced my hand.'

'But how did you learn that David had information to sell?'

'Don't you ever stop asking questions?' She sighed. 'It's my business. Suffice it to say that Ross has many good friends among the media and they keep us informed.'

'Fine, but did you actually know the strength of David's information, that he was prepared to trade the identity of Ben's father?'

'More or less, and I knew where he'd go with it.'

'Where was that?'

'Kyle Coker of course, and I'm convinced that he overplayed his hand very badly. He was way out of his class, he didn't have a clue how big the stakes were.'

'I realise that Coker's got his job and his reputation to protect, but surely he wouldn't go in for murder?'

'Probably not, but he's only the puppet. The man pulling the strings is Merv Sorenson and he's a seriously unpleasant man. He needs Coker's many schemes to succeed. He's got hundreds of millions of dollars of investment tied up with the American golf tour. Do you think he'd allow a fool like David Massey to hold things up? My guess is that David asked for some ludicrous amount of money, wouldn't negotiate and was taken out of the game. Be careful, Mr Ludlow, Sorenson plays for keeps.'

Chapter 35

Suzi had already settled the bill when I returned to the restaurant. I made some token protests when she said she must return to the villa and make sure that Ben was all right.

We agreed that Ben should not be told anything about his father until the Ryder Cup had finished.

As I saw it, Kyle Coker and Merv Sorenson had gone way beyond the bounds of normal business caution in their massive investments in golf resort developments. Their success partly depended on the continuing prestige and popularity of the professional golf circuit in America. That prestige had been eroded by the triumphs of European and Australian golfers in the major championships; and its popularity had declined owing to the pallid personalities of the players, featureless beneath their visors and anonymous in style.

Coker and Sorenson had seized upon the Ryder Cup as a means to rejuvenate American golf and to revive their business prospects. Hence the concerted dirty tricks campaign against the European players; hence David Massey's death. I tended to believe Louise Bentley's theory that he had dangled the bait of a very juicy story about the European captain, had not been offered the sort of money he required and perhaps had tried to negotiate with another party. Coker and Sorenson had reacted by having him murdered. Elementary, my dear Watson.

Thoroughly satisfied with my deductions I fell into a heavy sleep.

In the foursomes the next morning Ben, with his new partner, Dan Appleby, had been drawn against the American pair of John Brady and Jeff Malton. In so many ways these two Americans epitomised the malaise which was affecting American golf. No one could fault their good manners or sportsmanship but they were practically identical: in height, in gait, in accent and in the way they swung their clubs. There was a wide, slow takeaway, a strong drive with the legs to initiate the downswing and a high follow-through. It was admirable and rather boring, but I knew that the Americans would test Ben and his partner to the limit.

The captain had changed all the pairings, with the exception of Jack Mason and Ernst Tillman who were to go out last against Jerry Farrell and Travis Hanson. Since Nick Spencer was being rested, Jose Miguel was to team up with Tony Swan.

Ben and I, his partner and his caddie, left the practice ground in one buggy en route for the putting green shortly before eight o'clock, with Swan and Miguel and their caddies a few yards behind. It was only a matter of a few hundred yards to the putting green but we were all trying to conserve our energies with the prospect of a long day in the sun ahead of us.

With Ben at the wheel and Dan Appleby alongside him, we caddies were perched on the side of the vehicle. Halfway to the putting green I saw another vehicle coming towards us. It was unusual to see a jeep on a golf course, although I had noticed that they were sometimes used by the greenkeeping staff. I paid no particular attention since I was busy retaining my position on the buggy as it rattled across the bumpy surface. When the jeep was about twenty yards away I saw it pick up speed; to my horror it altered course and came straight at us.

Everything seemed to happen in alarming slow motion. I was conscious particularly of the huge front wheels of the jeep and the thick iron bars which protected its radiator. I shouted to Ben to jump for it but at the last moment he wrenched the buggy's steering wheel to the left and we ran down a shallow bank into sand and scrub.

There was a tremendous crash from behind us, the screech of twisting metal and then a series of thuds. None of us seemed to be hurt and we scrambled up the bank. Tony Swan's buggy was on its side, two of its wheels still spinning. I just glimpsed the back of the jeep as it careered away into the scrubland.

A crowd had gathered around the crashed buggy and there was much shouting and exclaiming. Fortunately, some stewards were already on the scene and one of them was on his radio calling for an ambulance. Jose Miguel was on his feet but massaging his neck ruefully; I headed for Tony Swan, who was still sitting on the ground with several solicitous spectators around him.

'Chris, help me up,' he said. 'I think I've just turned my ankle, that's all.'

'Stay there,' I said sternly, anxious that he shouldn't damage himself further. 'I can hear the ambulance coming. Let's be sure that's the only damage.' I could hear the approaching electronic shriek of its bell.

'OK. Who was the bastard in that jeep? Is anyone hurt?'

I looked over to the two caddies and received the thumbs up from both of them.

'They're all fine, Tony, but did you catch a glimpse of the maniac who was driving the jeep?'

Tony hadn't but, despite his cap pulled down over his eyes and despite his golf jacket zipped up around his ears, I knew that I had not mistaken the broad shoulders and lightly coloured moustache of Lee Brandel behind the wheel of the rampaging jeep.

By this time two medics had lifted Swan on to a stretcher, despite his protestations. Ross Bentley had arrived on the scene and, white-faced with anger, had dispatched Hugh Gregg to the practice ground to find Nick Spencer and Ramon Gonzales. I could hardly believe that Bentley was going to team two men who had been at each other's throats during the previous few months, but who is a humble caddie to question the judgement of an illustrious golfer such as Ross Bentley? Perhaps he was counting on their fiery personalities to ignite to the benefit of the European cause.

By the time the ambulance bounced away with Swan and Miguel on board, a host of policemen and security people were milling about and the starting times were sensibly delayed by thirty minutes. Everyone made brief statements but had nothing of note to say about the driver of the jeep. He had roared away into the scrubland and the vehicle had been found abandoned by the fifth green which was not far from one of the resort's service roads.

I kept my own counsel since I was already determined to do my own personal investigation of Mr Brandel.

After some fierce admonitions from Bentley to 'give it everything you've got', we were eventually up and away. It was evident that Ben had decided to assume the role of senior partner and even more evident that the American pair were at the peak of their form and determined to take advantage of any lack of resolve on the part of the British team.

It was no surprise that the Americans had a two-hole

advantage at the halfway mark and they increased it to three by winning the tenth hole.

The British pair had certainly not played badly, but that vital spark that can lift a man to a nearly invincible plane was missing. I resigned myself to Ben's first defeat in the Ryder Cup; until the twelfth hole when the whole character of the match changed. A remarkable piece of luck enlivened the British pair and produced doubts in the minds of the American golfers where none had before existed.

After their second shot, the Americans' ball lay in a greenside bunker, whereas the European ball, after a rather uninspired stroke by Ben, lay in a collar of thick rough on the right edge of the green.

Brady played a beautifully judged bunker shot which ran straight at the flag, hit it, seemed to go into the hole for a birdie and then horse-shoed out.

Dan Appleby surveyed his own shot, an intimidating one since the ball had dug deep into the grass and the green ran downhill from him towards the hole. Appleby hit the ball with a nervous jab and caught the top half of it; it was a dreadful stroke and the ball scuttled down the hill at great speed. I imagined that Ben would be playing the next shot from a similar position on the other side of the green in a vain attempt to prevent the Americans from going four holes up. But to everyone's amazement Appleby's ball hit the flag with a hearty clang and disappeared into the hole.

In an instant, the prospect of being in the hopeless position of four holes down had been transformed; the two British players were only two holes down and began to believe that the match could be rescued.

Don Appleby beamed at Ben. 'Just the stroke I'd intended,' he lied. Ben gave him a delighted slap on the shoulder and the European fans were cheering their men to the heavens. In contrast, John Brady let out a series of half-stifled curses. The initiative had suddenly passed to the European team; and they kept it by winning the next hole with a par to a sloppy one over par from the Americans.

Although Malton and Brady steadied the ship by halving the next two holes, Dan Appleby rifled an incomparable shot on to the green at the short sixteenth; the putt was conceded and the match was now level.

Over the final two holes even some of the spectators were feeling the tension. I saw several of them, both American and European, turn away their heads, unable to watch. Two well-made putts on the seventeenth green kept matters level and both teams made their pars on the final green to end an absorbing game which neither pair deserved to lose. There were smiles of relief and handshakes all round between players and caddies.

We had hardly registered the progress of the other games such had been our concentration but the latest situations flashed upon the giant scoreboard by the eighteenth green. Sandberg and Dave Curran had lost by one hole and Jack Mason and Tillman were one down after the fourteenth hole. But the real disaster was a crushing defeat for Spencer and Gonzales by seven holes down with six to play; they had been done by the infamous 'dog licence'. I hated to think what Ross Bentley would say to them at lunchtime but I thought he'd made a considerable error of judgement by pairing them.

It was more vital than ever that the Mason/Tillman combination brought home a point, or even half a point. Ben and I hitched a ride on a buggy to go back down the course to meet them and offer whatever moral support we could. We were in time to see Jack Mason hole one of those dubious 'arse-gripper' putts of about six feet in length. They shouldn't be missed but often are. The muted applause told us that the Europeans were still one hole in arrears; and so it remained over the next two holes.

The final hole is a long and difficult par four. The drive has to be carried over a bank which runs across the fairway about two hundred yards out, there is a wilderness of heather and scrub on the right and the green is on a plateau surrounded by bunkers. Even for a professional golfer the par is closer to five than to four. It seemed to me that Europe's only hope would be a severe error by one of the Americans.

Ben's friend, the cheerful Travis Hanson, without any preamble stuck his ball on a tee peg and smacked it firmly down the middle of the fairway. Ernst Tillman, a study in grey-faced tension and taut concentration, hit a wonderful soaring drive way past the Americans' ball. 'Great shot, Ernst,' Hanson said admiringly and patted his shoulder.

The crowd was quiet as Jerry Farrell lined up his long approach shot to the green. There were no shouts of 'You're the man' now, only silence as the spectators strained to see the flight of the ball. As far as I could tell, Farrell had a two-iron in his hands. He was as quick a player as Hanson; he took a look at the target, waggled his club twice and the ball was on its way. Very safe. It stopped on the right centre of the green, about thirty feet from the flag.

Forty yards ahead Jack Mason was weighing up his shot. Whatever he did he had to get his ball well inside Farrell's, he had to give Tillman a chance to make a birdie and save the match.

'What will he hit?' Ben asked in my ear.

'Five or six iron. He'll try and fade it in and stop it.'

'Dangerous. The flag's well left of centre.'

We watched as Jack took his stance to the ball, his solid figure motionless. Just as we expected to see a slight forward press of the right knee and the beginning of his swing, he walked away from the ball and called his caddie over. The result was a change of club.

'Oh God,' Ben prayed, 'surely he's not between clubs.'

When a golfer is uncertain about his club selection it normally results in only one thing; a bad shot.

Once again the crowd went silent. Jack Mason did not delay this time, but swung his club slowly back and smoothly through. The thud of his clubhead as it met first the ball and then the turf sounded beautifully solid and we all craned to watch the ball arc its way high into the sky. As it got halfway to its target, Ben said excitedly, 'He's overcooked it, it's got to turn.'

The ball certainly seemed to be heading for one of the bunkers on the left side of the green, but, as Ben spoke, the spin started to take effect and at the top of its trajectory the ball had moved on to a line between the edge of the green and the flag. It dropped quite gently on the green, hopped a bit more to the right and stopped about five feet from the hole.

Waves of applause and cheering rippled towards us from the stands around the green; Jack dropped his club and put his hands to his face in his relief; and Ben pulled me out of the buggy and did an impromptu jig.

Up ahead, in the middle of the fairway, the figures of Ernst Tillman and Travis Hanson trudged, alone with their thoughts, towards the green.

Hanson, as was his custom, did not dwell over his putt. It was on line but pulled up a foot short and was conceded. I didn't blame him for a less than heroic attempt; now that we were close to it, Tillman's putt looked around seven or eight feet from the hole, with a left to right borrow. To him, it probably resembled a putt down a marble staircase into a one-inch gap. In his normal meticulous way he studied the putt from several angles, took a few practice swings and slowly, slowly sent the ball on its way. It seemed to take an age to reach its destination and, as its speed decreased, it ran across the borrow smack into the back of the hole.

The normally undemonstrative German threw his putter in the air and embraced his caddie. A half. But it still left the Americans in the lead by eight matches to four.

Chapter 36

'Gentlemen, we are in danger of throwing this match away, of handing it to the Americans on a plate. Once again, we've been well and truly stuffed in the foursomes. I just don't believe it. We are just as skilful as the Americans, we have won as many major championships, I think, and in general we have youth on our side.'

Ross Bentley was standing with his back to the French windows of his villa and addressing his assembled players.

'Of course, the Americans have put us under pressure, not only on the course but off it as well. You all know about the accident this morning, but you'll be glad to hear that Tony and Jose will be fit enough to play in the singles tomorrow.

'Let me say a few things, briefly, about the Ryder Cup. It's one of the great events in golf, it has a special dignity that must be preserved. That's why you're all here, playing your hearts out, for expenses only. It must be a shock to some of you,' he said with a smile. 'You're playing for golf itself, for the honour of the professional game.

'That's why I've been disappointed in one or two of you. Petty rivalries have no place in the Ryder Cup.'

Nick Spencer's caddie, Scotch Willie, nudged me in the side and whispered, 'They didn't speak a bloody word to each other all morning. The air was poisonous. They were lucky to get a dog licence. The boss gave them the biggest bollocking of their lives.'

Bentley continued, 'Anyway, let's be positive. We need points this afternoon if we're to have any chance at all of keeping the Ryder Cup. The pairs stay the same this afternoon. Nick and Ramon will lead the charge, Ben and Dan will be the anchormen, Jack and Ernst will play second and Stefan and Dave in third position. Good luck, gentlemen, I want to look back on the second series of fourballs as the turning point.'

'Good luck,' muttered Scotch Willie, 'we need a sodding miracle.'

'Well, you can join in with Stefan, he's got a prayer meeting tonight,' I said.

'Yeah, I'll be there.'

A subdued Nick Spencer walked across the room and said, 'Come on, Willie, Ram's going to have a quick look at my putting.'

Scotch Willie raised his eyes to heaven, as if seeking divine inspiration, but I thought that at least the two of them were now speaking to each other.

If it wasn't a miracle that enhanced the European cause during the afternoon, at least there was a distinct improvement. No doubt we were assisted by some complacency on the part of the Americans, who probably saw their lead of four points as a reasonably secure one; after all they only needed six and a half points from the remaining four fourballs and twelve singles matches to win the Ryder Cup.

After nine holes the Europeans were ahead in two matches and level in two; this was the best session we had so far managed. Ben and Dan were having very little trouble with their opponents, Curtis Sawyer and Ken Binks, who were consistently outdriven by their young British opponents and could not match their putting on the slick greens. It was a far cry from a couple of decades ago, as Toby was quick to point out, when the American players were invariably longer hitters and better putters than their British counterparts.

The match finished out in the country with the British pair winning by five holes up with four to play. By this time Nick Spencer and Ramon Gonzales had confounded everyone by halving a very closely fought match with Jeff Malton and Marvin Gull; and Jack Mason and his German partner had registered their second half of the day. Up ahead, Stefan Sandberg was battling it out against Jerry Farrell and John Brady. Stefan's partner, Dave Curran, was clearly out of sorts but the European pair, mainly due to the Swede's brilliance, had a one hole lead.

As I stood by the seventeenth green, Toby detached himself from the crowd of pressmen and photographers, clapped me on the back and said, 'Well done. If the Swedish messenger of the gods can hold on, we'll still be in with a chance tomorrow.'

The European pair, however, could do no better than a par four whereas Brady sank a long putt for a birdie. Amid tumultuous applause from the American fans the players made their way to the final tee.

The Americans hit their shots safely down the middle but Curran carved his ball way right into the wilderness. As Sandberg addressed his ball, Toby muttered in my ear, 'If he's got an inside track to someone important, now's the time to ask his help.'

Whatever Sandberg's influence in high places, he hit a wonderful drive, under intense pressure, a smooth iron shot on to the green and made a careful putt to within inches of the hole to half the match.

'Nine and a half to six and a half in favour of the Yanks,' Toby said. 'We need eight points from twelve singles tomorrow. It could be done, but I doubt it.

Come on, let's go and have a drink. I've fallen in love with the champagne in one of the sponsor's tents.'

No wonder Toby had taken to the champagne; it was a vintage from over a decade ago, dark gold in colour and as smooth as Sam Snead's swing. Amid the familiar hubbub of such gatherings, Toby eased us into a corner of the bar and demanded, 'Now tell me about the accident this morning.'

'Some accident. We were lucky no one was killed.'

'What are California's finest doing about it?'

'The cops are no doubt pursuing their investigations, but since the jeep is owned by the club and was stolen for the express purpose of nobbling one or more of our lads, they're unlikely to get very far.'

'And have you any ideas?' Toby gave me an appraising look.

'Yes, I'm pretty sure I know who the driver was. He had his coat turned up and a cap on but I'd know those shoulders and that silly moustache anywhere.'

'So it wasn't Clint Eastwood? Kyle Coker, perhaps, in a false moustache?'

'It might as well have been Coker, but I'm pretty sure it was our old friend, Lee Brandel.'

'So that makes our theory pretty watertight.'

'Well, it certainly confirms that Brandel has been Coker's fixer, has done at least some of his dirty work. He may very well have killed David Massey or organised it.'

'So what are you going to do? Tell the police or what?'

'What. So far this is all deduction and speculation. Strong speculation but no proof, and the cops would probably call for the men in white coats if I accused Coker of master-minding a dirty tricks campaign against the European golfers, a campaign which included murder.'

'There's also my corner to fight. I badly need a good story to titillate the jaded fancies of my editor.'

'I'm going to deal with Brandel on my own. I'll get the truth out of him.'

'Why should he tell you anything?'

'Because if necessary I'll knock seven shades of hell out of him.'

'May I point out, dear boy, that you only have one hand in good working order; that Brandel is large and ugly and no doubt extremely unpleasant at close quarters. I'll bet he has bad breath and a kick like a mule too.'

'Thanks, Toby. But I'll have you to help me, of course?'

'Chris, I'd offer to assist, but as you know, I abhor violence.' Toby gave me a nervous smile. 'Come on, let's go to the press conference, Brandel should be there.'

'Where's your car, Toby?'

'In the hotel car park and that's where it's staying.'

'Fine, I just want to borrow something from it.'

With a few grumbles, because a detour of a couple of hundred yards was involved, Toby led me to his car. I opened the boot and rummaged around in the tool bag until I found what I wanted. A sizable adjustable spanner was the best bet; it should offer adequate insurance if Brandel needed some persuasion. I hefted it thoughtfully in my right hand and Toby averted his eyes while I tucked it into a plastic carrier bag and then put it in my pocket.

'For goodness' sake don't do anything stupid,' he said querulously. 'American prisons are said to be very unpleasant places.'

The purpose of the press conference was to announce the pairings for the singles matches on the final day.

There was much speculation about the likely tactics of the respective captains but the consensus was that the American skipper, Tony Bendix, with a requirement only to win five of the twelve matches, would probably put his best players out first in an effort to get the points on the board early. Ross Bentley had a much more difficult juggling act to perform.

As before, the sealed envelopes were handed to the press officer, who prepared to read them out. He was flanked on either side by the captains, by the presidents of the American and the British Professional Golf Associations and by various officials, including Kyle Coker and Neils Rutter.

I looked around the crowded room and eventually my eyes found Lee Brandel, on the end of a row near the front.

As predicted, Tony Bendix had put several of his strongest players at the front of the order and Bentley, anticipating this, had put Nick Spencer and Ramon Gonzales out first and second in the hope that they would win at least one match between them. Dan Appleby, Dave Curran and Mike Dolby came next.

'Sacrificial lambs,' asserted Toby.

'I hope not,' I replied. But Toby had a valid point in that Bentley had placed his least experienced players where they were likely to encounter some of the strongest American golfers.

'Bentley will settle for one point from those three,' Toby announced judiciously.

The European captain had completed his difficult balancing act by putting his most accomplished team members in the bottom half of the draw: Tony Swan in the eighth match, followed by Sandberg, Ernst Tillman and Jack Mason. Ben Massey was the anchor man and was drawn against the battle-hardened Jerry Farrell.

'Well, you and young Ben are going to have a lovely day, especially if it's level pegging when you come to the last few holes.'

'It'll be something for the autobiography, won't it, Toby?'

There were a few questions for the two captains, who answered them in a light-hearted vein, and then the journalists began to drift away. I kept my eyes firmly fixed on the back of Brandel's head and edged my way after him as casually as I could when he went towards one of the side exits. I used Toby as camouflage; I grabbed him by the arm and propelled him in the same direction.

'I want nothing to do with this,' he said in my ear. 'I'll get drummed out of journalism.'

'No, you won't, but I need your tape recorder.' I removed it from Toby's pocket and put it in my own and said, 'Just try and act naturally, go and have a drink and calm down.' Neils Rutter followed Brandel out of the side door and I went in pursuit of both of them.

I followed the two Americans through the same exit and saw them walking quickly away towards the hotel. Judging by their gestures they were not assessing the prospects for tomorrow's Ryder Cup singles. Far from it; their discussion seemed heated enough to make me wonder if I might have to intervene to stop some violence rather than start any of my own.

For a moment I wondered just how long I would have to wait in order to catch Brandel on his own; my ideal was to corner him in his hotel room. I was in luck because Rutter and Brandel paused on the steps of the hotel. I ducked behind a coach and watched as Rutter wagged his finger vehemently at my quarry and then, with a dismissive and seemingly contemptuous wave, walked off towards the villa complex.

Brandel shrugged his shoulders and walked into the hotel. I watched through the glass doors as he went up to the desk, got his key and headed for one of the lifts.

All I had to do now was find out the number of his room. Behind the reception desk stood a tall, dark-skinned girl with lively brown eyes and a dazzling smile. I did my best to equal her charm and, with my best English accent to the fore, asked her if I had just seen Mr Brandel entering the hotel. 'Is he staying here?' I asked.

'He is, sir, can I get him for you on the phone?'

'No, that's OK. It's just that we used to be good friends a few years back in London. Had lots of fun together.' I produced another of my *Daily News* visiting cards. 'I'd like to surprise him, just tap on his door and say hello. Can you give me his room number?'

'Sir, we're not supposed to let any visitors up there unannounced, it's against company policy.'

'Well, what can I do to persuade you to bend the rules a little?' I asked and tried out what I hoped was a quizzical smile, accompanied by the lift of one eyebrow. God knows what I looked like.

But it worked because the lovely Elaine, as the badge on her well-filled white blouse declared her to be, said, 'A drink in an hour when I get off duty would be fine. Room one zero one six.'

'It's a deal,' I said as I hurried towards the lift.

Chapter 37

Brandel opened the door to my first ring, looked at me blankly for a moment and said, 'Yeah, what do you want?'

'A few words.'

He made no move to invite me in, so I said, 'You interviewed me once and now I want the same courtesy.' To his surprise I shoved past him and, as he turned to protest, continued, 'I've got some questions about the driver of a jeep.'

'Get out, Ludlow, or I'll throw you out.' He flexed his shoulders rather self-consciously and I guessed that he might not be that well-versed in physical combat; probably his sheer size won him most arguments before a blow was struck.

Posturing is a waste of time in such situations; surprise is the crucial weapon. As Brandel watched, I removed the carrier bag from my pocket, pulled the spanner out, took one long step towards him and lunged low. My target was his right knee and, with an improvised action which resembled a low forehand shot on the squash court, I caught him a resounding blow on the side of the knee.

Brandel went down with a cry of rage and pain and I looked hastily around for the remote control for the television. On it went and I upped the volume to hide the noise.

His language was predictable in its concentration on the lower half of the anatomy and I interrupted him to say, 'That's just a start. I want to know everything about your activities on behalf of Coker. Everything. I'm prepared to cripple you just as you tried to cripple me and Ben and the others this morning.' I whooshed the heavy spanner through the air a few times. 'I'll start with your ankles and work up.'

With a show of bravado Brandel directed a few more insults at me and told me that I'd do ten years for assault. I walked over to the chair on to which he had levered himself, raised the spanner and whacked him hard on the point of his right shoulder.

His remaining courage fled and he shouted, 'OK, OK, you bloody lunatic. But let's have a deal.'

'I don't do deals with murderers.'

Brandel went an unpleasant shade of yellow under his tan. 'Murder? What murder?'

I put Toby's tape recorder on a table between us, switched it on and said, 'Tell me about David Massey, tell me how he was murdered.'

'You're off your head. I don't have a clue how he was killed, but it was nothing to do with me.'

'But you were in contact with him?'

'Sure, he had a story to sell and we wanted to buy. But I'm not saying anything more until we've got a deal.'

I agreed to forget that I had recognised him at the wheel of the jeep if he answered all my questions.

The story unfolded much as Toby and I had anticipated. Coker, with many unhappy sponsors, especially Merv Sorenson, needed a Ryder Cup victory to pep up the American golf scene.

'Coker and Rutter conned Sorenson into putting money into all those golf resorts. They're in hock for nearly a billion dollars. They need success because it breeds optimism and that brings sales, which they're

desperate for. They had to make sure of the Ryder Cup.'
Brandel went on to describe how he, as a journalist
who knew the British media scene as well as the American
one, had been deputed to find whatever scandal he could
about the European team and spread it.

'That ruck between Gonzales and Spencer was a nice
start,' he said, 'and then we revived the business of
Bentley's questionable putt in the Open. But we really
struck gold with David Massey. I couldn't believe my
luck, one of our stringers in London had an approach
from this kid, with some story or other.

'I didn't pay much attention, we had a dozen fellas
out there digging around, but when the name Massey
came up I thought it was worth a look.'

'And he told you that Ross Bentley had fathered an
illegitimate child?'

'Yeah, and we paid him some front money. Not a lot,
but he told us there was an even juicier story, one that
was worth a lot of money.'

'How much?'

'Oh, Massey had his head up his ass, he wanted half a
million bucks. But we agreed a hundred thousand, if he
gave us real solid evidence. We were ready to splash it
over every newspaper in Europe and the States.'

'And did he give you hard evidence?'

'No, though I think he had it. But my last contact
with him was the day before he was killed. He said he
had another bidder, a "punter" as he called it, but if we
went up to half a million it was still a deal.'

Brandel asked me for a glass of water and, without
taking my eyes off him for more than a few seconds, I
backed towards the room refrigerator and removed a
bottle of mineral water. You can't be too careful.

'So, what did you do?' I asked, after I tossed the
bottle across to Brandel.

'I reckoned the punter was a newspaper, so why should I care? If the story was published, that suited us fine and we wouldn't have to pay out.'

'But it wasn't?' I guessed.

'No. He said that your Ryder Cup sponsor was going to buy him off. Which made sense. So I had to talk to Coker to see how far he'd go and he rang back later and told me to forget the deal. He said Rutter would take care of it.'

'And David Massey was killed the next day?'

'Yeah.'

'On Coker's orders?'

'No chance,' Brandel sneered. 'He's no killer, but that faggot, Rutter, well he's a different matter.'

'Tell me more,' I said.

'Well, he's meant to be a financial genius and he may be, but he's bent, bent in every way you can think of. He's also nuts and I can imagine him arranging a murder, Massey's murder. He's been the driving force behind Coker. Rutter wants to make it big and he doesn't care how he does it.'

'What about Sorenson? He's got more to lose than anyone.'

'Sure, but he's no killer, he's just a business man.' I didn't question Brandel any more about Sorenson but his remarks sounded like special pleading and I wondered where his loyalties lay.

'One last question,' I said. 'Did you set up Jane Sandberg? Did you tell those lies about her to the NSPCC?'

Brandel's eyelids flickered desperately and he took a swig from the already empty bottle of mineral water. 'Not on your life. That was Rutter's idea. I haven't done anything illegal.'

'No? Attempted murder this morning for a start.'

'You can't prove that.'

'How about conspiracy? Apart from minor details like tampering with our measuring wheels, masterminding the wake-up calls in the small hours, arranging those hecklers at the California Classic.'

'I only did what I was told.'

'Yeah. History is littered with scum who only obeyed orders.'

'What are you going to do?'

'Nothing. Until the Ryder Cup is over and then we'll see.'

'Remember, we've got a deal.'

'And I'll stick to it,' I said wearily. I tapped the tape recorder. 'It's all there, isn't it?'

'It may be but it don't mean shit as evidence.'

'It's good enough for me, Brandel, and you'll do well to remember that.'

I was relieved to get out of Brandel's room. As I waited for the lift I realised that I was still clutching the spanner in my right hand. My knuckles were white and my arm was running with sweat. I shoved the spanner in my trouser pocket and hoped no one would notice.

If Elaine, the smiling receptionist, noticed, she said nothing. We shared a bottle of champagne, talked inconsequentially for an hour and then I went off to bed.

Tomorrow would be a big day.

Chapter 38

Toby's ungracious response to my nine o'clock telephone call was a loud groan.

'It's your wake-up call, sir,' I said in a falsetto American voice. 'You're on the tee in five minutes.'

'You woke me up, you young sod. Leave me to my agony.'

'A long evening?'

'Yes, with Mal Tomas, the photographer, amongst others. God, can he drink. We went through the card and back again. I'm too old for such sessions.'

'I'm coming over. I've got something for you to hear.'

'Well, if you must. But bring coffee . . . please.'

On the way to Toby's room I stopped at the hotel restaurant, ordered a full breakfast and lots of coffee to be sent to his room and picked up a copy of the local newspaper. It was devoted to the final day of the Ryder Cup and I skimmed its pages as I rode in the lift.

Toby, clad in a pale green 'Hollywood' T-shirt whose colour matched his face, and a towelling dressing gown, grunted a greeting at me and said, 'You're still alive, then. I don't think I am. What about Brandel? How many of the seven bells did you knock out of him?'

I put Toby's tape recorder on a table by the window, led him gently to a chair and told him to listen. I sat opposite him, half listening to my conversation with Lee Brandel and half reading an article by someone called Jim Burney in the newspaper I had bought.

The headline had a familiar ring: 'Brit skipper insults US golfers.' The story was familiar, too, as it harked back to Ross Bentley's well-reasoned comments about the relative performances of American and European golfers at the Open in Britain several months ago. The piece ended:

> Poor old Ross Bentley, British Open Champion back in the days of hickory shafts and flickering black and white TV pictures, ought to take a close look at the Ryder Cup scoreboard this morning and an even closer look this evening. Because that's when the Ryder Cup will be back where it belongs, in the hands of the American golfers, the finest in the world.

Jim Burney certainly had a taste for hyperbole. My reading was interrupted by a knock on the door and a large trolley, laden with all the delights of an American breakfast from fresh fruit through to crispy bacon, hash browns and pancakes with maple syrup and cream, was wheeled in.

After the waiter had gone Toby played the last few moments of the tape, told me to dig into the food while he re-started his heart with a black coffee and asked thoughtfully, 'Do you believe all that?'

'Most of it. Though I think Brandel might have been passing the buck in the wrong direction.'

'You don't think it's Rutter who was behind David Massey's murder?'

'I'm not sure, but the fact remains that he works for Coker, who runs the American pro tour. Coker's the commissioner, not Rutter.'

'OK,' Toby said, 'let's act now. While I have a shower you ring Coker, I've got his number here. Invite him to a meeting. This morning, preferably.'

'Are you mad? On the last morning of the Ryder Cup? Anyway, why me? You know him, you've got more chance of a result.'

'If there's a problem, tell him about the Brandel tape. Even better, play the sodding thing over the phone.'

It was several minutes before I forced myself to dial Kyle Coker's number. To my relief a woman answered and I told her that Ben Massey's caddie wished to talk to the commissioner. I heard some muttered questions and answers in the background and then the pleasant voice of Kyle Coker. 'What can I do for you, Chris? Do you need extra tickets, how can I help?'

I was taken aback for a moment or two and then said, 'I need to talk to you. It's about Lee Brandel.'

There was a pause and Coker said, 'One moment,' and I heard him put the phone down and close a door. 'What about Brandel?'

'He told me some fascinating facts about the way you and Rutter have been operating recently.'

'Facts, what facts? Brandel's told me that you threatened him with violence and he jerked you off with some rubbish to keep you quiet. Whatever he said has no credence whatsoever.'

'Nevertheless I taped it all. Why don't you listen to some of it?' I held the tape recorder to the mouthpiece and played the sequence during which Brandel admitted his part in the dirty tricks campaign, and his statement that Rutter had been responsible for David Massey's murder.

'How's that?' I asked Coker and saw Toby grinning at me from across the room.

'Inadmissible evidence. Crap,' snapped Kyle Coker aggressively.

'Maybe, but my friend Toby Greenslade will print it

in the *Daily News* anyway. You'll have a lot of explaining to do and I'm sure you'd rather do the explaining to us, in private.'

There was a long silence, then Coker said, 'My villa in ten minutes. We won't be disturbed.'

'You're coming with me this time, Toby,' I said.

'Wouldn't miss it for the world, dear boy.'

'Shall I bring the spanner with me?'

If Ross Bentley's villa had seemed gigantic and luxurious to us, Kyle Coker's residence was positively palatial. It covered the area of a hypermarket, had an astonishing design of circular towers, turrets and battlements which wouldn't have looked out of place in sixteenth-century France, and was handily positioned to overlook the eighteenth fairway of the championship course. As I rang the doorbell, Toby gestured at the name which was picked out in elegant lettering alongside the door: Villa Kyle.

'He's got it made,' Toby said, as the door opened and the solid presence of the commissioner was revealed. He looked cool and there was hardly a hair out of place among his thick, white locks; the dark blue suit was set off by a cream-coloured shirt and the American Ryder Cup tie.

He looked every inch the millionaire and the interior of his villa, furnished in a strange blend of Californian rococo tempered here and there by antiques which had probably been shipped out from England, confirmed his financial status. So did some of his pictures; I spotted a Jackson Pollock and a Jasper Johns among the many paintings on his walls.

Coker walked us through the living room, a journey which seemed to take several minutes, and out into the garden.

'This is a palace you've got here,' Toby said politely.

Coker ignored him and said, 'We'll sit in the shade over there. It's private.' He made no attempt to offer us a drink and, as soon as we were seated, said, 'If this is some seedy attempt at blackmail it won't work.'

'You've been mixing with petty crooks too long, Mr Coker,' I said. 'All we want is some semblance of the truth from you. Listen to Brandel's tape and then perhaps we can talk.'

As the conversation was replayed, thin and metallic, on the small tape recorder, Coker seemed to retreat into his chair; as if he were hoping, by an effort of will, to disappear and leave the indignities of the last few months behind him. When the hiss of the tape indicated that the interview had ended, Coker rubbed his face with his hands. It was a resigned and very tired gesture.

He began to speak very quietly and I wondered whether the tape recorder, now switched on again, would pick up all his words. 'I didn't want to get involved in all this, but it seemed like a harmless bit of insurance, a bit of gamesmanship. After all, I was confident that America would win the Ryder Cup.

'But Neils said we had to make as damn sure as we could that the Cup came back to us. We've got one hell of an investment in these resorts. Eagle Cliffs, of course, Harbour Dunes up the coast, four places in Florida, Arizona, Texas. The whole pack of financial cards only stands up if we sell the villas and the condominiums and if the people come and spend their money with us.'

'And it's not happening?' asked Toby.

'Hell, no, and golf is going through a terrible time. If only we had an Arnie or a Walter Hagen around, instead of this army of methodical nonentities. People can't identify with these guys, there's no excitement and the interest in the game is dying.'

'So you allowed Rutter to go ahead with the nasty stories, the dirty tricks,' I said.

'Yes, in the end. Insurance, gamesmanship, call it what the hell you like.'

'Would you call accusations of child abuse gamesmanship?' I asked harshly.

'No. I felt desperately sorry for the Sandbergs. I fear that was one of Neils' ploys. He went too far.'

I held up my left hand, which was still strapped up. 'Just as he went too far by getting some thugs to try and break Ben's fingers. Fortunately for him they got the wrong man.'

'Don't you think it's going a little far to send Brandel out in a jeep with a plan to maim some of our players?' Toby asked.

'It's all out of my control now,' Coker said.

'But you're the commissioner,' I shouted angrily.

'Maybe, but I never could control Neils Rutter. And the stakes are so high. I've committed millions of PGA money to these schemes. Poor Neils has sunk all his own money into the projects and borrowed a lot more.'

'Did he borrow from Sorenson?' I asked.

'Yes.'

'And Sorenson put up the bulk of the money?'

'Yes.'

'And how did he make all his money?'

'Nobody quite knows. He appeared from nowhere about ten years ago. Started buying up radio and television stations, newspapers and magazines, he's even got stakes in some of the Hollywood film studios.'

'Do you think Sorenson is laundering money for some organisation or other?' asked Toby.

'Maybe. Could be American or Japanese, maybe,' Coker said.

'So he and Rutter could have arranged David Massey's murder?'

'Not Neils. He's a financial genius, he's erratic and over-ambitious but he's not a killer. We've known each other a long time, been friends for a long time.' Coker was speaking very softly and slowly.

'Did he persuade you to put all this money into these schemes?' I asked.

'Yes. I couldn't deny him anything.'

'Were you lovers?' I asked and saw Toby's head lift in surprise. I surprised myself. It was a wild guess, triggered only by Brandel's contemptuous reference to Rutter as 'that faggot'.

'Yes, I love him.' He caught his breath and out it all came; the outpourings of a man who had lived too long under a terrible strain and had got himself caught up in things way outside his experience and control. 'Oh, yes. Neils has been my lover for more than twelve years. I have a wife and children, ex-wives, even the occasional mistress. No one has ever suspected a thing. And you've no idea what a relief it is just to tell you that, whatever the consequences.'

There was silence for what seemed at least a minute, and then Coker said, 'It would be stupid of me to ask you to respect my confidences, I'm sure. You're a journalist, Toby, and have your own furrow to hoe. But my relationship with Neils doesn't have to be part of the story, does it?'

'No, why should it be?' said Toby. 'Most people have parts of their lives that they want to keep secret. But the rest of the story . . .'

'I'll deny,' said Coker quickly. 'I didn't want any part of all that unpleasantness. Golf doesn't need it and the ironic thing is that we didn't need it either. We're going to win the Ryder Cup and that will probably save us from our financial problems. In the short term, anyway.'

Coker stood up and we followed him silently through the beautiful garden and through the vast house, our footsteps echoing on the marble floors. At the front door Coker paused and said, 'You will leave Neils out of all this, won't you?'

Toby said nothing, shrugged, and we walked away. Out of earshot, he said, 'Fat chance. He can deny away but this is one fantastic story. Are they telling the truth?'

'Oh yes. I'm taking it at face value. Except for the David Massey death. I still believe Rutter was involved, but with the connivance of Sorenson.'

'Sorenson sounds more likely, doesn't he? If he's a part of some organised crime outfit. A single bullet through the head sounds very Mafia.'

'Well, let's try and nail Rutter,' I said. 'I'll oil that spanner of yours. But first I've got to help Ben to win the Ryder Cup. See you later.'

Chapter 39

My orders were to meet Ben at his villa at 11.30, so that
we would have time for an hour's practice before his
match began at one o'clock. I did not want to speculate
how he was feeling, since my own stomach was already
in turmoil and I was only carrying his bag. In one way I
hoped that the whole fixture would have been decided
by the time we began the final nine holes; in another I
hoped we would experience the full heat of an epic
finale.

I had time to watch the early combatants hit their
shots from the first tee. But the crowds were so huge
that I only just got a vantage point by clinging to the
downslope of one of the many grassy embankments that
were dotted around the course. I felt intimidated by the
enthusiasm and excitement shown by the fans.
Everywhere I looked were stars and stripes banners and
emblems, and cries in support of the American team
crashed about my ears. The few European fans seemed
hopelessly outnumbered, even though I spotted the
formidable figures of the Blackstocks in a prime
position by the first tee: despite the heat, Lionel was
wearing a full John Bull outfit, with a red tailcoat and a
top hat with a Union Jack band, and his wife, Daisy,
was arrayed in a Union Jack dress.

Even the resplendent Blackstocks had to give best to
the wives of the American players; arrayed in white
shirts, red and white striped sweaters and dark blue
skirts with white stars and each waving a miniature

American flag, they made an unnerving spectacle, especially when you took in the *Dallas* hairstyles. Between them they carried enough gold in the form of necklaces, earrings, bracelets and bangles to save a Third World state from starvation.

Five minutes before eleven o'clock a spreading ripple of shouts and applause greeted Nick Spencer and Marvin Gull as they made their way on to the tee. Spencer was talking animatedly to his caddie, Scotch Willie, and looked as relaxed as anyone could in such circumstances. As the players were announced to the crowd Ramon Gonzales pressed his way through the massed ranks of spectators, bounced up on to the tee and gave Spencer a handshake. They stood talking quietly together, as if they were now the best of friends.

Spencer, first to play, hit a fluid one-iron a long way down the right-hand side of the fairway into the perfect position and Gull followed him with a three-wood. The game was on.

I stayed to watch Gonzales drive adequately down the middle and then saw Dan Appleby, who looked very nervous and drawn under his white cap, push his drive into trouble well wide of the fairway.

It was time to meet Ben.

Suzi greeted me at the front door and gave me an enthusiastic kiss. I squeezed her buttocks lecherously and she breathed theatrically into my ear, 'Not now, darling, save it for later.'

'How's Ben?' I asked as we drew apart.

'He's asleep on the terrace.'

'Asleep?'

'It'll do him good. He's been sick three times already.'

'Four times,' came Ben's voice from the back of the villa. He strolled into the room and grinned amicably at us. 'Time to go, Chris. Now you will follow me, won't you, mum? But sort of stay out of view, if you can. Otherwise, I'll get even more nervous.'

I wondered how nervous he'd get if he knew that the captain of the team was his real father.

Suzi kissed me on the cheek and embraced her son. 'You can do it,' she said, 'don't worry.'

We took a buggy up to the course where security men in their own buggy waited to escort us to the practice ground. Half a dozen American players were warming up on one side of the range and their European opponents had segregated themselves on the other side. The seats behind were full of spectators, many of them with binoculars, and the lines of fans stretched out on either side. As we arrived Jose Miguel departed for the first tee amid shouts of good luck from his team-mates. The quiet Spaniard put his whole being into his golf and I knew that Ross Bentley regarded him as one of his best bets for a point.

Ben took up his position alongside Tony Swan and asked him how his ankle was bearing up.

The tall Englishman grimaced slightly but said, 'No problem. It's strapped up and I've had an injection in it. If this was the Greyhound Derby I'd be banned for life. But I'd play on crutches if I had to.'

One by one the players drifted away to hit some putts before taking their places on the first tee. As we did the same, I checked one of the scoreboards and saw that almost all the matches were evenly balanced, either level or just one hole either way. Dan Appleby was the only European golfer in trouble; he was three down after eight holes.

Ben went through his putting routine and, as ever, was striving only to locate his touch, that elusive amalgam of timing, sensitivity and rhythm, that is so essential if a golfer is to have any confidence on the greens. No wonder putting is regarded as the game within a game, almost as one of the black arts; an inability to putt consistently has ruined many an otherwise brilliant golfer.

There seemed nothing whatever amiss with Ben's stroke and he was ready enough to end his preparations when Ross Bentley arrived on the edge of the practice green to wish him luck. I stayed close to make sure that the captain didn't drop any hints about long-lost fathers but he remained true to his Ryder Cup role.

Ben handed me his putter and said, 'I think that's enough, Chris. Could you do me a favour and just nip over to that bar and get me a Coke?'

I put the putter back in the bag and did his bidding. There was no great hurry, we had ten minutes to spare before our match began and I knew that Bentley would do his best to relax his player. As I returned a scoreboard near us whirred into action and gave us the latest position. The Europeans were down in only two matches, and in one of those Dan Appleby had reduced his arrears to two holes, we were ahead in four and level in the rest.

'It's going to be one hell of a close-run thing,' Bentley said. 'The odds are still on the Yanks but if we can put a few points on the board early on, who knows. It may well go to the wire, Ben, and that suits me because I know you won't fail.'

Bentley shook Ben by the hand, jumped into his buggy and weaved his way through the spectators on his mission to encourage and cajole the rest of his team.

'Well, if he thinks we can win, so we can,' Ben said thoughtfully. I heaved his golf bag off the ground and did my automatic check of the clubs: no more than fourteen in number, including two woods, two wedges, nine other irons from one to nine and a putter. Except that there wasn't a putter.

I looked blankly at the bag for a moment and felt the sweat prickle on my face and body. I looked again, just in case the putter was hidden under one of the clubhead covers. It wasn't there. I looked desperately at Ben, who was waiting a few yards away and chatting to a group of spectators.

'Ben, have you got your putter?'

'No, you put it back in the bag.'

'It's gone.'

'Gone? It can't have gone.'

Ben strode across and checked every club in his bag; we removed several of them in the hope that we were wrong. But the club had disappeared.

'Stolen?' asked Ben quietly. 'Dirty trick number umpteen?'

'It looks like it.'

'Chris, I'm on the tee in five minutes. I'll take the bag.' He waved over a European official in a buggy. 'You race over to the professionals' shop and buy me a putter. You know the one I use, I'll trust your judgement about feel and balance. See you on the tee.'

I sprinted the hundred yards or so to the shop as Ben took a ride on the buggy in the opposite direction. This was a great way to start the most vital game of golf in my caddying career. I'd be lucky to *have* a caddying career if this was ever made public. 'Oh yes, Chris Ludlow, he's the caddie who let his boss's putter get stolen just before the Ryder Cup singles.' I could hear the mocking voices. If I was near to panic, how did Ben feel?

The shop was packed with customers, browsing amongst the plethora of Ryder Cup souvenirs. I grabbed an assistant by the arm and said, 'Where are the putters? Show me.'

Not surprisingly he was taken aback as I pulled him across the shop. 'Sorry. I'm Ben Massey's caddie. His putter's been stolen.'

'Oh yeah,' his look said but he allowed himself to be manhandled and pointed my way to a rack of putters. Three of those which Ben used lay in the rack and I tried them one by one. The handle was too thick on one, the balance seemed all wrong on another and the lie of the blade on the third was too upright. I was beginning to panic as I looked at the huge choice available. Which one would suit Ben? I looked at some putters of the same manufacture as Ben's stolen one and decided that, in Ben's absence, I would have to back my own judgement and choose one which felt good to me.

After trying three or four I found the right one: a beauty, perfectly balanced. I pushed my way to the counter and brandished it at the assistant. Where the hell was my wallet? It was safe in Ben's golf bag.

'Can I pay you later?' I asked helplessly.

The assistant looked at me with a cynical grin on his face. As he opened his mouth, I forestalled him by taking my watch off my wrist and thrusting it at him: 'Keep that as security. It's gold and it's a Patek-Phillipe.'

I didn't brook any argument but threw the watch at him and headed for the door.

Chapter 40

Amid the justifiable protests of the many fans who had gathered around the first tee, I pushed and excused my way to Ben's side. He had already hit his ball into a good position on the right of the fairway and his opponent, Jerry Farrell, did the same, though his shot finished about twenty yards ahead of Ben's.

I handed the new club to Ben who eyed it suspiciously, as well he might. I knew that he had used the same putter for several years. It was an old and trusted friend to him and now, in the most important match of his young career, he had to strike up an acquaintance with an alien being. Ben gripped it, lined it up on the tee and swung it tentatively. To my relief he said, 'It feels fine, it'll be fine.'

The Blackstocks were still stationed by the tee and I spotted Suzi in the crowd just behind them. I looked back at the crowd as we moved off the tee and had my first sighting of the religious fanatic who is often seen at major American tournaments and who always manages to get his banner into camera shot. On this occasion the banner read, 'Genesis IV 10.' I wondered what it meant but didn't have a bible on me to check the quotation.

Ben's swing, as graceful and steady as anyone could wish, propelled his ball on to the green but Farrell, unperturbed, put his ball to within ten feet of the hole. Ben had twice that distance to go, downhill across a left to right slope. This was a feel putt if ever there was one and I prayed that the putter would work well for him

325

and inspire him with confidence. The stroke was slow and smooth and Ben's ball started down the slope and, halfway to the hole, began to turn. It wavered slightly as it hit a spike mark and then continued on its course and dropped neatly into the hole.

'What a lovely putter,' Ben said quietly. Farrell missed his easier putt by several inches. We were one hole up and in good heart. I nudged Ben as we stood on the second tee and nodded at the scoreboard. Nick Spencer was three in the lead after fourteen holes and Gonzales was two up. Europe was ahead in five other matches and only behind in two. The prospects were good and even better when Ben sank a putt of around twelve feet to take a two-hole lead.

There have been many remarkable matches in the Ryder Cup, great golfing deeds accomplished in the fury of battle, but the quality of the golf produced by Ben Massey and Jerry Farrell can rarely have been surpassed. Like the doughty battler he is, Farrell hit back with two birdies and an eagle of his own in the next few holes to go one ahead of Ben and, at the halfway mark, the match was level. Between them the players had notched up six birdies and two eagles.

As the spectators realised that a battle royal had been joined they began to desert the other matches to join in the fun. The atmosphere was tense enough at the start and the swelling crowd, stretched twenty or more deep down the fairways and clinging to every vantage point, rushing frantically from green to tee, made me feel almost claustrophobic.

On the tenth tee the scoreboard told us that both Nick Spencer and Ramon Gonzales had won their matches. Even more encouraging was that Dan Appleby had fought his way back to halve his match. As Ben prepared for his tee shot I saw the scoreboard change again and a great cheer went up from the European fans; Dave Curran had also snatched half a point in his match.

Ben hit yet another solid drive down the tenth fairway; the ball was crunching off the middle of his club. As he gave me his driver I nodded at the scoreboard. 'We're only one point behind. Bentley's prayers are being answered.'

'Yeah, well keep praying. Perhaps we need that guy's help, too.' Ben gestured at the bearded man of god with the placard; he had managed to worm his way to the front of the spectators again.

The initial fury of the two contestants' exchanges had now calmed and they managed to halve the next holes in straightforward, even docile, fashion. But the American team were far from finished; Mike Dolby and Luis Moreno were both defeated but this was relieved by the news that Jose Miguel had beaten Curtis Sawyer by a two-hole margin.

On the thirteenth tee we were joined by Toby. 'Keep going, Chris. The Americans need two points from the last five matches to win.'

Farrell responded to this information by making birdies at the next two holes but Ben kept the match level with two of his own at the fourteenth and fifteenth holes.

On the next tee a huge wave of cheering rent the air as Tony Swan beat John Brady on the final green and the noise multiplied as Stefan Sandberg's victory over Larry Sussman was flashed up on the scoreboards.

'We're level in the whole match, for the first time,' said Ben.

Such equilibrium did not last because Travis Hanson registered a narrow win over Ernst Tillman, just when Ben and Farrell halved the short sixteenth with par threes.

By this time the whole crowd had compressed itself between the seventeenth and eighteenth holes. The Americans needed one point to win the Ryder Cup whereas the European team required both points for victory. Ahead, we knew that Jack Mason was one hole in the lead against Jeff Malton.

On the seventeenth tee I caught sight of Suzi, squashed between two broad-beamed Americans, both of whom were carrying cans of beer. She gave me a thumbs up and all I could do was gulp and smile weakly back. Both Ben and Farrell successfully threaded their drives between the menacing fairway bunkers. This was no time for heroics and they both hit irons conservatively to the centre of the green.

By this time Ross Bentley had joined us and, as the two golfers conscientiously holed out for their par fours, he walked with us to the final tee, his radio to his ear. 'Malton's missed his birdie putt,' Bentley muttered to us. 'Jack's conceded the par four. He's got a putt of thirty feet. Oh God, I'm glad I don't have to face these shots any more.'

Bentley was sweating heavily and his knuckles were white around the radio. 'It's on its way,' he said. A great cheer came rolling back from the eighteenth green and then it changed into a deep groan.

We had reached the tee but, owing to the undulations of the ground, could only see the bobbing heads of the players, the caddies and the various officials. 'He's four feet past,' Bentley muttered. Although he was sweating, his face looked grey. 'If he misses . . .'

The various permutations flashed through my mind. Two halved matches meant a win for the United States, but the win and a half meant a tied match and, as the holders, Europe would retain the trophy. Not a satisfactory outcome and certainly not the sort of negative thought to plant in Ben's mind. My analysis was checked by another great roar from the crowd around the eighteenth and we could see a forest of arms waving.

'He's done it,' shouted Ross Bentley. 'He's done it.'

'Come on, Ben,' I said quietly. 'We need a birdie.'

He nodded and smiled. The crowd were eerily silent and the only sounds I registered were the slight sighing of the wind and the discreet flapping of a flag on a nearby green. Ben adjusted the glove on his left hand, ran his right hand through his hair, took a deep breath and addressed his ball.

Ross Bentley was shielding his eyes and looking away up the rolling fairway. Toby, who as a journalist was allowed inside the ropes, deliberately turned his head away as Ben began his swing. In the circumstances his shot deserved the applause it received. The ball landed on the right side of the fairway and was well beyond the ridge which runs across the fairway just over 200 yards from the tee and menaces the drives of less gifted golfers. The only problem which I perceived was that a high mound cut into the fairway just ahead of Ben's ball and might well interfere with the line of his shot to the green.

'Bread and butter drive,' Ben muttered, 'when I needed Sunday roast.'

Farrell produced the latter and his ball finished in the left centre of the fairway, about thirty yards beyond Ben's.

The crowd stampeded down the edges of the fairway and, followed by Ross Bentley and the American captain, Tony Bendix, in their respective buggies, we trudged towards Ben's ball.

As I feared, the mound, cunningly placed by the designer, prevented Ben from hitting a direct shot to the green. He walked back and forth trying to assess the angles. Since the hole had been cut, once again, on the left edge of the plateau green, I knew that Ben had been planning to draw his second shot from right to left in order to get close to the flag.

'I daren't risk a draw,' he said. 'I'd have to go over the highest point of the mound. It'll have to be the fade. How far to the pin?'

'Hundred and ninety yards.'

'Four-iron, then.'

The marshals had moved the crowd away from the slopes of the mound with great difficulty and that unnerving silence settled again over the crowd as Ben fidgeted into his stance. The safe shot was a left to right fade to the centre of the green; but if Ben aspired to a birdie he had to flirt perilously with the deep bunkers in order to land the ball on the left edge of the green.

The rhythm and stability of Ben's swing and the healthy smack of iron on balata told me that he had made a perfect contact. The line of the shot told me that Ben had gone for broke and the ball ripped through the air towards the bunkers on the left of the green. It should turn at any moment as the spin took effect, and so it did. My fingers were digging into my palms as I watched, Ben motionless beside me. Thump went the ball into the edge of the green and I waited for its roll down the slope towards the hole. The ball hovered for a moment and then rolled slowly and inexorably off the edge of the green into the bunker. The misjudgement had been only a matter of a few inches but I knew that Ben would be seen, despite all his heroics on the previous two days, as the man who lost the Ryder Cup for Europe.

The British spectators were silent while the Americans mixed shouts of delight with sympathetic applause.

Ross Bentley held his head in his hands in his anguish. Without expression on his taut face, Ben stared at the ground.

Jerry Farrell, relieved of any necessity to try and make a birdie, hit a smooth shot to the centre of the green. Tony Bendix jumped off his buggy and embraced his player and Farrell acknowledged the thundering cries of congratulations from his fans.

When we reached Ben's ball in the bunker I knew that he would be fortunate to play it out to within twenty feet of a hole which was no more than fifteen feet from the edge of the deep and steeply faced bunker. Not only that but the green ran sharply downhill from Ben and there was a noticeable borrow from left to right. My mind wound itself back to memories of the unfortunate Tommy Nakajima who, in the Open Championship, had taken four shots to extricate his ball from a bunker at the infamous road hole at St Andrews. Ben's shot looked even more difficult.

Since Farrell's ball lay further from the hole, he putted first and laid it to rest no more than a foot from the pin. Ben conceded his par four and, with a broad grin, Farrell threw his ball into the crowd. The applause went on and on; to all intents and purposes the Ryder Cup had returned to America for the first time for a decade. Stewards and officials, and Farrell himself, gestured the crowd into silence and Ben prepared to play a shot whose immense difficulty had been magnified by its circumstances.

With no margin for error, Ben had to cut the ball steeply into the air and try and land it on the edge of the green. If he played the shot perfectly, there was a chance that the ball might stop within ten feet of the hole, but the slope of the green was so severe that I thought such a result unlikely. There was a real danger that Ben would not even get the ball out of the bunker, so close was he to its face.

We looked one last time at the line of the shot and tried to compute the effect of the spin which Ben would impart with the open face of his sand-wedge, and the speed and the angle of the slope.

Ben stepped back into the sand and said, 'OK, it's got to go in. I wish I'd gone to Stefan's prayer meetings now. Will you hold the flag for me, please, Chris.'

As I stood with the flagstick in my hand, I could just see the top of Ben's head. Tens of thousands of people around the green were craning their necks to witness the final throes of the drama. All the players, the two captains and the officials of both teams were scattered around the edges of the green. Ross Bentley had his head in his hands yet again; and Stefan Sandberg had his hands clasped together, in prayer, I hoped. I wondered whether my mother and father were watching on television.

In total silence, Ben took one more look over the edge of the bunker and then I saw his club as it reached the top of its arc. The swing was slow and smooth, Ben's head motionless. As long as the ball comes out, we've got a chance, I thought. A putt for a half to tie the scores and the Ryder Cup stays in Europe.

I watched intently as the clubhead began its downwards journey; I heard a sort of whoosh as contact was made with the sand; and then everything went into slow motion as a shower of sand came over the edge of the bunker followed by Ben's ball. Out it came, steeply up into the sky, spinning, spinning. I swore later that I was able to count its every revolution and even read the maker's name. An American writer once compared the flight of a golf ball to man's aspirations for immortality; in those moments, as I stood waiting on the eighteenth green at Eagle Cliffs, I think I understood what he meant.

The ball pitched about four feet from the edge of the green, jumped in the air and began to roll across and down the slope. As the spin imparted by Ben's sand-iron ceased the ball began to gather pace. It couldn't possibly stop anywhere near the hole, I knew it was going to miss on my right; I removed the flag and stood back. When it was eighteen inches away I thought the ball would hit the edge of the hole and spin away down the slope. It was rolling ever faster but took one more slight turn across the slope and with a clunk, the ball hit the back of the hole, jumped in the air and then settled in the bottom of the cup. A birdie — victory! Glory for Ben and a surge of delight for me.

Ben came hurtling on to the green, flung his arms around me and danced us both around the green. I saw Jerry Farrell, who had played superbly throughout the match, with shoulders slumped and head down. I remember very little after that except that we were engulfed by the European players and officials, and by the fans. Ross Bentley and Ben were carried shoulder high from the eighteenth green and hordes of journalists and radio and television interviewers were bellowing questions at Ben, at Ross, at anybody connected with the European team.

You couldn't hear let alone think straight in the hubbub and confusion, and champagne corks were popping like toy machine guns. Someone grabbed me around the shoulders and shoved a bottle in my hands and I drank deeply, the lovely nectar bubbling and foaming over my face and down my shirt. Ben upended a bottle over my head and amid a scrum of people, shouting and cheering and clapping us on the backs, we eventually reached the sanctuary of the clubhouse.

I was thoroughly enjoying an embrace from Suzi when Toby, hair tousled and shirt unbuttoned and with what looked like a litre glass of champagne in his hand, tapped me on the arm.

'Sorry to interrupt, dear boy, but I've just seen Rutter heading rapidly in the direction of Coker's place. I think we should seize our opportunity. I have a nasty feeling that his next stop might be Peru or somewhere like that because a helicopter is warming up on the back lawn. You'd better exert your forceful personality and demand answers to leading questions.'

Moments later we had abandoned the party and were heading across the eighteenth fairway towards Coker's palace. Crowds of brightly dressed spectators were still scattered across the course, and had joined forces, British and Americans alike, in impromptu parties. As I said bitterly to Toby, 'A caddie's work is never done.'

'Nor is a golf journalist's,' he replied.

Chapter 41

Toby and I scrambled over the stone wall which divided Coker's property from the golf course and watched three men come through the French windows of the villa and advance on the waiting helicopter. Although we couldn't hear their words it was apparent that a top-class barney was in progress. At one point Neils Rutter seized Merv Sorenson by the arm and began to scream at him, his face thrust forward and only a few inches away from Sorenson's; Kyle Coker was making calming gestures and eventually wrenched Rutter away.

Standing amongst a grove of apple trees on the edge of the garden, we were not obviously visible to them and I whispered to Toby to edge a bit closer to the helicopter. There was no one in it.

'Who's the driver?' I asked.

'No idea. We'll see in a minute. Aren't you going to do something?'

'Who do you think I am? Superman?'

The men had cut diagonally across the lawn to within ten or twenty yards of the helicopter when Rutter stopped again. We could hear his words now as he screamed at Sorenson, 'You won't liquidate anything, you bastard, I'm going to liquidate you.'

Forty yards away we watched in impotent amazement and horror as Rutter produced a handgun from his jacket pocket and fired it from a range of a few feet into Sorenson's body. The crack of the gun was not much louder than the pop of a champagne cork. As Sorenson fell to the ground I noticed that Toby had moved smartly to the right to take cover.

I didn't think that Rutter, nor even Clint Eastwood, could hit me with a bullet from a handgun at a range of around thirty yards, so I stepped forward a few yards and yelled, 'That's murder number two, Rutter, when are you going to stop?'

Rutter jumped with surprise and turned in my direction, his gun raised. I saw Coker grab at his arm and shout, 'No more, Neils.'

Despite Toby's warning not to get any closer I stepped forward a few more yards. Rutter extended his arm and I heard the crack of another bullet. Involuntarily I ducked and felt foolish; the bullet smacked into a tree some distance away.

'You killed David Massey,' I shouted.

'No, I didn't, asshole,' Rutter yelled back.

He grabbed Coker and walked him towards the helicopter; Coker turned and shouted, 'It's true, Chris, we had nothing to do with his death. Not us, not Sorenson.'

We watched as Rutter urged him into the helicopter and sat at the controls.

'Biggles Rutter heads south,' Toby said as the blades whirred and the aircraft lifted away. It hovered briefly over Villa Kyle and then headed towards the ocean.

'Let's try and help Sorenson,' I said.

'Let's not, he hasn't moved. It's time to merge with the crowd and . . .'

There was an almighty thump from the direction of the ocean and, as we looked past the villa into the heavens, we saw pieces of helicopter flying in all directions and then the whoosh of exploding fuel. We stood there gaping at the sky for several moments and then Toby pulled me back into the cover of the apple trees. 'Biggles' final sortie. As the Californians say, "I'm outta here." Let's go, we don't want any part of this.'

The spectators who had stayed on the course were all looking away from Coker's villa and towards the scene of the helicopter explosion. We dropped over the wall under the cover of some bushes on the edge of the course and rushed up to a group of people. 'What's happened?' asked Toby and we joined in the general speculation.

After a few minutes we wandered off towards the clubhouse. Toby said, 'I've got a fantastic story and I won't be able to use half of it for fear of being accused of withholding evidence. There'll have to be a lot of "sources close to the US Commissioner speculate" and all that rubbish.'

'Do you think that was an elaborate suicide pact?'

'I hope so because that was one of the fleet of helicopters which was going to take the European team to the airport tomorrow.'

'I believe those two,' I said thoughtfully.

'About what?'

'That they didn't kill David Massey.'

'Who did?'

'It's suddenly clicked into place, Toby. Who would most want to stop David broadcasting the fact that Ross Bentley had fathered an illegitimate child by an under-age girl? And not just a few months under age — anyone can make a mistake, your honour — but a chit of a girl of fourteen.'

Toby stopped and looked at me, horror, surprise and amusement struggling for supremacy on his features. 'You don't mean who I think you mean, by any chance, do you?'

'I do and I want to talk to her.'

'You'll need to do more than bash her on the knee with a spanner to get the truth out of her.'

By this time we were shouldering our way through a gathering tide of people who were flooding on to the course as news of the accident spread. A security man tried to rush past us and Toby seized him by the arm and said, 'Someone's saying there's a body lying in one of the villa gardens over there. The big villa with the turrets.'

'Holy shit,' the man said, and dashed on, shouting into his radio.

We strolled back into the clubhouse where the party for the European team was going with a tremendous swing. If the revellers had heard the explosion above their own noise, nobody cared. Nick Spencer was standing on a table and trying to conduct a group of supporters in a ragged chorus of 'You'll Never Walk Alone' and even Stefan Sandberg had a glass of champagne in his hand.

'Be careful with that stuff, Stefan,' I said with a smile.

'The Lord Jesus turned the water into the wine,' he replied, and I noticed that his Swedish accent was more prominent than usual.

'Do you have the bible with you?'

'Of course.'

'Genesis, chapter four, verse ten.'

'I don't have to look that up,' Stefan said softly. ' "And he said, what hast thou done? The voice of thy brother's blood crieth unto me from the ground." '

I thanked the Swede. So, even the God-botherer had been in there doing his bit to embarrass Ben.

I spotted Ben and Suzi in a corner, their backs to the throng, and Toby and I made our way between the shouting celebrants towards them. 'You're both looking very serious,' I said. 'Come on, we've just won the cup, you're a hero, Ben.'

'I've just acquired a father, too,' he replied.

'And he's not sure that he wants one,' Suzi said.

'Look, since I was tiny I'd got used to not having a father. And I'd come to terms with it. I'm not sure I want Ross as a father.'

'Ben asked him where he'd been when he really needed him,' Suzi reported. 'Poor Ross, he was so elated. The Ryder Cup and now Ben as a son.'

'I wasn't really fair to him because he didn't even know about me,' Ben said gloomily.

'So, what are you going to do?' Toby asked.

'Nothing. We'll see what happens. No acknowledgements in public . . .'

'And that means this is off the record, Toby,' Suzi said. 'No exclusive, no amazing revelations. You'll keep quiet. Agreed?'

'Scout's honour,' Toby said.

'Ross is going to help Ben in any way he can,' Suzi continued. 'We'll all spend some time together.'

'A ménage à trois?' asked Toby brightly. 'You and Louise and Ross?'

Ben and I laughed as Suzi kicked Toby, not so playfully, on the ankle.

'Where are the Bentleys?' I asked.

'They were chatting to Tony Bendix and his wife in the far corner, I think.'

I made another circuit amongst the madcap celebrants. Tony Swan, egged on by Nick Spencer, was doing a headstand against a wall and drinking champagne upside down. I eventually forced my way through to where the Bentleys were still talking to Tony and Candace Bendix. I wondered how I could lure Louise away; it had to be achieved with tact. Oh, sod it,

I thought, and said to Louise, 'May I talk to you a moment, Mrs Bentley, it's very important.'

'What, now?' she asked, one eyebrow raised questioningly.

'What's the problem, Chris?' Ross asked. 'Surely it can wait.'

'No, it can't, I'm afraid, but it'll only take a minute or two. It's about Ben.'

That did the trick. Louise shrugged and suggested that we went on to the terrace. Although a few people were drinking and chatting, most of them were enjoying the fun inside. I steered Louise to a table at one end of the terrace.

'If this is about Ben, I've nothing to add. We've sorted everything out and discretion will be the watchword.'

'No, Louise. It's about David and why you killed him.'

She looked at me for a moment and smiled. 'You've done some good detective work, Mr Ludlow, you've been quick and clever. I didn't realise you were also mad.'

She got up from the table and tried to walk back towards the party but I barred her way.

'Let me pass,' she said vehemently.

'No, you'll listen to me. David was selling information about your husband, that he had made Suzi Massey pregnant when she was only fourteen. He had reasonable proof; birth certificates, your letter to Suzi when Ben was eighteen, Suzi's bank statements.'

'That wasn't enough to prove anything.'

'It was enough for David Massey. And it was enough for you. That's when he made his fatal mistake. He had a deal with Brandel and Coker but, instead of taking the money and running, he tried to play them off against

340

you. You were the other bidder for the story and the incriminating evidence. That didn't occur to me at first. I thought Sorenson or Rutter had eliminated David because he was being a nuisance. But it was you and you could afford the money to shut him up, just as you could afford to pay Suzi a monthly retainer and pay Ben's school fees.'

'Then why didn't I just pay up? Why on earth would I kill the boy? What a ludicrous idea.'

'Because you didn't trust him. Just a couple of days ago you admitted how you had taken care of Suzi and Ben and hidden the facts from your husband. Do you remember?'

Louise nodded and I continued, 'Well, you dropped your guard and referred to the "loathsome David". That puzzled me because I could think of no reason for your ever meeting him.'

'That's hardly the basis for an accusation of murder.'

'No, but it was a vital part of the puzzle, especially when I became convinced that neither Coker nor Rutter had been involved in David's death. You didn't trust him but you arranged to meet him, though certainly not at Ben's house. You would never have risked being seen near him. No, David must have rung you after Ben went off in a hurry. It was an unexpected chance for you to carry out your tentative plan to kill him. Let's see, you probably parked in that supermarket car park about a mile down the road and then walked your dog to Ben's house. You do have a dog, don't you? And perhaps a wig or certainly a headscarf. Nobody would notice a lady walking a dog in that part of Surrey. And then you shot David Massey. Nice and clean, one shot through the eye.'

'You have a vivid imagination, Mr Ludlow. Now I'd really like to rejoin my husband.'

'One last thing, Louise. You were left with the problem of the whereabouts of the documents that David had stolen. They weren't on him, because you searched his pockets, no doubt. So a few days later you called Suzi to offer your condolences and to check that your mutual secret was safe. And she told you that the police had returned them to her without comment. Problem solved.'

Louise Bentley rose to her feet and I rose with her. She looked me steadily in the eyes and said, 'Prove it, Mr Ludlow.'

Without another word or a backward look, Louise Bentley, elegant and self-assured, walked away from me along the terrace.

A selection of bestsellers
from Headline